# HER INHERITANCE FOREVER

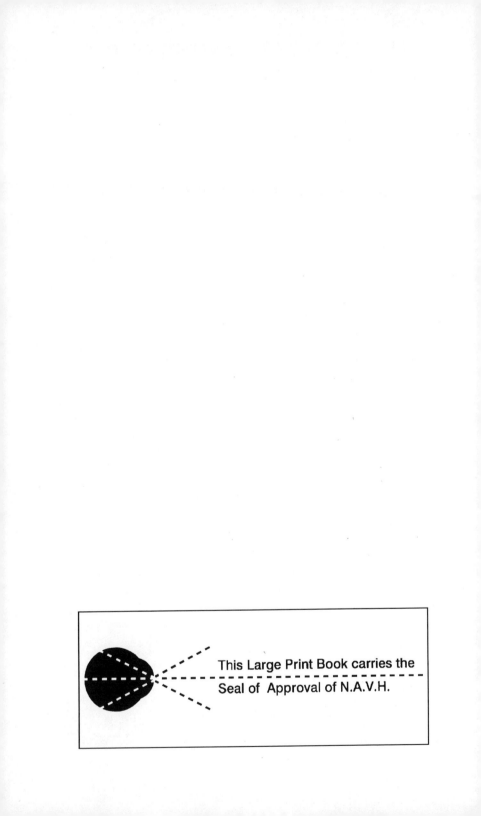

This Large Print Book carries the
Seal of Approval of N.A.V.H.

# TEXAS: STAR OF DESTINY, BOOK 2

# HER INHERITANCE FOREVER

## LYN COTE

**THORNDIKE PRESS**
*A part of Gale, Cengage Learning*

GALE
CENGAGE Learning·

Detroit • New York • San Francisco • New Haven, Conn • Waterville, Maine • London

**GALE**
CENGAGE Learning™

*LARGE TYPE
F
COTE, L*

3 1257 01867 2310

**LIBRARY OF CONGRESS CATALOGING-IN-PUBLICATION DATA**

Cote, Lyn.
  Her inheritance forever / by Lyn Cote.
    p. cm. — (Thorndike Press large print Christian historical fiction) (Texas, star of destiny ; bk. two)
    ISBN-13: 978-1-4104-2229-3 (alk. paper)
    ISBN-10: 1-4104-2229-1 (alk. paper)
    1. Frontier and pioneer life—Fiction. 2. Texas—Fiction. 3. Large type books. I. Title. II. Series.
  PS3553.O76378H47 2010
  813'.54—dc22                                              2009043343

Published in 2010 by arrangement with Avon Inspire, an imprint of HarperCollins Publishers.

Printed in Mexico
1 2 3 4 5 6 7 14 13 12 11 10

*Dedicated to my friend Leslie.*
*Thanks for your help and encouragement.*

*Thanks to the librarians at the San Antonio Public Library who helped me with the battles of Goliad and San Jacinto.*

*To Texas history buffs:*
*In this novel, I've taken dramatic license*
*with two facts. I'll*
*explain them and the reasons why I*
*"adjusted" history in my*
*historical note at the end.*

The Lord knoweth the days of the upright: and their inheritance shall be forever.

They shall not be ashamed in the evil time.

Psalm 37:18–19 KJV

# PROLOGUE

*Spring 1835*

Señor Scully's wavy golden blond hair gleamed as the last of the sun's rays streamed in the west window behind him. Alandra had just hesitantly entered the crowded vaqueros' sleeping quarters where he sat. Now she looked down at Señor Scully's hand, which he'd just unwrapped from a makeshift bandage. Sinking into a chair at the table, she sucked in breath. "What were you doing to cause this wound?"

Sitting across from her, the Anglo cowboy tried to hide the long cut with his other hand. Fortunately, the skin was lying over the wound like a flap. But it looked as if someone had neatly sliced the skin back to take a closer look at the bones. She hoped her billowing queasiness was not visible. The other vaqueros leaned or sat around on the bunks and chairs, pressing in on the two of them.

This was the first time she had been left in charge at the Quinn rancho. Both the Quinns and Ash's family were away, so of course, she should have expected something like this. The Mexican vaqueros would not make a fuss over her treating a wound, would expect it of her. But this Anglo . . .

She fought to keep her composure. She could not recall ever feeling this *aprensivo,* squeamish.

Scully growled at her, "I told the others I can take care of this —"

"I am the *doña.*" She drew herself up proudly.

"That's right, and a lady like you shouldn't be even looking at something like this." He hid his hand under the table.

"You are wrong. This is for me to do." Ignoring his objection, she reached for his hand.

He jerked away. "You're just a girl —"

Why was he causing such a fuss? The other vaqueros whistled and scolded the Anglo. A rush of hot embarrassment overwhelmed her. She rapped the top of his head with her knuckles.

"Hey!" He half rose and looked at her resentfully.

"That is what Tía Dorritt does when Carson acts like a child," Alandra said, trying to hide how fast she was breathing.

"I'm not letting a green girl touch —"

Stung, she leaped forward to rap his head again. He stepped back.

"Scully, are you going to dance the fandango with the señorita?" one of the other vaqueros teased. "Or let her doctor your hand?" The others chuckled and whooped.

Alandra flushed up to the roots of her hair. "Sit," she ordered, and pointed toward the chair he had left. "Now."

Scully's green eyes blazed. The power of the man, so much anger, so much strength, rushed toward her, enveloped her. He glared, looking like a bull ready to charge.

*"Toro, toro,"* the grinning vaqueros chanted as if this were a rodeo.

Alandra tried to ignore *le frivolidad.* She devoutly wished she did not have an audience. "Señor Scully," she ordered, "let us get this thing done."

She sat back down with dignity. Bending over, she opened the wooden chest at her feet, trying not to reveal how her hands trembled. She went about laying out the brown bottle of iodine, the silver needle, and the silk thread.

Still hanging back, Scully weathered a few

13

more moments of the chanting. Then, with ill grace, he capitulated, dropping down onto the hard chair and placing his hand on the scarred table in front of her.

"*Una momento,*" a vaquero said. He brought out a half-full bottle of tequila and poured a dram into a glass, shoving it toward Scully. "Drink. For medicine."

Alandra nodded. The tequila would help the pain.

Scully shook his head. "I don't drink hard liquor."

"Stubborn —" Alandra began.

"*Toro, toro,*" the vaqueros chanted again, teasing the Anglo.

Still glaring, Scully took the glass and downed the shot.

The vaquero poured him another.

Meeting no one's eye, Alandra acted as if she were unaware of this. She threaded the needle, telling herself she could do this, must do this. *I am the* doña. *I take care of the people.*

The vaqueros watched her every move. Their concentration weighed on her. She held her lower lip with her teeth, holding in her sick feeling. She carefully, slowly, stitched, trying to think of cloth, not skin. Scully remained the stoic Anglo throughout — until she poured iodine over the wound.

14

This forced a yelp from him. The vaqueros joined him, and all of them yowled and yipped like coyotes. Then they called out their approval and applauded her.

Still nauseated and shaky, Alandra packed up the nursing supplies and rose to leave. Politely, Scully stood, but the tequila had done its work. He swayed on his feet.

Amid more catcalling, she pushed him back down. "Come to the big house in the morning, Señor Scully. I'll need to check for *infeccion.*" Just before she marched out the door, she looked back. Two of the vaqueros were helping Scully to his bunk. So the proud Yanqui, the *severo* Anglo, was human after all.

# ONE

*Mid-February 1836*

In the dim light, Scully let Quinn and Ash, crouching, move ahead. Not even he could hear Ash and Quinn creeping over the coarse grass, rocks, and sand. Scully made sure of each of his own footfalls.

Ahead, he saw one small fire. It must have been of dried mesquite since it barely revealed any smoke against the nearly dark sky. The three of them eased around in the shadows. Every sound from the camping Indians and their horses made his nerves tighten more and sharpened his listening. Then he heard it — rocks sliding down the hill.

And worse, the Comanches heard it too. Suddenly they were scattering away from the fire, grabbing rifles. How many?

Scully glimpsed Quinn lift his gun. A half-naked Comanche moved into the firelight. He held the señorita clamped against his side. With his other hand, he held a knife to the señorita's hairline, about to scalp her.

*No.* Scully aimed and fired. His bullet smacked, plowing deep into the Indian's forehead. The man was lifted off his feet. The force carried the señorita with him into the shadows beyond the fire.

Scully burst into the camp then, his tomahawk held high. The Mexicans came charging into camp too. Yelling. Gunshots. An arrow whizzed past Scully's head. A few sharp shrieks. The sound of horse hooves. And then all was silent.

Scully halted at the campfire and looked around. The other Indians and their horses had melted away into the sudden nightfall. He scanned the gloomy darkness for the señorita's paler skin and found her. He hurried to her side. Kneeling, he lifted her from the ground. Her slender body was limp on his arms; her hair tumbled loose. "Are you all right?"

She stared up at him, her eyes wide with shock. A thin line of blood showed where the knife had etched her flesh. "Why did you shoot?" she demanded, suddenly coming alive. "You could have gotten me scalped."

He ignored her obvious hysteria and drew her closer to the fire to see if she'd been harmed. Touching her was strange but necessary. Added to the thin red line, her cheek was bruised and her face was smudged with dirt. Tears formed furrows on her cheeks. But her clothing hadn't been torn. Quinn came to them. "The rest have scattered. How is she?"

"Tío Quinn," the girl moaned, reaching for him.

Quinn knelt beside her. "You're alive. You're fine. We'll take you home now."

She pulled away from Scully, and Quinn hugged her.

Scully drew back. That was proper. Quinn and his wife had raised the girl from when her brother died. Ash had explained that *tío* was Spanish for uncle, and Mrs. Quinn was Tía Dorritt. Years before, Scully had hired on when Quinn was in Louisiana at the end of a cattle drive. The first time he'd seen this señorita, she'd been just a young girl.

Scully listened to their muted exchange as she told Quinn, no, she hadn't been compromised. Relief like silent thunder rolled through him. Trying to forget the unaccustomed feel of her, soft and light in his arms, he returned his hatchet to his belt and reloaded his rifle.

Then he lifted his canteen to drink and stopped. "Here give her some water." He wiped the mouth of the canteen with his buckskin sleeve and handed it to Quinn.

She took the canteen but gave Scully a fierce look. "You could have gotten me killed, shooting like that. What if you'd missed? He might have scalped me." Then she drank long from the canteen.

"I don't miss." Scully stood up and turned his back to her. He knew she was not using her normal sense. Still, the señorita's thankless attitude pierced and pricked him as if he'd swallowed a cactus. Ladies like her, frail and fine, didn't belong on the frontier. Quinn could have run both ranches, his own and hers. She'd inherited Rancho Sandoval when her brother died. The señorita could be — should be — in Mexico City, where living was easier.

Quinn stood up and handed the canteen back to him. "That was a good shot, Scully. You did right. He was going to scalp her. He thought he could do it and still escape. He was showing off."

Scully shrugged in response. Now that they'd found the señorita unmolested, a new question occurred to him. "What I want to know," he said, turning around to face Quinn, "is why this bunch kidnapped the señorita."

Quinn gazed at him in the faint light. "I

want to know the same thing." He raised his voice. "Did anyone capture any of these renegades?"

Ash came into the faint firelight, his dark skin making him almost invisible except for his glistening eyes and the silver in his hair. "Thought you might want one able to talk." Ash held up a limp, unconscious Comanche by the shoulder.

"Good." Quinn helped the señorita to her feet. "Ash, tie up the renegade and gag him. When he comes to, we'll persuade him to tell us why this happened. Was anyone injured? Did we kill any more of them?"

While the other vaqueros searched, Scully dragged the body of the dead Comanche away from the fire and began covering it with rocks. But in case any other young brave wanted to show off, Scully still watched the shadows of night around the señorita.

A quick survey of the area revealed no others. Quinn whistled to his mount. "If I thought our horses could make it, we'd head back now. But they need rest. Ash, Scully, and I will take the first watch, the rest of you bed down for a few hours." He repeated this in Spanish.

Quinn settled the señorita wrapped in a blanket near the warmth of the fire but

21

beyond its light. He gave her more water, some pemmican, and the Mexican flatbread. Finishing his task, Scully found he couldn't look away. He watched her, the girl they'd spent hours searching for. She leaned her head in one hand as she ate. She lifted his canteen to her mouth again, and he watched her swallow. Then as she looked over Quinn's shoulder at Scully, her expression soured.

Irritated, he drifted away, farther from them, listening and watching. He found a concealed spot and settled back on his heels. He blinked his dry eyes. It was going to be another long night. The Comanche renegades wouldn't have taken her if they'd meant her no harm. But why had they taken her in the first place? Who would want harm to come to the señorita?

Saddle sore, Scully admitted to relief at seeing the outline of the jacales and adobe buildings of Quinn's rancho against the cool gray afternoon sky. And Quinn had pulled the rescue off. He rode with the señorita behind him, beside Scully.

Since the night before, neither Scully nor the señorita had exchanged as much as a glance. Somehow this had settled like a sunbaked brick in his stomach. He wiped his forehead with his sleeve. *I'm just tired.*

When they reached the ranch house, Quinn dismounted and helped the señorita off the horse. Quinn's son Carson came around the side of the house with his mother. Ash slipped from his saddle to be greeted by his wife and son.

*Family.*

Along with the other vaqueros without family, Scully turned his horse toward their long low adobe house behind the barn.

"Wait, Scully," Quinn said.

Scully let the others pass him. "What, boss?"

"I want to know why this happened. Put the Comanche in the unused storehouse. Make sure he's bound tight and can't escape. All we have to do is pen him up a few days and he'll tell us anything to get free."

Scully nodded. The tactic made sense. He pushed up the brim of his hat. "Will do." He turned away again.

"Scully," Quinn added, halting him. "Come to supper at the house tonight just before dark. Until then rest."

Against his will, Scully glanced at the señorita, who was clutching Mrs. Quinn's arm and mounting the few low steps into the adobe ranch house. She glanced back at

23

him, looking as if she wanted to say something. What?

Then the vaquero who'd been leading the Comanche handed Scully the end of the rope attached to the prisoner's wrists. Scully headed for the unused storehouse back near the corral. What was this all about? Why did Quinn want him to take supper in the main house? Vaqueros were never invited to eat with the family. Certainly he had never been. He shut his mind to this. Wondering was always fruitless. He'd find out tonight.

That evening, Scully appeared at the door of the hacienda. He had slept most the day, just waking in time to bathe. He'd dressed with care in his newest buckskins, a red bandanna around his neck and his blond hair tied back with a leather thong. It was an honor to be invited for dinner in the hacienda. Curiosity about why he had been invited had tightened in his stomach. His guess was that it had something to do with the señorita. But what?

Ash's wife, Reva, plump and pretty, beckoned him inside with a smile of welcome. He doffed his hat and stepped over the threshold. Instantly, the aromas from the kitchen hit his empty stomach, along with the warmth from the welcoming fire on the hearth.

Mrs. Quinn walked forward with her hand held out. He'd gotten used to the fact that though she was an Anglo woman she often wore bright Mexican-style dress at home. Tonight it was blue with fancy embroidery around the neck. But whatever she wore, Dorritt Quinn was always a handsome woman. "Thank you for coming, Scully."

"Thanks for having me, ma'am." He grasped her hand for just a moment. It always surprised him how small women's hands were. He scanned the candlelit room, seeking the señorita, then he stopped himself. Now that she was safe here, she was not his business. Then he glimpsed her through the doorway, near the table. Their gazes connected and she primmed up her mouth like a spinster schoolmarm.

Smiling, Mrs. Quinn took Scully's leather hat and jacket, hanging them on the pegs alongside the arched Spanish door. "Come. We are ready to sit at the table."

He followed her into the midst of large open room its massive-fireplace to his right. She led him to the left side, where the round, polished oak table gleamed in the candlelight. Under his feet was a wide-stone floor. Raised on dirt floors, he always looked

25

with wonder at this floor. He'd heard that Quinn had ordered the stone all the way from a quarry in Mexico.

The beamed ceiling was higher than in most houses because Mrs. Quinn said it made the rooms cooler in the hot Texas summers. The walls of the house were thick white adobe. And the furniture was of pine, oak, and leather. Silver candlesticks glowed in the low light. There were feathers and pinecones in a polished wood bowl atop a glass-covered bookcase, and near the windows sat several cactus plants in brightly painted clay pots. Mrs. Quinn had a way of making plain things look elegant. Scully liked that. He drew in a deep breath of satisfaction. This wasn't a house — it was a home. And the nearest he'd ever get to one.

Summoning everyone to the meal, Quinn seated his lady at the round table. She looked up at Scully and motioned toward the chair to her right. "Scully, will you please seat Señorita Alandra?"

Scully tensed. He'd never seated a lady before. And now he had to do it for this Tejano lady who was still irritated with him — only heaven knew why. Following Quinn's example, he moved forward and pulled out the chair. The señorita didn't look back, but slipped in front of him and sat down. He slid the chair closer to the table, drawing in the sweet fragrance from her glossy black hair, now twisted into a neat figure eight and pinned up at the nape of her neck. This morning it had been loosed, looking wild like the mane of a black mare.

*"Gracias,"* the señorita murmured.

"Welcome, miss," Scully muttered. She always had that edge to her voice when she talked to him. Still uncomfortable, he sat beside her, where Quinn had waved him.

Then Ash and Reva with their son Antonio, and the Quinn's son Carson, with his other friend Emilio Ramirez, gathered around the table too. The three friends, Antonio, Carson, and Emilio were close in age, gangly and just leaving off being boys and becoming men. The skin of each showed their heritage. Carson was tanned from the sun and Quinn's Cherokee blood. The other boy, Emilio, had the Tejano complexion and Antonio was the darkest and favored his father Ash.

"We'll give thanks first," Quinn said, and bowed his head. "Dear God, thank you for loving us and bringing us safe home. And thank you for keeping our little Alandra safe. And thanks for this fine meal. Amen."

Scully looked up. It always surprised him when Quinn prayed. He didn't look like a praying man, with his long tail of hair and buckskins.

In the door behind Mrs. Quinn a plump Tejano girl in a bright turquoise skirt, waiting to serve the meal, grinned at him, flirting. In several trips she carried in bowls of hominy, beans, flatbread in rounds they called tortillas, pickled red and green peppers, and a large beef roast, crusted with black pepper. As she placed a dish in front of him, the girl smiled at him. He acted like he hadn't seen it, but Ash winked at him.

The señorita glowered at the girl.

Ignoring this, Scully accepted bowls of food and passed them on with care. The proud señorita beside him made him feel that he didn't belong here. And in truth he didn't — he had lived a rough life. But an honest one. The serving girl came to him and filled his glass from a clay pitcher. She managed to brush up against him, and he felt his face burn.

The señorita sniffed and averted her eyes.

The girl finished serving and left the room. Scully wished he could too. Sitting beside the señorita made him feel as awkward as a mule harnessed with a thoroughbred.

"Tío Quinn," the señorita spoke up right away, giving Quinn a pointed look. "I am not your *little* Alandra anymore."

"I beg your pardon," Quinn said. "I keep forgetting you're all grown up." His voice was light but his eyes were serious.

"I am nineteen and I am running my own rancho," the señorita said, lifting her chin.

Quinn smiled and raised his glass to her. "You are indeed. Again, *mi culpa.*"

Scully was still amazed that an unmarried woman would tackle running her own cattle ranch. But Tejanos, like Comanches, did things differently. He began eating then, savoring the rich flavors and the tenderness of the beef. Mrs. Quinn always raised a few cattle on corn at the ranch, and he'd come to love the taste of corn-fed beef.

As he chewed, he had the feeling that he was being watched. He turned his head and caught the señorita quickly looking away. Why was she looking at him? Wasn't he eating proper enough for her? He wiped his chin with the white linen napkin, then continued eating, staring at the bookcase on the far wall.

Finally, Quinn cleared his throat. "We've got some talking to do," he said, "and Scully, I wanted you to hear this because I'm going to need you to take on a new responsibility."

Scully nodded. He had no doubt this

would have something to do with the kidnapping.

Alandra wondered what Quinn meant by that. Why was the *distante* Anglo vaquero here at all? She shut her eyes for a moment. A night and day of fear had weakened her. Though she had fared well, her body still ached from her rough treatment by the renegades. And at times the terror of the first few hours still caught around her lungs, making it hard to breathe. But stretching her shoulder muscles bit by bit, she shoved this down again. *I was not hurt. I am alive.*

Then she noticed that her fork was shaking, her hands betraying her. She pressed them together in her lap. Tears tried to well up in her eyes. She blinked rapidly and took in breath slowly, willing herself to calm, to show no aftereffects of her fear.

Unwillingly, she looked toward Scully again, and found him watching her in that remote way of his. As always, she was intrigued by the gold wedding band he wore on the little finger of his left hand. Had the man lost a young wife?

Quinn cleared his throat again. "Scully, I want you to go to Rancho Sandoval and work for Miss Alandra."

Alandra's head snapped up. "What?" Beside her, she sensed Scully go very still.

She swung toward him, examining his cool green eyes, the mirror of his soul, according to what Dorritt had taught her. The Anglo cowboy appeared just as shocked as she was. And just as hesitant to be thrown together. This Scully never missed an opportunity to let her know that he didn't think she could run a ranch.

She looked to Quinn, holding in her distress. "With respect Tío Quinn" — and she did respect this man who had protected her and raised her — "but I am the one who hires men for Rancho Sandoval." Her stomach started jumping. Quinn's words had unleashed everything she wanted to forget about last night.

Quinn looked even more serious. "Yes, you do. But Dorritt and I agree that there is something strange about this kidnapping. It doesn't follow."

Ash nodded, pushing back his chair. "I agree. There was no reason for these renegades to skirt Quinn's thousand acres and single you — the Sandoval — out. The Comanche don't care about wealth like you have. They care about horses and guns, not gold or deeds."

"Then why did they take Lonnie, Pa?" Carson demanded, his changing voice cracking, making him turn red.

It warmed Alandra to hear Carson's outrage and worry, and his use of his nickname for her. He was the closest person to a younger brother she had. But it chilled her to confront this question. Why had she been taken?

"I don't know," Quinn admitted, folding his hands and resting his elbows on the table. "I questioned the renegade late this afternoon but he still wouldn't tell me anything. I don't know if he even knows anything. I'll keep trying till I think it's hopeless." He shook his head. "I just didn't see anything like this coming. Since I came to an agreement with the Comanche when I built this house, they've stayed away from us . . . and from Rancho Sandoval." Quinn lifted his cup of coffee and shook his head. "Doesn't make sense."

Alandra looked down, afraid her face might betray her. She must not let fear rule her life. She was the *doña* now. "But —"

Quinn interrupted. "Alandra, that's why I want Scully to go home with you —"

*No. Not this stiff Anglo.*

She protested, "But I have Emilio's father, Ramirez —"

"Ramirez is a good man, a good foreman." Quinn cut her off. "But while the Comanche don't bother Anglos, they don't mind

32

attacking Mexicans. If Scully — an Anglo who's been my top vaquero for years — is at your rancho, the Comanche will think twice. His reputation is known to them. The fact that he took out the brave last night in the dark from that range is enough to make any other renegade shy away. Don't think that story won't spread."

Alandra thought on what Quinn had said, clasping her hands tight together. She could not argue even one point. All Mexicans resented the fact that while Comanches, the most feared tribe in Texas, seemed to look upon Anglos as *adversarios* to be careful of, they had no problem raiding Mexican or Tejano ranches. Since the Quinns had run her ranch while she grew up, it had come under Quinn's protection. But perhaps the Comanches thought that this had ended when she took over management of her ranch. And, yes, Scully's reputation as a fighter and vaquero had been established even before last night's daring shot.

The sound cracked in her ears again. The knife blade cut into her forehead. A scream crawled up her throat. She stared down, holding everything in, aware of Scully's attention on her — as if he knew what she was feeling.

Breaking the abrupt silence, Carson asked,

"Pa, do you think someone will try to kidnap Lonnie again?"

But Dorritt, not Quinn, replied, "If we don't know *why* she was kidnapped this time, how can we know that, son?"

"We don't know who to take aim at," Quinn added, hitching up one shoulder. "Who we're up against."

"Well," Ash drawled, "I recall one person who hated Alandra's brother enough to try to shame him and kill him."

Alandra froze. Scully's hand resting on the table next to her plate suddenly clenched.

Sitting beside Ash, his wife Reva nodded. "I remember that lying snake too."

Alandra swallowed a gasp, her pulse racing. Then her words gushed out. "That is not possible. My cousin has been gone all these years. My brother — may he rest in peace — hired men to hunt him till they finally gave up. He told me he thought our cousin must be dead."

Dorritt took her hand. "Yes, but your brother could have been wrong. Your cousin might still live —"

"And you think he still hates me?" Alandra murmured, a shudder ripping through her.

"And that isn't all the bad news," Quinn added.

"What do you mean, Pa?" Carson asked.

Alandra held her breath. She had some idea what Quinn was about to say, but at his words, she wanted to close her eyes, jump up and run away.

# Two

"We need to talk about what's happening all around us," Dorritt replied, instead of Quinn. "It will certainly affect us all no matter who wins this rebellion."

"You mean what happened in Bexar in December?" Scully asked. The trouble in Texas had been going on for nearly a year now. He didn't say it out loud but he didn't see how the battles between the Mexicans and the Texians would affect him.

Mrs. Quinn nodded. "Yes, the Mexican General de Cos surrendered to the Anglos. But San Antonio de Bexar, with the old fort — the Alamo — is too choice a stronghold to be relinquished. I have every certainty that General Santa Anna will try to win it back."

"Santa Anna," Ash said, "scares me."

Scully didn't believe any man scared Ash, but Ash saying this caught his attention. This was serious, then.

Looking down, Ash slid an arm around his wife's shoulders. "More than a decade ago, Santa Anna was with General Arredondo when he massacred the American adventurers, the filibusters, who were trying to take Texas for the U.S. Not only the filibusters, but every man with them. Over three hundred slaughtered."

A horrified silence pressed down over all of them around the table. What kind of man had three hundred people killed?

"*Angloamericano* settlers," Quinn spoke up, "have never had any real intention of becoming Mexicans. But as long as they were left alone north of the Rio Grande, they were fine, enjoying the land that is making them rich from slaves and cotton. But I don't think the powers in Mexico City are going to let things go on as they have been."

"They want to make the Anglos knuckle under," Ash added.

"And the Tejanos too," Emilio spoke up for the first time.

Scully had been surprised that many Tejanos, Texians of Mexican descent, didn't like being classed as Mexican, what he had mistakenly called them at first.

"What do you think will happen?" the señorita asked, sounding worried. But

Scully noticed she purposely turned her head away from him.

Mrs. Quinn laid a hand on the señorita's arm. "We don't know, but we can't bury our heads in the sand. We have to be alert and careful. We want you to go home and be with your people. But this is the other reason we want Scully to go home with you. War is dangerous even to those who take no part in it. Innocents always die. History has taught us that awful lesson." She pressed her lips together.

*And we don't want it to happen to you, Alandra.* Scully heard Mrs. Quinn's unspoken words. And they dropped inside him like a handful of lead shot. War. He knew what his decision about this should be. But it was hard, very hard.

After the evening meal Alandra stepped out onto the wide porch into the chilly, starry night to get away from all the concerned faces and to think. She pulled her dark wool rebozo tight around her. Barely recalling the meal she had just finished, she wished everything could be the way it had been three days before. But even that would be no remedy. This fight between Mexicans and Texians had started nearly a year ago.

Scully followed her outside, no doubt on

38

his way to join the other vaqueros. She did not want this man on her land. The thought of him being sent as a guard irritated her like an ill-fitting sleeve catching her with every move.

Then her mind dragged her back to the night before. Fresh, sharp, and appalling sensations slashed through her flesh. Awakening to a hand clamped over her mouth, being dragged from her bed, gagged and bound with bands of buckskin and bundled out her window.

Twisting, clawing, punching, she had fought the Comanche every step of the way. But she had been overpowered, helpless. In the moonlight, her captor had grinned at her, amused by her efforts.

Another rush of raw terror made her stumble. Scully caught her before she fell. For just one moment she clung to him. His sinewy arm was as stout as a tree limb. *Show no weakness, especially to this Anglo.* She stiffened and pushed away from him. "*Gracias.* I am afraid I am still a little fatigued." *Still a little terrified.*

She drew up all her reserves, all the endurance that she had gained from life here on the frontier. Her brother had been strong to the end, and she would be too.

But had someone wanted to bring her end

early? She looked away, willed away the telltale moisture in her eyes. *I am the* dueña *of Rancho Sandoval. I am strong. I take care of my people, myself.*

Against her will, she looked up at the Anglo. He was taller than Quinn and Ash and had the same slender but sturdy build. Scully always put her in mind of a mustang, tamed enough to accept a bridle but still wild. And proud.

She drew in breath. She probably owed this man her life, or at least her scalp. She should try to explain why she reacted as she had when he had saved her from the renegade. This task made a bitter taste in her mouth. No, she couldn't speak of her panic that night. Men always deemed showing any emotion as a sign of weakness — a reason to dismiss a woman as less than a man.

But it would be ungracious not to express her thanks. She cleared her throat. "Please, señor, I wish to thank you —"

He cut her off. "Don't mention it."

Alandra glared at him. She'd forgotten this man was no gentleman. A gentleman knew how to accept an expression of gratitude with grace. She primmed her lips. "Then I bid you *buenos noches,* señor."

He started down the steps but then halted. He looked up. Their eyes connected and held. "You don't think you need me at your rancho, right?"

She did not want to need this man, or any man. And why was he speaking like this? Usually this Anglo did not speak unless asked a question. Why was this vaquero so silent, so *reservado,* now speaking to her? Pity?

Offense stiffening her spine, she turned her back to him and leaned against the nearest porch post. She said to the night, not to him below her on the steps, "You do not want to come to Rancho Sandoval, do you, Señor Scully?"

"No, I don't."

His bald answer made her react perversely, and she heard him take another step away, leaving. To detain him, make him wait on her, she glanced over her shoulder at him. He had come to this rancho while she was still a girl and yet he remained a stranger. "Where do you come from?" *Why are you here?*

He eyed her a moment before replying. "Born in Kentucky."

She held him still with her gaze. She would force him to reveal something more of himself. "Is your family still there?"

"Don't have family."

His stark reply touched that tender place

41

where the ache of never having known her parents and her deep love for her late brother still lingered. She pressed a hand to her heart as if able to staunch that deep emptiness. Her stiffness vanished. "I have no family, no blood relatives either."

In contrast to her sudden softening, he made no response other than a slight nod.

She studied his profile in the candlelight glowing from the windows. Then she stared away into the night. She shivered. The terror crouched inside her, waiting to seize her again. Two nights ago her life had changed. Or at least her perception of it.

Before that night, she had taken safety for granted. Who would harm the mistress of Sandoval, Quinn's adopted niece? Now she wondered if she could ever feel that safe again.

But even if her dread lingered, why couldn't her own people protect her? She did not want this man, this *distante* Anglo, as her protector. She did not want to believe that war might come to Rancho Sandoval.

She rubbed her arms, warding off the penetrating night chill, but her voice did not betray this. "Tío Quinn thinks you should come to Rancho Sandoval. But I am the one who must decide whether I agree or not."

"Oh?" he countered in that low, expressionless voice.

She stared down at him, putting him in his place. "Yes, but I understand you take your orders from Quinn."

She turned and walked back inside. Instantly, two different emotions — one after the other — crashed over her. First, the familiar hacienda welcomed her — the glowing fire on the hearth, the sight of Quinn reading his Bible aloud while Dorritt, nearby, knitted cotton yarn into socks and listened to her husband. And on the floor in front of the fire, Antonio and Carson, sprawled on their bellies, played chess while Emilio watched, teasing the other two. Home.

The second emotion — unadulterated fear — swallowed up the first. She stood outwardly calm, but vibrating inside as if she had been struck hard enough to knock her off her feet. And she hated herself for this new frailty. Were her aunt and uncle right about Señor Scully needing to be at Rancho Sandoval to protect her? Was her long gone cousin behind her kidnapping? But why? To gain what? Could anyone hate that deeply for years on end?

Dorritt looked up at Alandra and smiled.

"Come and sit beside me, *querida.*" Dorritt guessed how uneasy and off-kilter Alandra, almost a daughter to her, must feel. Long ago, she herself had been kidnapped too. Then she had broken with her own family and married Quinn, the half-breed frontiersmen, against their wishes.

Alandra sat down on the chair beside Dorritt and they listened to Quinn's sure, deep voice, reading Psalm Thirty-seven, Dorritt's favorite.

Dorritt became aware that Scully had followed Alandra and now lingered in the doorway. Alandra must have noticed him too, because Dorritt observed the young woman smoothing stray hair back from her face while she pointedly avoided looking toward the door. Dorritt hid a smile. Quinn ended the psalm and looked up.

Scully turned and let himself out. With an unaccustomed pang, Dorritt watched him go. Alandra was in danger and war had begun. Would they remain untouched if the war came near? Any of them? How would it all end? She reached for Quinn's hand. Silently she repeated: *The Lord knoweth the days of the upright: and their inheritance shall be forever. They shall not be ashamed in the evil time . . .*

The stench of stale sweat filled the small storehouse. Pistol in hand, Scully stood beside Quinn just inside the closed door. Every day for three days they'd brought water and food and questioned the renegade. They needed whatever he knew about why the kidnapping had happened. The prisoner, just a kid — bound hand and foot — glared at them in the murky light. Even though Scully knew very little Comanche, it was easy to follow the exchange just from the tight expressions and harsh sound of the voices.

The prisoner still bared his teeth like a cornered wolf. But his eyes looked exhausted, desperate. He was barely older than Carson.

It made Scully uncomfortable and he averted his eyes. The face of the señorita came to him — her terrified voice. No one would be allowed to hurt her again. His jaw firmed. This Comanche had been a fool to go against Quinn and those he protected.

Quinn stared at the prisoner and then asked another question. Scully looked up. This time the words appeared to hit the Comanche harder. The kid looked suddenly scared, as if he'd been gut-shot.

Quinn's mouth was a straight tight line. "I just told him — until he tells me what he knows about why Miss Alandra was taken, he's not getting out of here. I said I do not intend to kill him. So if he doesn't tell me what he knows, he will die of old age here. But if he tells me, I will believe him and set him free."

Scully knew that being locked up was worse than torture to a Comanche. He watched the kid struggle with his bonds and try to control his obvious panic.

Quinn stared at the kid and asked him another question. Then Quinn translated in an undertone, "I just asked him if he thought any of his friends would be coming to free him."

Scully nodded, his own gut tightening. That was enough to sober any living creature. To be shut up in this four-by-four cell for good. No way out. And no one coming to his rescue.

Quinn nodded to Scully and turned toward the door.

The Comanche spoke up, sounding desperate, as if the words were being dragged up from the deepest pit inside him. He glanced up at Quinn and then away and spoke some more, looking ashamed.

Scully understood the kid's reluctance to tell what he knew. But what did it matter? Scully was certain that his own shot had killed the leader of the renegades. Maybe this young brave had learned his lesson and would go back to his tribe and steer clear of Quinn.

The memory of the señorita's small hand on his arm for a few moments last night flowed through him. He shrugged his shoulders, as if that could relieve the tension the memory brought.

Quinn replied to the brave with another question. There was a long silence while the Comanche stared into Quinn's eyes and then nodded. Then Quinn said, "He's told me all he knows."

"You believe him?"

"Yes."

Scully looked at the Comanche and wondered how Quinn could be sure. "What do we do now?" he asked, rubbing his taut neck.

"We take him away from here and set him free."

It was what Scully had expected. Quinn always kept his word. But he sensed the incident wouldn't end here. This kidnapping was like a rock dropped in water, rippling, disrupting their peace.

Uneasiness tugged at Scully. He ignored it. Or tried to.

Beside Quinn, Scully rode several miles to the west of Quinn's rancho. The renegade, still bound by the wrists, sat behind Scully. Finally, Quinn pulled up and said, "We'll let him go here." He said something to the prisoner that sounded like a warning, then the brave slid from Scully's horse.

Quinn tossed an old knife far past the Indian. As the kid ran to retrieve it, Quinn shouted something. Then he turned his horse and galloped away.

Spurring his horse, Scully caught up with Quinn and they rode together, the wind blowing around him, evaporating his sweat. When they were out of the sight of the Comanche, Scully couldn't stop himself from asking, "What did you say to him?"

"I told him you or I would kill him on sight if we ever saw him again on our land or Alandra's."

Scully nodded. He didn't ask what the Comanche had finally revealed about the señorita's kidnapping. Just waited.

They had nearly reached the rancho when Quinn slowed his horse. Scully fell in closer beside him. "The brave told me that a Mexican paid the renegades to steal Alandra," Quinn said.

48

"What Mexican? Not a Tejano?"

"Mexican. The brave said the man was older, had gray hair mixed with black. The Mexican gave them no name. Promised them horses and gunpowder. Said he wanted Alandra kidnapped and brought to him south of here."

Scully's heartbeat sped up. The señorita was still in danger. "South? Where exactly?"

Quinn calmed his horse, startled by a black-eared rabbit dashing in front of them. "This brave said he didn't know the exact location they were to meet the Mexican. All he was told was that it was just south of the Nueces River."

"Deeper into Mexico," Scully commented, gripping his saddle horn. The señorita's terrified expression came to him again, setting his teeth on edge. "You think it's that scoundrel, that cousin of Sandoval, who did this?"

"I have no way of knowing if it's the cousin, but I can't think of any other Mexican who would hate our Alandra enough to pay to have her kidnapped. And her cousin did kidnap me and Dorritt all those years ago."

This was news to Scully. Mendoza must be quite a crafty snake to have kidnapped Quinn. A foolhardy one to boot. "You think this Mexican is still using the same trick, then?"

Quinn frowned. "I don't know. But I still can't see what he'd gain by kidnapping Alandra now. He wouldn't gain her property. As soon as she turned eighteen, my guardianship ended and she inherited Rancho Sandoval. She immediately made out a will. She didn't want any shirttail relation to gain her inheritance."

"I didn't think she had any relations," Scully couldn't stop himself from saying. *Her family is no business of mine.*

"Her parents broke with family in Mexico City. Her mother was a mestiza, and Alandra's father's pure Spanish Creole family refused to accept the marriage."

Quinn emphasized the word "pure," showing disapproval of such pridefulness. So the señorita's mother had been part Indian. But then so was Ash and Quinn. Squinting in the glaring sunlight, Scully pondered the fact that he'd been taught to look down on half-breeds. Yet who could look down at a man like Quinn?

Quinn went on, "If Eduardo Mendoza is behind this kidnapping, his hatred of Alandra would be the only cause I can come up with. Unless . . ." He halted and frowned darkly. "Unless he thought he could force her to marry him."

Scully froze. "Force her? How?"

Quinn just looked at him. And Scully answered his own question. The cousin could force himself on Alandra and carry her off to Mexico City. If a man was evil enough, he just took what he wanted. Scully fumed.

Quinn cleared his throat. "I've waited to give you a chance to think this all over. But when Alandra goes home, I need you to go to Rancho Sandoval with her." He stared into Scully's eyes.

Scully didn't turn away. He didn't want to refuse, but he didn't want to go. Both carried equal weight with him. He voiced the first objection that came to mind. "I'd be the only Anglo there. Ramirez, her foreman, speaks English like the señorita, but hardly anybody else does."

"You work along with the other vaqueros here fine."

"I picked up what I needed from them."

"I think you've learned to understand Spanish, you just don't talk it much. You can learn to, if you needed to."

Scully's horse, restless from the slow pace, needed some quieting, so he stroked its neck and made soothing sounds. Then he realized that he was just as restless. He wanted to do what Quinn asked; he'd been doing that for years. But leaving Quinn's rancho stuck in his craw. He liked working for Quinn, as fair and honest a man as could be found, and the ranch was so well run.

Quinn took off his leather hat, wiped his brow, then settled the hat back. "Since you hired on with me in '26, you've gone from a greenhorn with cattle to my top hand. I've been planning that when Ash wants to retire, you'd take over here as foreman."

Scully's face burned and he couldn't stop it. To have a man like Quinn want him as foreman was more than he'd ever imagined. He looked away.

"But that's a ways off. And Ash might outlive us both. A man never knows what will come with each new day. That much I've learned in life."

Scully nodded solemnly. *Too true. A man is as grass that withereth.*

"I'll have to think through and talk over what I've learned with my wife. But will you go to Rancho Sandoval? Especially now when there could be more danger? Just until we find out who wants to harm Alandra."

Scully noticed again that Quinn always respected his wife's counsel and didn't mind others knowing it. Leaving Quinn's rancho would be hard. He didn't owe Quinn anything more than a day's work for a day's pay, but this place was special, as close to a home as he'd had since his second ma died. One of those sudden flashes from long ago raced through him. It was dark and he was all alone — He blotted out the memory.

"Come on," Quinn urged, shifting in his saddle. "Let's get home. And you'll eat at the main house again tonight."

Scully gave Quinn a questioning look. But he did not ask why he'd been invited to eat in the main house again. He didn't look forward to sitting beside the proud señorita once more. But Quinn always had a good reason for whatever he did.

Scully rode the rest of the way in silence. The image of the señorita with the Comanche blade to her skin stirred him, riled him. Who wanted her out of the way and why?

That night after everyone had gone to bed, Alandra stared out the window of her old room, unable to relax. A lone candle flickered within glass in a wall sconce. She wondered how she could refuse to take Scully to her rancho. She didn't want to offend Dorritt or Quinn. Until her brother's death, when she was seven, these two had lived with her at Rancho Sandoval. Then when Quinn had finished building this

53

house, they'd moved here, bringing her with them. Quinn and Ash, with Ramirez, had run the two ranchos as one from here. Alandra rubbed her tight forehead. It was beginning to ache.

The night was quiet. Voices singing an old song and the sound of a guitar wafted from the vaqueros' house behind the hacienda, near the barn. Señor Scully came to mind once more, unbidden. She began pacing barefoot. At dinner tonight he had barely looked at her, much less spoken to her. His presence, however, had made her more sensitive to everything. And try as she did, she could not ignore the man. She paced to the door and back.

Then it occurred to her that since she'd arrived here three days ago, she had not once ventured farther outside than the wide front porch. She halted, staring outside into the night. *I have been acting afraid.* This realization shamed her and moved her to action. *I cannot let the fear win.* But her pulse raced as she put on her shoes and tugged her rebozo down from the peg by the door. Then she hurried through the quiet darkened house, slipped out the front door and down the front porch steps.

Just before her foot touched earth, her heart actually lurched. Then she was running, the terror suddenly goading, driving her, mindless. With a jolt, she bumped against the rail of the empty corral. This stopped her. Panting, she gripped the rough railing as if she were drowning.

She forced her eyes to stay open and made herself breathe in and out evenly. Her pulse slowed bit by bit till it was normal again. Still she clung to the railing.

A flicker of movement caught her eye. A man was standing in the darkness, watching her. Panic clawed her. She nearly cried out. Then she noted how tall the man was and the moonlight glinting on a gold ring on his little finger. Señor Scully. Relief weakened her knees. And a moment later her irritation sparked.

"You need anything, miss?" he asked in his low voice. "Somebody scare you?"

*Yes, the man whom you shot three nights ago.* She clenched her hands. "I am fine," she lied. "I was merely in the need of some fresh air, señor."

"Yes, miss."

*I do not want you, señor, at Rancho Sandoval. I do not want to believe the war will come to my home. I do not want to believe that I need protection, and not from you.* The final truth disturbed her more now than the others. *"Buenos noches."* She forced herself to release the railing and walked back toward the house. Feeling his gaze upon her the whole way, she made her decision.

And it was not an either or solution. She need not go against Dorritt and Quinn. And she need not have Señor Scully at her home. She would merely remain here a little longer. In time, when her aunt and uncle calmed down, she would return home. Then Ramirez and her vaqueros could and would protect her ably. The war that had come to San Antonio de Bexar would not come to Rancho Sandoval, a day's ride south. A fresh confidence made her steps quick and sure.

She marched inside and headed directly to Quinn and Dorritt's bedroom. She'd raised her hand to knock when she heard Dorritt speaking her name: "Alandra is not one who likes to explain things, such as where she's going and when she'll be back."

"I know," Quinn said, his reply muffled by the door, "but Scully must know where Alandra is whenever she leaves the walls of her casa."

"But when Alandra was kidnapped, she was in her bed," Dorritt objected. "Are you sure Scully can protect her? Maybe she should stay here with us?"

Quinn answered, "You're right. That

might be best."

Though the same idea had been in her mind, hearing Dorritt say she should stay sparked Alandra's temper. She bristled. *Do they think I am a little girl still?*

Quinn continued, "If she won't stay, Scully will just have to guard Alandra's window at night."

*After he hears my prayers and tucks me into bed?* Again Alandra was about to knock, and again she stopped herself. A fresh round of terror washed over her. The Comanche grabbing her, mauling her. *Stop, please stop.* She pressed both hands against the door frame, holding all her anguish inside and silent.

Dios mio, *help me.* She wiped tears away with her fingertips, drawing in breath to gain control and clarity. The kidnapping had changed her. It had not weakened her, but it did make her starkly aware that someone wanted to harm her. This was real; she could not deny it.

Her way opened before her. She could not stay here like a little girl, giving into fear. But neither could she be foolhardy. Inhaling deeply again, she finally knocked on the door.

There was a pause and rustling inside. "Who is it?" Quinn asked.

"Alandra."

The door opened after a moment, and she saw Quinn in his buckskin breeches and Dorritt in a white cotton nightgown. The sight of them together in such an intimate setting left her feeling strangely bereft. "I'll go home tomorrow and will take Señor Scully with me."

The two of them stared at her, then exchanged glances. Dorritt came and put her arms around Alandra. "I'm sorry this has happened."

*I am also, dear Tía Dorritt.* She kissed her aunt's cheek and turned to go to her room.

"I'm glad you're taking Scully," Quinn added, touching her shoulder as she left.

She didn't turn back; she just bid them a brief good-night. Scully would come to Rancho Sandoval. But she was the *dueña* there, the lady, and he was the cowboy. And if he tried to start running her ranch, she'd make that unmistakably clear to him.

An unaccountable blush warmed her face.

Oh, when would she be free of peril and his protection? When would her life return to normal?

Late the next afternoon, as they approached Rancho Sandoval, Scully rode stiffly beside the señorita. Behind them rode the vaqueros

58

who had helped in her rescue.

She glanced sideways at him. "We will have to talk over with Ramirez why you have come home with me."

"I can handle that," he said.

The señorita's eyes flashed. But before she could snap out a reply, her eyes widened at the sight of people pouring out of the hacienda, barn, *corrales,* and jacales — all waving and calling.

Within minutes the rest of the Sandoval vaqueros — shouting and waving their sombreros — galloped out and surrounded Scully and Alandra. They escorted the two of them to the casa. When Alandra dismounted, she was enveloped by her people.

Scully watched the hubbub. Spanish flowed from everyone in that fast string that blended all their words together. He remembered something he'd heard in the cantina in San Antonio de Bexar — an Anglo had joked that Tejanos never seemed to be in a hurry until they opened their mouths. Obviously the man had never seen a vaquero in action.

Then the señorita turned and motioned toward him. "Señor Scully has come to improve his Spanish, so we must all help him by only letting him speak *español.*" The señorita slanted a taunting look at him and then repeated this in Spanish, grinning as if telling a joke on him.

Scully slid from his saddle, not amused.

Ramirez approached the señorita. "Does Señor Quinn believe that our *doña* is still in danger?" The people around the señorita looked worried.

"Yes, he does," Scully said.

"Stop," the señorita ordered him. "I do not want to discuss this here and now."

Ignoring her, he looked around. The eyes turned to his were all worried. His jaw hardened. He'd come for one reason — to protect the señorita. And he couldn't be bothered trying to speak only Spanish now. This was too pressing for games. "Ramirez, will you tell the people that —"

"I am the *doña* here," Alandra objected, radiating displeasure. "I can and will tell my people what I want them to know."

Scully grimaced and touched his hat brim to show a measure of courtesy. But there was more at stake here than who was in charge. "Yes, miss, this is your rancho. But I need everyone to know that they should keep their eyes open in case they see anything unusual or anything that doesn't look right."

The señorita stared at him for a moment and then repeated his words in Spanish. The worry on the faces still turned to him deepened.

"Have any of them seen any strangers anywhere nearby?" Scully continued, hooking his thumbs into his belt.

The lady translated this and was answered with blank stares.

*No help here.* Scully frowned. "Miss Alandra and Ramirez, we need to talk. And then I want to take a ride around your land to see if I can find anything out of the ordinary, any sign that anyone has been trespassing. Anything that looks suspicious."

The señorita spoke to her people. Then, with a swish of her skirt, she led Scully and Ramirez through the door into the interior courtyard of the house. Soon they were seated at a black wrought-iron table beside an interior spring and its stone fountain. Nearby, a rounded clay fireplace sat in the midst of the courtyard, radiating warmth.

Scully had been here before but never sat amidst the green palms around the stone fountain. This restful and gracious setting didn't jibe with a violent kidnapping and its unknown motives.

Ramirez was older than Scully, shorter and more compact. A good foreman, Scully knew, he had been trained by Ash and Quinn to take over here when the señorita came of age and took control of her inheritance, Ramirez was a man he knew he could work with.

"What does Señor Quinn say about this bad business?" Ramirez asked as he accepted a cup of coffee from the housekeeper.

Scully sipped his own strong black coffee, letting the señorita explain in rapid Spanish why he had come with her. Quinn was right. He could understand Spanish.

Then Ramirez turned to him. "So am I to go on running the ranch, but you come to protect our *doña?*"

Scully nodded, edging forward. "I need you to pick out men to take turns guarding her window at night."

"I had already planned that," Ramirez replied.

"You had?" The señorita sounded surprised.

Scully ignored her comment. "I want at least one man with me to ride around the rancho and see if I find anything suspicious."

"What do you mean?" Alandra demanded. "I thought you came to protect me."

"I did. But part of my protecting you is finding possible evidence of anything that is out of the ordinary hereabouts. I know your land, and Quinn taught me how to track. I will leave a plan of where I'm going so a man can be sent to bring me back at the first sign of danger. If you stay here in your casa and the yard, your vaqueros can defend you. Every man must be armed and ready for anything, Ramirez."

The señorita didn't look happy but she said no more. Scully repeated his request for someone to go with him.

Ramirez considered this. "My son. Emilio is young but a good shot."

Carson Quinn's friend. What he'd seen of the young Ramirez had been favorable. He'd come with them today.

"Good." Scully rose. "We'll need some supplies for a couple days." He turned to Alandra. "Do you have a map of the rancho?"

"Sí, in my office." She rose too.

"Let's go see it, then." His tone left no room for argument.

Alandra fumed at his high-handed ways. But she couldn't deny the fear that still nagged at her stomach. She wavered a bit as she got up.

"Are you all right?" he asked, touching her sleeve.

She tugged free. "I am fine." And she did not want to make a scene in front of Ramirez, who stood waiting for her to dismiss him. She lifted her chin said, "That will be all, Ramirez. *Gracias.* Please do as Señor Scully has asked."

Ramirez bowed and left her.

She led Scully to her office on the far side of the courtyard. She spread out the map of her nearly seven thousand acres on her desk. It took him only a few moments to point out where he would be going. Then he moved to the door. "I can count on you not to stray far from the house, then?"

Coming home had moved her, made her more serious; she murmured in reply, *"Por supesto."* Of course.

He stood there eyeing her, then nodded. "I'll be back within two days or less. Stay safe," he said, and left.

So brief. So Anglo. On the ride here, he had spoken less than ten words to her. Did it hurt his tongue to speak?

When she heard him close the front doors behind him, she wandered out into the courtyard to the nearest wall. She pressed her forehead against the cool rough adobe, something she had done even as a child. Her brother had always told her that their parents' love had built these walls and that she could feel it if she pressed her hands against it.

This hacienda, this land were all that

survived of the parents she had no memory of and the late brother she had adored and who had adored her. Home again. She had been gone less than a week, but the exhausting, frightening time away felt so much longer, a century at least.

When her housekeeper and maids had rushed out to embrace her, joy beyond words had bubbled up within like a spring of fresh sweet water. Now the sound of the fountain's water and the greenery of the courtyard soothed her. *En casa.*

Then her peace was shattered — the memory of rough hands on her skin, dragging her out her window, touching her. . . . *Stop! I am not afraid.* She sucked in air. That was still a lie, but she had to fight the paralyzing dread with her every thought.

Alandra walked through the hacienda then, room by room, until she came to her bedroom. This was where it had happened, where her peace had been torn apart. She forced herself into the room, lay down upon her high bed and stared at the ceiling.

Fiery then icy waves of panic washed over her again and again. She clenched her whole body to end the trembling that made the bed beneath her creak. She did not win completely. But she did not give in and bolt.

Dios mío, *why have you let this evil come*

*upon me?*

Quinn's voice answered her: *Wait on the Lord, and keep his way, and he shall exalt thee to inherit the land: when the wicked are cut off, thou shalt see it.*

*But I have such* miedo, *Father. Take this fear from me.*

# THREE

Hours after Scully had left, Alandra was just finishing her evening meal. Her housekeeper Maria was keeping her company when the shout came, *"Forasteros!"*

Strangers? Who could be coming? She rose and went outside to see.

The dusty black carriage with two outriders was unfamiliar. and heading straight for Alandra. The arrival of a carriage was infrequent enough to stop everyone at Rancho Sandoval in the midst of what they were doing. All her people were coming out of their jacales, the barn, and the hacienda. And after the kidnapping, this strange carriage approaching and heading straight for Alandra unnerved her.

She clasped her hands in front of her, afraid they might shake and give her away. Maybe it was merely strangers passing through, stopping for water or directions. With her casa behind her and her people gathered around, Alandra stood her ground, holding herself straight and strong.

The carriage halted just feet from her. A man dressed as a servant of a wealthy family, sitting beside the driver, jumped down, opened the door, and dropped the carriage steps. A young Spanish-looking, well-dressed gentleman who looked to be in his mid-twenties stepped down and then held out his hand for a young lady. When she had alighted, an older gentleman appeared and descended.

All three stared at her. The young gentleman sported a neat mustache on a face that looked permanently peeved. The older gentleman resembled the younger, but was not as slim or tall. The lady was dressed all in black and wore a mourning veil that concealed her face. A widow perhaps.

"Welcome to Rancho Sandoval," Alandra said, her voice fainter than she wished. And her body rippled with a silent warning through every nerve. "What brings you to *mi casa?*"

"Are you Alandra Maria Ynez Sandoval?"

The older gentleman had spoken, and his question disconcerted her. How did he know her full name? She studied them again. Though they looked a bit travel worn, their clothing and carriage spoke of affluence. But that was never a guarantee of character, Tía Dorritt had taught her. "I am." She stared straight into his eyes. "Have you a message for me?" Sometimes private individuals carried messages north from Mexico City. "Who are you?"

The older gentleman moved forward, his arms open wide. "I am your uncle Benito Ignacio Sandoval, the brother of your father." He tried to embrace her.

Alandra stepped back, pushing him away with both hands. His words repeated themselves in her mind. *My father's brother?* She took another step back. Memories of her brother and what he had told her about their parents' forbidden love flooded her with aversion. "Why have you come?"

"Cousin," the younger gentleman scolded, stepping forward, "We are in the wilderness, but where are your manners?"

"And where is your proof that you are who you say you are?" she snapped, taking an instant dislike to him. And another step back. "I do not know you." *I do not care to know you.*

The younger man halted and looked to her left. She followed his gaze to see that Ramirez, with rifle in hand, had come to stand beside her. Following Ramirez's gaze, she looked around. All her vaqueros, each armed, had surrounded the carriage. And they looked dangerous. She said a silent *gracias*.

The young gentleman flushed. "This is not the way to welcome guests to your home."

"You are strangers and in the wilderness," she said, copying his phrasing, "and this is the way we welcome strangers. Now if you are family, you must be able to convince me of that." *And convince me why I should welcome a visit from you.*

"Must we do that out here in the wind?" the lady asked, speaking for the first time. Her voice was quiet and controlled.

Alandra considered the request. The sun was very low, the wind brisk, and it was February. Sitting down was an appealing notion. She glanced at Ramirez. "You will come into the courtyard with me and bring three vaqueros with you."

Then she turned to the strangers. "You may come into the courtyard, but your men must stay out here with the carriage. And my vaqueros will make sure of that."

Alandra did not wait for a reply, but turned and strode into the courtyard just inside her front doors. Ramirez barked a few terse commands and followed her. That they had only the two drivers and two outriders gave her something more to think about. If they had come all the way from Mexico City, how had they traveled through Mescalero and Comanche territory with only four men? Had they left more men somewhere nearby?

The three strangers entered and looked around the courtyard, which many had called lovely, an oasis of palms and lush pink and red azaleas, as well as aloe and yucca plants, in the arid country south of San Antonio. A clay fireplace warmed the courtyard. And Alandra did not want to take the strangers into her casa.

She motioned to her housekeeper to bring refreshments, and sat on one of the black wrought-iron chairs around a matching table, facing the front door. Ramirez stood behind her, and the vaqueros stationed themselves around the courtyard, their rifles resting in their arms.

"Please be seated," Alandra invited. Her tone was neutral and she faced them squarely. Their claim of family was questionable. But what did it matter if they were her relatives or not? They had no power over her. And she was protected, though she wished that Scully were there, a sentiment she wanted to ignore. She didn't like feeling as if she needed his protection.

The three moved toward the chairs near hers, glancing repeatedly at the armed guards. "Before I sit," the young man said, "allow me to introduce myself. I am your cousin Fernando Juan Adolfo Sandoval, the son of Benito." He gestured toward the other man and then the lady. "And this is a cousin from my mother's side, a recent widow, Señora Isabella Maria Pilar Esteban. She has come to act as your chaperone."

Wondering why she needed a chaperone in her own home, Alandra nodded her greeting and motioned again for them to be seated. The housekeeper and two maids brought in pitchers of water, basins, and white linen towels for the guests to wash their hands. After that was accomplished, the servants returned with fresh coffee, warm tortillas, and green chilies.

All through this, Alandra watched the three. The lady swept back her veil, and Alandra saw that she was young to already be widowed. Meanwhile, Alandra did not appreciate how the eyes of all three roamed over her home, not in simple appreciation, but with the look of a buyer appraising a purchase.

She spoke up, looking toward the one who said he was her uncle, "Señor, please explain our relationship and why you have come all this way." Then she lifted her coffee cup and watched him over its rim.

The older gentleman did not look happy at her giving him an order, but once again his eyes moved from rifle to rifle. "As I said, I am Benito Sandoval, your father's brother."

She gave him the shadow of a mocking smile. "Then why would you expect a warm welcome from me? If you are indeed my uncle, you must be aware that my father's family broke their connection when he married my mother."

"Blood ties cannot be broken, and the dispute over your mother's mixed blood is all in the past. That took place when we were all still under the Spanish crown, not independent Mexicans."

Alandra did not know why the change in government in Mexico City should have anything to do with the fact that her grandparents had disowned their son because he — a Mexican of pureblood Spanish blood and called a Creole — had married a mestiza. In Mexico, the social classes followed bloodlines, the more pure Spanish blood a person had, the higher their status. She herself was a mestiza because of her mother's mixed blood. But to call her that to her face was considered an insult. So this man's explanation of why she was acceptable now made no sense, but she let this pass and sipped her hot sweet coffee. They would be gone soon enough.

Since there were no inns between San Antonio, the town Anglos called simply Bexar north of her and Laredo far south on the Rio Grande, she had entertained travelers on their way between Mexico to San Antonio before. She did not have to like these people to shelter them for a night in her home. "So what has brought you this far north?" she asked.

After pressing the white linen napkin to his lips in a fastidious way, the older man replied, "We have business to conduct in San Antonio de Bexar."

"Bexar is only a day's ride north," she said. Indeed, considering the lateness of their arrival, she would be expected to entertain them at least one night.

Her cousin Fernando nodded in an overly gracious manner and smiled. "When we mentioned Rancho Sandoval on the way here, we were told that it was one of the finest haciendas in all of Texas. And I see that we were not misled."

Alandra copied the man's nod. "My parents loved this place." She looked around

74

and smiled.

"We heard that they had passed away —" Benito paused to cross himself. "— and that your brother was prospering on this land. But that he died young."

Alandra was feeling her fatigue now. This stilted polite talk with people she wished would disappear was as tiring as riding hard. She should not have sat down until she reached her room for the night. "I am afraid that I have passed an exhausting few days, and I am too tired to entertain you as I would like." She would make an attempt to hurry them on. "Perhaps you should proceed to San Antonio and then stop for a visit on your way home?"

The widow shuddered. "Oh, please, señorita, I must rest from the journey. How can you be so cold as to send your family away in the chill evening?"

"We could not reach the city before dark," her cousin Fernando said stiffly.

Alandra sighed. "I take it that you will stay the night, then?"

"That is most gracious of you, cousin," her uncle Benito said sardonically.

Her lips pressed together, Alandra waved her hand and her maids came out. "Please see that the guest rooms are ready. We will be retiring soon."

The housekeeper and maids hurried to the guest wing of the house. Her uncle went to the door where his servant waited and asked him to bring in their luggage. The sight of a trunk and several valises dismayed Alandra. But she said nothing. It was obvious that her relatives wore a great deal of their wealth on their backs, so she should not have been surprised at the amount they needed to take with them on a journey.

When her housekeeper returned, Alandra rose to escort her guests to their rooms in the wing on the opposite side of the courtyard. There, she ordered two vaqueros to stand guard at the doors of the two rooms. This visibly stung both men. But she was not going to let three strangers roam over her house, filled with silver and gold ornaments and costly tapestries.

Both Benito and Fernando glared at her. Benito growled, "We will not submit to having guards at the doors of our bedrooms. We are guests, your family, not common criminals."

Alandra had already considered this objection. But she would not have these strangers prowling through her house while she slept. "You have not convinced me that we are related." They started to object and she raised a hand. She did not have the energy

76

for a skirmish. "I have another reason for exercising caution. Earlier this week I was kidnapped by Comanches."

Isabella gasped. The father and son exchanged horrified glances. "Señorita, you have been compromised," Isabella whispered.

Alandra flushed. She held her anger on a tight rein and forced herself to say with disdain, "Your attitude shows that you do not understand living in Texas. Tío Quinn," she said, emphasizing the only family tie she did acknowledge, "rescued me in less than a day and brought me safely home."

"But if people find out," Isabella said, still looking and sounding aghast, "your reputation would be ruined."

Bristling at this insult, Alandra glared at the woman. "My reputation is my business. If I say nothing happened to 'compromise' me, the ranchers around will believe me. The only reason I have brought this up is that having been kidnapped just a few days before you appeared on my land has made me suspicious of strangers. You understand then why I must be cautious."

"No, I don't understand," Fernando said vehemently. "What do Comanches have to do with us?"

"Because a captured Comanche said that

a Mexican with gray hair" — Alandra glanced at Benito's graying hair — "had promised them guns and powder if they kidnapped me and delivered me south of the Nueces River."

"And you are accusing me of doing that?" Benito demanded, his face flushing in anger.

"No," Alandra said coolly, "I am merely explaining why I am very cautious about strangers —"

"We are your family," Fernando insisted.

"You are strangers. You have shown me no proof of relationship. So if being guarded is unpalatable to you, you may leave. If you stay, you will suffer a guard at your door and window. The choice is yours." She stared at them, waiting for their decision. She knew what it would be. But she wished, so wished, that they would instead leave in a huff.

After a brief staring contest, the three of them turned and entered the two guest rooms, Isabella to one and the men to the other.

*"Buenos noches,"* Alandra bid them. None of them returned her farewell, but shut the doors in the faces of the guards.

Alandra was drained, flattened. After instructing Ramirez, who had followed her to post guards on her door and windows too, she turned toward her own bedroom on the other side of the darkened casa. And behind her, at her own request, walked her own guard. She could hardly believe that in her own home she couldn't feel safe without an armed guard at both her door and window. She had thought she would feel better, safer, coming home. But to the threat of further danger from a mysterious Mexican with gray hair was now added peril and uncertainty from inside her own hacienda.

She bid the guard a polite good-night, went into her room and closed the door behind her. She walked to the window and opening the shutters slightly glanced outside. Her guard there touched his hat brim in deference to her. She nodded her thanks and pulled the shutters tight against the cool night air. Though she wondered if she would get any sleep, she let her maid come in and help her dress for the night.

When the girl left, Alandra sat on the side of her bed, listening to the sounds of the night. In equal amounts, fatigue and a nervous restlessness tugged at her. Though feeling exhausted, she could not lie down and rest. Instead, she rose and, barefoot, paced the cool tiled floor.

Why had Scully gone scouting around when new trouble might have come right to her front door? But though she wished that he were there, she decided against sending for him. Her vaqueros were sufficient to protect her. And what could he do that they could not? Still, she longed for someone to back her up. Though she felt this was a weakness, she couldn't deny it.

The next morning, Alandra found the three visitors already at the breakfast table overlooking the courtyard. She longed for the coming spring and the warm days of taking breakfast in the courtyard. Maria, the housekeeper, poured her coffee as Alandra helped herself to the covered plates on the sideboard and then sat at the head of the table. "I hope that you passed a quiet restful night."

Fernando pulled back his lips in a dismal attempt at a smile. "Except for the guards at the window and door, our night passed comfortably."

Alandra merely nodded and began eating.

"I do not know how you bear living in a place where savages still roam free," the lady said with a shudder.

"Usually the Comanches do not bother me or my nearest neighbors, the Quinns. These were renegades, and my friends came after me and brought me home." Alandra shrugged.

Benito smiled in a way that made her even more cautious than she already was. "We are hoping that you will show us around your prosperous ranch today."

Alandra paused, her fork suspended in midair. "Really? I thought you were on your way to San Antonio to take care of some business. I do not want to keep you."

"We have been traveling for over a week, *mi prima*," Fernando replied. "We are much fatigued and wish to rest a day. And as my father said, we would like to tour your rancho."

Alandra eyed them. Something was going on here beyond what was being stated. If they thought they were being subtle and putting her at ease, they were quite mistaken. All her inner alarm bells were ringing in warning.

She nodded. "If you wish to stay another day, of course, you may. As long as you realize that you will be accompanied wherever you go and will be guarded at night."

Benito shook his head at the other two, who smiled as if she were amusingly eccentric. "As you wish," her uncle agreed.

She concentrated on eating breakfast. And since she added nothing to the conversation other than assent or dissent, they soon rose

from the table. "With your permission —"
Fernando bowed to her with blatant mockery. "— we will go outside and take a look at your fine horses."

Alandra nodded. Two of her vaqueros stood at the door, waited for the Mexicans to pass them, then followed the three out through the courtyard. Alandra sipped her strong sweet coffee and nibbled at her eggs with green chilies. Her so-called relatives mocked her even as they tried to impress her. And with his pomaded hair and starched white neck cloth, Fernando had branded himself as a dandy. She disdained men who wanted to be "pretty."

Ramirez appeared at the door. She nodded to him to enter.

"Señorita, I have been waiting to speak to you since dawn." He kept his voice low, as if not wanting to be overheard.

Alandra's uneasiness surged. She waved him to come and sit beside her at the table. He did so, holding his hat in front of him and leaning close to her. "Señorita, the guards I posted at the door of the caballeros speak English as well as Spanish. I thought these strangers might speak in English, thinking that none of us speak it. So I told the vaqueros to listen at the door and window to hear if they could discover anything about why they have come here. And why now, right after you had been kidnapped."

Alandra stared at Ramirez.

He looked stricken and began to apologize, "I am sorry if I did wrong —"

"What did they hear?"

Ramirez's expression became set and grim. "The two talked about what they planned to do when this rancho was theirs."

Alandra's mouth opened as she looked at Ramirez. How could these strangers take her land? Suddenly she could not sit still. She swept out the front door toward the *corrale*. Ramirez followed her at a trot. When she reached the *corrale* fence, she turned to him.

"What do you want me to do, señorita?" her foreman asked, looking troubled.

She did not want to admit that she had no clear plan. Her shock still simmered. "How can I know if these people are really my relatives from Mexico City?"

Ramirez shrugged.

She stared at the paddock where a vaquero was training a colt. Unless these three planned to murder her and inherit the rancho, they must have some other way to gain the property, some document or legality she did not know about — yet. She realized then that while Ramirez could run the day-to-day operation of the cattle ranch for her, he could be no help in a legal dispute. So she made the only request she could think of for real help, more than even Scully could give. "Please send someone to the Quinns' rancho to tell them what has happened here. Ask them to come here and help me."

Ramirez nodded and hurried away. Alandra leaned against the fence, watching the vaquero teach the colt to accept a halter. She longed for Scully to return soon. Why had she let him leave her to scout her property? Part of her irritation with him was not his fault. She did not like having to ask for help. A young woman running a rancho by herself with only a foreman to help was unheard of. No one in San Antonio had believed a woman planned to run her rancho herself.

Dorritt and Quinn had never made her feel less competent because she was a female. But she knew they were the exception rather than the rule. And though Señor Scully, an Anglo, was not happy to have come to protect her, he had never shown disdain for her. Again, an exception.

Even her own people, Tejanos who lived nearby, were guilty of discounting her ability to run this rancho without a man. When she'd turned fifteen and became old enough to enter San Antonio society, the fact that she intended to run the rancho herself had been dismissed as immature and improbable by both Tejano and Anglo males. The women had been no better.

She had resisted them as the colt was now resisting the vaquero who flicked his whip and spoke sternly to the horse. Many worthy San Antonio señoras had tried to match her with eligible bachelors capable of running Rancho Sandoval. Many suitors had traveled from as far away as Santa Fe. But she had been raised by Dorritt Quinn, who taught her that she was capable of anything if she worked hard enough.

The colt tried to pull away from the vaquero, veering toward her. Just as she had eluded all the offers of marriage. She wanted to be the *dueña,* the *doña* of Rancho Sandoval, for several years to show them all she could handle her inheritance. And then when she chose to marry, she would marry for love, as her parents had, marry a man who respected her as Quinn respected Dorritt. She had decided years ago she would marry without consideration of making a good "match."

The vaquero smiled as the horse whickered near Alandra, seeking her attention, trying to evade the lesson. She stroked the colt's black nose and murmured to him.

She wondered again about the two events in less than a week that had destroyed her peace and put her in jeopardy. Could these people, professing to be her relatives, really be behind her kidnapping? Did that make sense? If so, why?

She scolded the colt and ordered him to obey the vaquero, who led him back to the center of the paddock. After the colt tried many more maneuvers to escape, the vaquero succeeded in getting it to wear the halter. Smiling, Alandra turned toward the hacienda she loved.

This vague threat against her and her land might prove to be more dangerous, more desperate, than being carried away by Comanche renegades. For years the wicked had just been a word in the Bible and the distant memory of her cousin. Now, over the past week, she'd begun to understand what wicked and evil truly were.

"Señorita."

"Miss Alandra."

The two voices roused Alandra in her bedroom, sitting in the chair by the window where she'd finally dozed off. A day spent trying to smile at her oh-so-proud-and-elegant relatives and at the same time discover why they had come had exhausted her. She sat up and blinked. Who had called? More danger?

She rose and opened the shutters. She looked out into the chilly night lit by the bright nearly full moon. She saw Emilio Ramirez and his father. And then she glimpsed a tall form. "Señor Scully?" she whispered.

Heartfelt relief swirled through her, very similar to the relief she'd felt when she heard Quinn's voice in the renegade camp. She was not standing alone against this new danger. She could not stop herself from saying, "Thank God, you have come."

"Ramirez here thought we should wake you at your window and not take the chance of anyone knowing I'm back till you want it known."

"I did not expect you to return till tomorrow."

"Emilio's horse came up lame so we turned back early. What's this about strangers coming saying they're family? And why didn't you call us back early?" Señor Scully asked.

Alandra decided not to take offense at his questioning her. Ignoring it, she shuddered, pulling her wool rebozo around her against the cool air coming in through the open window. "Meet me in the courtyard," she said. She hurried to slip on her sandals and then crept out her door and through the hallways.

Scully was waiting for her, standing in the moonlight.

She waved him to a chair near the clay stove, where she stirred the embers to flame. She then sat down across from him, leaning forward with her elbows on her knees. She plunged into her explanation but kept her voice low. She did not want to be overheard. "These *strangers* came the day you left, and Ramirez says they want to take my land." Each phrase she spoke made her spirits drop. Scully said nothing, merely took off his hat.

She gazed at the moonlight highlighting his reddish blond hair. What would he say?

"How do you want this handled, miss?"

Alandra imagined tomorrow morning, Scully with rifle raised, ordering the three strangers off her land. But if they had some legal way to take what was hers, it was not that easy. This problem could not be settled with force, as the Comanches had been. "I will have to find out how they think they can take my land. And if they are who they say they are."

"How will you do that?"

Ramirez came in, probably delayed by stabling the horses. He took off his hat and stood near them.

Alandra rubbed her taut forehead. Scully's questions irritated her. Yet she could not fault him for them. He was doing just what he must, getting the information he needed. And he was listening to her, not discounting her fears. Or treating her like a frail, weak woman. "They may know of some legal peculiarity. This war complicates everything, now that the Anglo rebels control San Antonio. I do not know if the Mexican government officials are still there or still able to act legally."

"Maybe I should let these strangers know you're not alone," Scully offered. "I'm here to protect you and your rancho. And added to Quinn and his lady, you have other powerful friends, the other Tejano landowners in Bexar. Maybe once these strangers realize that, they will give up and go home."

Even in the midst of this horrible conversation, it surprised Alandra to hear so many words pouring from Scully. He rarely said more than three words at a time. And the words he spoke were most welcome. "You must come in and stay in the house, Señor Scully. You will sleep in the room across from mine. And take your meals in the

89

house. Then you will take the measure of these strangers yourself."

Silence greeted her request. Finally, Scully asked, "Would that be proper?"

Irritation lashed her. "I do not want these strangers to deem you a hired hand and show you no respect. You must be seen as someone who can stand up to them."

"But I *am* just a hired hand."

His statement goaded her. "No, you are not. Quinn would not have sent 'just a hired hand' to protect me." Instinctively she sensed that Scully was more to the Quinns, perhaps more to her. She shut her mouth, letting this truth sink in. Was the *distante* vaquero Scully a friend to her too? Or was she just so afraid she'd turn to anyone?

Ramirez finally spoke up. "It is too bad that you have not a husband, señorita. They would not treat you with no *respeto* if you had a husband to fight for you."

The need for comfort nearly overwhelmed her. Scully was there in front of her, strong and male, a fighter. She nearly reached for his hands. No. She stiffened, pulling herself together. She looked to Ramirez. "Help him move into my late brother's room. Good night."

Scully rose. The men nodded politely, wishing her goodnight also.

Alandra went back into her room, closed the door and then the shutters. She fell into bed. Help had come. Just let them try to outfight and outfox both her and Scully. She pulled up the quilt and in a moment was asleep.

At the end of the midday meal in the courtyard, with gloomy clouds overhead, Scully sat silently beside Alandra. He stared at the three intruders. "Do I have to keep repeating myself? You have overstayed your welcome. Two nights free lodging is enough. Now the señorita doesn't want you here any longer. I can't put it plainer than that."

Alandra had tried the polite, subtle approach at breakfast but was met with evasion. The three had ignored every inquiry meant to move them back onto their journey. So she had asked Scully to tell them to leave.

"We have documents we can show you," Benito said finally, reluctantly, "if one of your servants would go out to the carriage and bring in the ornate box under the driver's seat?"

Documents? Wondering what they could have brought with them that might prove a family connection, Alandra nodded and one of the vaqueros left. She sipped more coffee and said nothing. *Documents.* Uncertainty rumbled back to life in her stomach. She pinched off a piece of a sweetmeat and nibbled it.

The vaquero returned with the box and gave it to Benito, who unlocked it with a key attached by a fine gold chain to his waistcoat. He opened it and drew out a sheaf of parchment. "This is the will that your father drew up before he left Mexico City with his mixed blood bride." He paused, looking into her eyes. "In it, you will find the reason that we are here." As he handed her the many-paged document, the man almost smirked.

Letting the insult to her mother pass, Alandra accepted the papers but did not bother to read them. "Tell me what the reason is and then I will read the document and see if I agree with your interpretation."

Benito, his son, and the señora exchanged obvious disgruntled glances. It was plain to see that they were not used to an independent female. Benito cleared his throat. "Very well." Though his look said that she was unladylike in the extreme, he began, "Your father's will states that if his male heir had no issue, then all his land and possessions would come to my son."

Alandra felt her mouth drop open. Shock

pierced her like a frozen arrow. "Are you mad? That is not Spanish or Mexican law. I am the daughter of Esteban Carlos Sandoval and his only surviving heir. English law favors male heirs, not Spanish law."

"You are correct," Benito said with a smug smile. "But this will alters the normal inheritance practice. Wills are written for that very purpose. Since your father was leaving Spanish society and moving far away, your grandfather allowed his son to make this disastrous marriage without family retaliation."

*Family retaliation.* The phrase was an ominous one, stirring crosscurrents in her. What had they threatened her parents with, beyond being disowned? And was this visit family retaliation?

Benito continued, "Your grandfather gave your father the money to buy this land and made your father agree then to bequeath it back to the Sandoval family if his male heir left no male heir to carry on the name of Sandoval. This land is to stay in the hands of a Sandoval." He paused to give her a pointed look. "And you, as a female heir, will change your name when you marry."

Though churning inside, Alandra brushed this nonsense aside with a wave of her hand. "Rancho Sandoval is mine. You are mad if you think you can come here and take my land, my inheritance, with this." She tossed the paper onto the table in front of her.

"There is no need for you to lose your inheritance," Benito said with an aggravating grin. "Fernando will marry you and the two of you will keep this rancho, these six thousand acres, in the Sandoval family."

"What?" Scully objected.

Sudden fury surged through Alandra so intense that it made her actually feel hot around her collar. She stood, and so did Scully. "I am the *dueña* here. A mere piece of paper cannot change that."

Señora Isabella shook her head in disapproval.

"Isn't that what my father just said?" Fernando snapped. "This mere piece of paper changes everything." As courtesy dictated, both men, though angry with her, had risen as she did. She felt Scully agitated, restraining himself.

But Fernando continued, "Do you think we would come here if we could not prove this in court in Mexico City? You, a mestiza, without social or governmental connections, expect to keep this land in spite of this will?"

His contemptuous expression infuriated her. And his using the word mestiza. No one had ever said that word to her face. She burned, hot waves coursing through her. He had nearly threatened aloud that he would make certain that the courts accepted this document. And there was nothing that she, an inferior, a half-breed, could do about it. Her hand itched to slap his sneering face.

"This sounds mighty convenient to me," Scully said in a rough voice.

Ignoring Scully, Fernando summarily dismissed her with a wave of his hand. "*Mi prima,* you have never even been to Mexico City. How far do you think you will get taking legal action against our family? You may be powerful here." He now glanced with disdain at Scully and the armed vaqueros near the door. "But you have no power where it counts. And be warned, since women rarely understand the legalities of any document, they rarely win in court."

The final insult that she would lose because she was a stupid woman nearly did her in. She clenched her jaw and for just a second imagined her vaqueros shooting all three of these intruders where they were. Of course, she would never do that. It was only her rage at this man's effrontery.

Scully cleared his throat. "Miss?"

Catching Scully's cautionary tone, she slapped a cap on her fury. *I must not show*

95

*emotion. It will only make this Fernando more sure that he can defeat me, a weak emotional female.* She inhaled deeply, sobering enough to respond with intelligence, not passion. She smiled at Scully. "*Gracias,* but I can handle this."

Picking up the parchment document again, she looked steadily into Benito's eyes. "I will study these. Until then, you will be where? The inn in San Antonio?"

Benito took a step closer to her. "Of course, you may read the will, but I must keep that document in sight until I lock it back in my box. And if you want us to go to San Antonio, we will. And there we will set this document before the magistrate immediately. We do not wish to go to court against a blood relative, but we will if we have to."

"Nice of you," Scully muttered. "Decent."

Alandra glared at Benito. She knew she could order them off her land, and Scully and the vaqueros would enforce it. But she was unsure of her legal ground. She must read the documents carefully and consider if they were legal, and if so, how to counter them. This was not just about her, but about every person who lived at Rancho Sandoval, some twenty families.

She sat down and began reading, ignoring

the three strangers. The document was long and involved, but it did indeed transfer her ranch to Benito's son if her father's male heir died childless. When she was done, she looked at the three of them, sitting across from her. And she wished, oh so much, that she could wipe the self-satisfied grins off the father and son. Glancing sideways, she glimpsed Scully's stony expression. The Anglo was not convinced either.

A thought occurred to her. "My father and brother have been dead many years. Why do you come now to make this claim?"

"Fernando was not ready to take a wife," Benito said, his tone condescending.

Why had her father signed this unwise document? As she looked into the smug expressions of the two men, she wondered if a pistol had been held to her father's head while he had signed this.

Alandra held herself with a tight rein. With Scully at her side, she rose again and handed the parchment back to Benito. "I will consider this. You may stay another night."

She looked to her housekeeper. Then she turned and again ordered two vaqueros to stay with the visitors at all times. Alandra looked to Scully then, and the two of them walked outside.

"What do you want to do now?" he asked, looking dour.

She did not want to admit that she had no clear plan. Her anger still simmered. She pressed her hands to her hot cheeks, trying to cool them. "I cannot believe that the document is real."

They heard the sound of riders coming then, and looked up.

# FOUR

Scully and Alandra halted, waiting for riders to approach. In spite of the cool sunshine, the sight of friends warmed him. But why hadn't Quinn and his wife come? Caution flared in Scully's middle.

All three riders swung down from their saddles and walked toward the señorita. To Scully, it looked like the start of a duel. Antonio, Carson, and Ash confronted the three Creoles who had followed Alandra and Scully outside. The meeting was as tense as a bowstring. Uneasy, Scully let his hand settle over the pistol on his hip, ready.

*"Buenos tardes, señorita,"* Ash said with a nod. "We heard you had company."

"Who is this *negro?*" Fernando asked with disdainful glance at Ash.

Scully didn't like the man's tone or expression. But Ash was able to take care of himself. Scully grinned, waiting to see what he would do with this arrogant Mexican.

Carson moved forward and gave the *señorita* a quick hug. "Alandra, we came as soon as we could. Ma wanted to come but she couldn't."

Scully didn't like the sound of that. What could have happened to Mrs. Quinn in two days?

The Mexican Creole repeated his question, "Who is this *negro?*"

Ash held out his hand, a challenge. "I'm Ash, Quinn's foreman."

"And *mi amigo,*" Miss Alandra added, slanting a look at Fernando sharp enough to strip the skin from his skull.

Ash held his hand out for a few more moments and then, grinning, put his hands on his hips. "I hear that you're family of Señorita Alandra's who's come to visit." His mouth twisted into a mocking smile.

Carson stepped forward. "My father is Desmond Quinn and I am called Carson." Doffing his hat, he bowed to Isabella. "Sir —" Carson then bowed to Benito. "— my father and mother asked me to welcome you to Texas."

"Carson," Alandra said, "my relatives have just shown me documents which they insist are legal." She pursed her lips. "These documents say that they have inherited Rancho Sandoval, not me."

Carson looked to Scully, who nodded in return. "May I see these documents?" Carson asked.

"You are a mere boy," Fernando said dismissively, not even looking at him.

Carson flushed at this comment. "Still," he persisted, "my father, who was appointed Alandra's guardian, would wish me to —"

"Señorita Sandoval is the only one who is concerned in the document," Benito cut him off. "I am not showing the document to anyone else."

"Not even a judge?" Ash asked with another taunting grin. "From what I hear, you people sound like you already own Rancho Sandoval. But that is something you will have to prove."

Scully didn't know how Ash did it, but he'd come out on top in this verbal skirmish. The three Mexicans looked as if they'd just bit into an unexpectedly spicy green chili pepper. And wanted to spit it out but couldn't.

His chin heavenward, Fernando turned away. He offered his arm to Isabella and they headed with formal dignity back into the casa.

Benito shook his head at the señorita, ignoring Ash and the others completely. "It is good that we have come, Alandra. Here on the frontier you have had to mix with all kinds of low company. Fernando and I discussed this after breakfast." He cast a disdainful look at Scully.

Scully had been aware that he had been an unpleasant surprise to these two at the breakfast table that morning. He'd kind of enjoyed putting their teeth on edge. And had been as "Anglo" as he could.

"We must remove you from the company of those who are beneath you." Benito glared at Scully.

"Well, that puts us all in our low places." Ash chuckled.

Flushing, the older gentleman ignored Ash and continued, "Alandra, the sooner you leave this place, the better. Tomorrow we will all go to the church at Bexar and you and Fernando will be married. Afterward we will return here and Fernando will confer with your foreman about the running of the ranch in Fernando's absence. Then we will leave for Mexico City as soon as possible."

Scully moved closer to the señorita. He gripped the handle of his pistol.

Benito turned his back to Scully. "Alandra, you will take your place in Mexican society. You will no longer count *angloamericanos,* mestizos, and Negroes as friends." He actually snapped his fingers. "Come now. You must begin choosing your clothing for your wedding and instruct the servants to begin boxing up all the portraits and valuables for the trip south."

Alandra looked up into the man's face, defiance firing her dark eyes.

Scully was glad she wasn't looking at him like that. He had seen friendlier expressions on Mississippi River pirates.

"Perhaps, señor," the señorita suggested, "you should go inside for your health. The wind today is particularly sharp." Then she turned to Ramirez. "Please go inside and tell my people to ignore any orders these strangers give them. And then join me at your house, *por favor.*"

Then haughtier than even Señora Isabella, the señorita strode away toward the Ramirez house. Scully moved with her, proud of her.

"Pa's not going to be happy." Carson hurried to catch up with Scully, and so did Ash's son.

"I too am not happy," the señorita snapped, but followed it with a grin for the boy.

"Don't you let those coyotes bother you," Ash said, walking with them. "They can't make you do anything you don't want."

Scully noticed that the señorita was wring-

103

ing her hands. That wasn't like her.

"Carson, why didn't your mother or father come?" she asked, sounding as concerned as Scully felt.

But Ash replied in a lowered voice, "Mrs. Quinn is expecting and is having some troubles. She didn't think she should be riding right now. And Quinn, you know, wouldn't leave her, and neither would my Reva. Her ma had a change of life baby too, that younger brother of hers that's just a year older than Carson here."

*"Qué?"* Alandra whispered, looking surprised. "I didn't know."

Scully felt his neck warm, embarrassed to hear this. And worried too. Mrs. Quinn, though a handsome woman, was not in her first youth.

Slowly, Alandra digested this information, worry opening inside her like a half-healed wound. "Does she need me?"

"Ma said that you shouldn't worry about her," Carson replied. "She will be fine. She just couldn't come and she felt bad about it. Really bad, Lonnie."

Alandra stopped and put her arms around Carson, who was as close as a brother to her. "I know she'll be fine. Tía Dorritt is a strong woman." *And she has shown me how to be strong too.* The starch came back to her spine. *These interlopers will not win.*

Just as the five of them reached the open door of Ramirez's small adobe house, her foreman and his son caught up with them. "Please come in, señorita." He motioned for her to enter first. Señora Ramirez was making tortillas, and seeing guests she wiped her hands on her full white apron.

"Please, señora, go on with your work," Alandra said with a smile. When she was a child, this good woman had given her sweets many times. "I am sorry to intrude. We needed a place to talk without interruption but we can talk outside. It is no problem."

There were two benches under the overhang of the roof, and Alandra moved to the one beside the door. Tightening the white rebozo of the softest wool around herself, she stared out over the ranch she loved, the browns and tans accented with lush greens, set against the low-feeling cloudy sky.

Carson, Emilio, and Antonio picked up the other bench and set it down to face the first. Alandra sighed, feeling overwhelmed, as if invisible weights were being loaded upon her head and shoulders. Soon everyone but Scully was sitting there, sipping coffee that Ramirez's wife brought out. Scully stayed on his feet beside her.

Alandra looked up at him. "Why are you

standing?"

He nodded toward the nearby barn where the four men who'd come with the three Mexicans were lounging. "Keeping an eye on them."

Alandra frowned. Perhaps they had orders to report anything they saw or heard to Fernando and Benito. "We will all speak quietly and in English."

Scully nodded. And Alandra turned back to the men opposite her. She did not know how to start. There was so much to discuss, so much at stake.

Ramirez spoke up first. "Señorita, tell us what you want us to do. Shall we run these strangers off your land?"

Alandra wanted to say, yes, do it now. *But I cannot act rashly. That would be unwise.* She bit her lower lip and then said, "I fear that would not stop these people. If it were not for the rebellion here, I would go straight to San Antonio and enlist the aid of the governor and magistrate there. But I do not know how things are in Bexar now. And what may happen next."

There was a moment of silence while the men evidently thought this over. She sighed and rubbed the back of her neck. This week she'd been living a bad dream. Wicked men had come into her life, to steal her, to rob her, to destroy her peace.

"You think the Mexican judge and all would back them?" Scully asked.

Before she could reply, Ash spoke up. "It all hangs on what happens in this rebellion. If the Mexicans win, I think these strangers will win. But if the Texians win, that might end their case. The señorita is right. It's hard to know what's going on with courts in Bexar and what will happen in the end."

Alandra tried to imagine Texas not under Mexican rule, Texas under the control of Anglos. What would that mean? How could she even hope that her own people would lose Texas? Few Anglos respected Tejanos.

But she could find no fault with Ash's reasoning. This attack on her right to her inheritance might hang in the balance, awaiting the outcome of the fighting, the rebellion.

Scully stood beside her, a silent but commanding presence. Strength seemed to flow from him to her. She sat up straighter.

Carson added, "These three are from Mexico City and I don't doubt they have powerful friends in the courts and government."

"They said as much to me today." Alandra choked on revulsion, recalling their open threats. The thought of her father's family and their power and influence in the Mexican capital made her hands grip the rough bench on either side of her.

Ash's mouth twisted as if he'd tasted something sour. "And there is always the chance that it will stand up in any court because it is valid."

Alandra opened her mouth to object.

Ash held up a hand to stop her. "Señorita, we don't know what pressure was put on your father to sign that document. I've heard of sad, terrible things that happened to Creole *ricos* who wanted to marry against their family's wishes. They might have threatened your mother's life."

Alandra nodded. "I have considered that." The thought of what her parents had suffered to be together made her feel as if a spigot had been turned and all her strength was being drained from her again. She had never faced such pressure. *They left Mexico City so Carlos and I would be free.*

"I've heard you talk about these people before. Who are *ricos* and Creoles?" Scully asked.

"*Ricos* are the wealthy. Creoles are highborn Mexicans, sons and daughters of the pureblood Spaniards," Alandra answered. "Only Spaniards from Spain were allowed to govern in Mexico City under the crown.

This is one of the main reasons that Mexico wanted independence from Spain. Creoles were not permitted any role in their own government."

Ash nodded. "Now that Mexico broke with the Spanish crown, the Creoles and light-colored *ricos* run everything. But the Mexican Creoles feel just like Anglos about anybody who has mixed blood. If you're not white, you're not worth anything. If the dark skin doesn't show, as it doesn't in Alandra, it can be ignored. But if a man looks dark, he's beneath them."

Scully made a sound of distaste.

Alandra too hated every horrible but accurate word Ash spoke. She had not liked it when they had called her mestiza, an insult. She had never thought much about her mother's mixed blood. It had not mattered in her life. Still, she knew she must concentrate on the fact that this was about her land, her inheritance, not her blood. "If the document is real, what am I to do?"

Suddenly she felt as helpless as the day they had buried her brother. "I cannot lose my land." *My life.* "I cannot let my parent's rancho go to the very people who drove my father and mother out of Mexico City. Never." Her breathing came faster.

Scully muttered in agreement.

"We won't let that happen," Ash said, reaching to touch her shoulder with his dark gnarled hand. "Quinn won't let that happen. He promised your brother he'd take care of you and keep the land till you were ready to run it yourself. You're not alone in this."

"Right," Scully agreed.

"But what can I do?" she murmured. She shook her head, warning away tears.

Scully moved closer to her, his palm settling onto her shoulder. The large hand spoke of strength and staying power. And she did not draw away.

Ash patted her hand. "We've got to take action before they do. You heard how they are in a hurry to tie you to them even tighter with marriage to —"

"They can't make her marry someone she doesn't want to," Scully interrupted.

Ash gave an ugly laugh. And so did Ramirez. "Two men who want to gain over six thousand acres with all the gold, silver, horses, and cattle that go with them? Will they refuse to use force?" Ramirez asked, his son Emilio beside him.

Ash joined in, "And two men who will be able to get support from the Mexican Army and who have enough money to bribe a priest to perform a marriage against the wishes —"

"That isn't right," Scully objected, sounding personally insulted.

His outrage on her behalf helped calm Alandra. "I have heard rumors," she said, "about dishonest priests. *And* forced marriages in Mexico City and Spain." She put both hands to her eyes as if she could block out these troubles. "What am I going to do?"

"Well, I think that we need to beat them at their own game." Ash lowered his voice even more. "They say you're going to leave for Bexar tomorrow. I say we leave tonight and get there first."

"How will that help?" Alandra lowered her hands, looking into Ash's grave, lined face.

"If you marry someone else, you can't be forced to marry that fine gentleman." Ash nodded soberly toward the main house.

"Marry? Me? Who would I marry?" she asked, tingling with shock.

Ash looked at the man standing beside her. "Scully will marry you."

Alandra gasped.

"What?" Scully straightened.

Ash held up both hands. "Hear me out. It can be a marriage in name only. But it will stop these three from bribing the priest to perform a marriage against the señorita's wishes. This is a very real danger."

"No." Alandra shook her head.

"Señorita Alandra," Ash said, lowering only one hand. "We need to take this step by step or bad is going to happen. First, we must protect you from a forced marriage. And if you're already married, they can't marry you to someone else, especially if your marriage takes place in the church in San Antonio where they might try it. It will spike that gun."

Alandra glanced at Scully, who stood frowning down at her and Ash. She tried to come up with a counterargument and found she could not.

Ash leaned forward, resting his elbows on his knees. "There's another reason. You're going to need time to find out if these people are who they say they are and if this document is genuine. If you have a husband, he can to go into court to make your claim that this document is illegal. Fortunately, legal matters can get stalled for years. And it will buy you time to find what you need to prove your case."

"But I don't need a husband. In Spanish law, women can own property and can sue in court," Alandra insisted, tangling her fingers together.

Ash tilted his head. "Unfortunately, a man — and a man with such light skin like Scully

— will be listened to in court, in either a Mexican or an Anglo one, more than a woman. It's men who run the courts, not women. And whites, not those of us with mixed blood."

Alandra wanted to argue. Her brain worked frantically, trying to come up with anything that could stand against Ash's logic. She could not. This was the way of the world — white men had the advantage always.

Ash sat back, stretching out his long legs. "Also, Scully is the kind of man who will not be taken lightly by anybody around here. They all know him and his reputation. They also know that Quinn would back you and Scully. And that Quinn's friends with the Comanches. Quinn would never use that power against them, but they don't know that."

Alandra could not remain seated. She popped to her feet and began pacing. Her heart throbbed as these ideas flocked into her mind. "I wish I had never seen these people. Why is this happening?"

Carson shrugged. "Ma says this is just the way life is."

Ash's son Antonio spoke for the first time. "What I want to know is — did these Mexicans have the señorita kidnapped?"

Ash groaned and stretched. "They might have. They might not. It doesn't seem to make any sense at all. I mean why kidnap the señorita if they have legal grounds to take her land?"

"Maybe they don't have legal grounds," Scully said. "Maybe the will is a forgery."

Alandra rubbed her arms, chafing while these men discussed her future.

"And there is always the unpleasant possibility that the document might be real," Ash said. "But we can't be bothered with that now. We have to stop them from marrying the señorita off to Fernando, and the best way to do that is to get to the priest first."

Alandra stared at Ash, not daring to glance at Scully. "There must be another way."

"Well, you'll have to think of it then, señorita." Ash slanted a look up at her. "I can't."

"I can't marry. I'm too young," she pleaded. "I wanted to run my rancho and be my own woman first. Not *marry.*" Her refusal came out too strong to be polite. *But that is how I feel. Marry? No!*

"Well, I'm not champing at the bit to get married," Scully declared. "I heard everything you said, Ash, but there's got to be someone else that can be the groom. I'm not the marrying kind. Who would put the two of us together in harness?"

She threw up a hand. "And haven't I just said that myself!"

Ash raised both hands. "I thought we were going to keep our voices down." He grinned.

Alandra turned her back on him and folded her arms. *No.*

Scully cleared his throat. "Carson, what do you think your parents would say to this?"

"They and Ash usually agree," Carson said.

Alandra tapped her toe on the hard earth. She wanted to refuse to consider this, but she could think of no better plan. The danger was real, and her ranch was a considerable motive for these men to break the laws of God and man. The silence stretched between them.

Finally, she glanced toward Scully, but found it impossible to meet his gaze. "Are you agreeable to this marriage in name only?"

The Anglo remained silent, though she felt his intent gaze like a ray of heat. "If that's what it takes to protect you." He sounded reluctant.

And she felt herself oddly insulted. But

that was ridiculous. It did not matter one way or the other how he felt about marrying her. Because they were going to be married in name only. "I hate to do something deceitful. We will be going into a church and taking vows. How can I take vows that I do not mean?"

Ash nodded. "It does you honor that you consider this point. But we must take action. If there had been a way to prevent you from being kidnapped, we would have taken it. This is a way to prevent you from being forced into a marriage you do not want. Which is worse? Taking vows that you may revoke? Or being forced to marry someone, forced to take the same vows against your will? And if Fernando forces you to take those vows, you can be sure that he will consummate the marriage. Then there is no possibility of annulment. You will be trapped for life. And all your land will be his — whether the will is valid or not."

Under the sky glowering with gray clouds, Alandra heard her late brother's voice: *You will inherit the land, little sister. And with it you inherit the responsibility to our people. You must put their welfare first. They came out of Mexico City with our father and mother and into the wilderness. You cannot let them down.*

Feeling a light mist on her face, she gazed

116

around at the jacales and adobe huts and thought about the families who lived in each one. *I know what I must choose.* "I will wait by my bedroom window tonight in my riding habit. I will leave everything else to you."

With that, she turned and walked back toward her house. Each step she took vibrated through her. The decision had been made. Never before had her responsibilities weighed so heavily upon her. She dragged in breath. *Father, if there is another way or a better way, please let me or Ash think of it before tonight.*

Scully forced down a yawn. The sky glowed with the gray of near-dawn, the sun just below the horizon. The night before, right after dark in the near full moonlight, the five of them — Scully along with Alandra, Ash, Antonio, and Carson — had walked their horses a mile from the barn before mounting and heading north toward Bexar and its church and Mexican fort.

Now they entered the silent town, just waking. The señorita in her dark riding habit had rarely spoken during the nearly twenty mile ride.

He found himself glancing at her, and made himself look ahead. *I'm marrying this woman today.* No matter how many times he repeated these words, he could not catch hold of them, make them feel real.

"Whoa," Ash murmured.

Scully and the others all pulled up on their reins.

"I think we better go to the inn and stay there till the town wakes up. Then we'll go and get the wedding done."

"Why wait?" the señorita asked.

Was it because she was afraid her relatives might appear before the wedding and prevent it? Or was the thought of marrying him, even though it was a sham marriage, irritating, shaming her? And she wanted to get it over before the town awoke? Scully stared ahead, away from all the faces, his neck hot under his bandanna.

Ash went on, "We don't want to arouse any suspicion that this is something out of the way —"

"Ash, that would be possible if this were not me, the *doña* of Rancho Sandoval," the señorita said. "If this were to be the wedding expected from me, it would have taken months of preparation and it would be a huge fiesta. Whether I go now or later to the church to be wed, it will be deemed extremely odd, my marrying in such a hasty clandestine way. Better that we accomplish

118

this before the town wakes up for the day. Let us go now and have done with this."

*Have done with this.* Scully didn't know why those words pricked him.

Ash yawned and rubbed his eyes. "I'm getting too old for this kind of running around. But you're right. We'll go directly to the San Fernando church."

"No, I have spent this night thinking. First we will go to the Veramendi palace."

"Why there?" Ash asked.

"I attended the wedding of Ursula Veramendi to Jim Bowie in 1831. She has passed away but her family will help me, I think. Lieutenant Governor Veramendi let his daughter marry an Anglo. I think I can convince him to persuade the priest to perform this hasty wedding to Scully. I need someone to persuade the priest since there isn't time to post the banns."

"Banns?" Scully asked. "What are they?"

Ash hit his forehead. "I forgot about them."

"In church on each of the three weeks before a wedding ceremony, the upcoming nuptials are announced during mass. It gives time for anyone who has an objection to the marriage to come forward."

"Really?" Scully asked.

"*Sí.*" Alandra started down Commerce

Street in the sparse light. And that's all she said. Scully shook his head as they all fell in behind her. Never had he imagined something like this happening to a plain man like him.

When they reached the gates of the imposing house, Alandra called out in a commanding voice, *"Atencion, por favor! Atencion, el guardia!"*

A small window opened in the heavy wooden door. *"Quién?"*

"It is I, Señorita Alandra Sandoval. Open. I am here to see Veramendi."

The man stared at them and then called for help. The barred gate was opened and her party rode into the courtyard. The señorita thanked the gatekeeper and they all slid from their horses. Soon, the housekeeper was opening the door to the casa and grooms came running to take their horses to the stable.

Scully kept his face straight. This marriage wouldn't be real. It was just a way to protect the señorita, and that was the job Quinn had given him. He tightened his resolve to do this thing regardless of the twisting in his gut.

The morning air was cool and damp. The hours in the saddle made Alandra, his bride, move a little stiffly, slower than usual. The housekeeper led them through the wide double doors.

Soon Veramendi came out in a richly embroidered dressing gown. "What is wrong? Is someone dying?"

"No, *señor*," the señorita said, "I am here to get married and I need your help."

The man halted and gawked, open-mouthed, at her. "Married? Why?"

Ash cleared his throat. "Earlier this week Señorita Sandoval was kidnapped by renegade Comanches." He cleared his throat again. "Under the circumstances, Quinn and I thought it best she marry immediately. And privately."

Veramendi's mouth opened and closed twice. "How dreadful, señorita." He hurried forward. "How dreadful."

The señorita looked upset, her face was flushed. She probably didn't like the explanation Ash had given for the rushed private ceremony. He was implying that she'd been "compromised" and needed to be married in case there was a child. Scully could understand her embarrassment. But he also saw why Ash had used it, since it should satisfy anyone as reason enough for a quick marriage.

"Who is the groom?" Veramendi asked.

"I am." Scully watched for and got the

shocked reaction he'd expected. Why did the Tejanos think they were better than the Anglos? His mind brought up the reverse. Why did the Anglos always think they were better than the Mexicans or Tejanos? No wonder they were all in the midst of a revolution.

The señor came out of his shock and took Alandra's hand in both of his chubby ones. "Señorita, I'm certain many men of honor in this district would be happy to marry —"

Scully fumed at the slur on his honor.

"Señor Scully is a man of honor," Alandra interrupted him.

Veramendi looked embarrassed. "I did not mean to cast doubt on Scully's honor. He is well known as an honest man of valor. I merely meant that . . ." The *señor* looked as if he didn't know how to untangle the unintended offense.

"I am to marry Scully, Señor Veramendi," the señorita said, sounding pained. "It has been decided between me and the Quinns."

"Where are they?" the señor asked, looking around the dim room for them.

Ash spoke up. "Señora Quinn is enceinte and unable to travel at this time. I will act as the *padrino* for Alandra. And our wish is that you will register Alandra and Scully as married today in the legal records."

122

Alandra nodded. "I . . . we wish to marry and then I will return to be with Tía Dorritt." She looked around. "Please, señor, we have ridden all night. I want to marry and then we can go to the inn and rest. We will leave as soon as we are able. Tía Dorritt needs me. But I also want to go to the church and ask God's blessing on our union."

"This is a very unsettled time, señorita," Veramendi said, patting her arm. "Our son-in-law James Bowie is at the Alamo and I think that war must come here soon again. In light of this and . . . your situation, I will do just as you and the Quinns have asked. I will register the marriage and then we will go to the priest for his blessing. In normal times, this would not happen, but in the midst of war . . ." The man shrugged.

Scully thought that Veramendi had mentioned Bowie to remind him that he had given his daughter permission to marry an *angloamericano*. This man must not think all *angloamericanos* were beneath him. Scully let his brief irritation dissolve in the cool morning air. And Scully realized that the blessing at the Church was necessary to stop Fernando from trying to force a marriage on Alandra — in these days of war.

In a very short time Veramendi had

dressed and registered the marriage, with Ash and his secretary as witnesses. And then they were hurrying through the waking town of San Antonio de Bexar to the Church of San Fernando. Bringing up the rear, Ash led the horses with Antonio and Carson. The two teens, who would wait outside with the horses, went forward to push open the church door, which groaned and creaked, sounding loud in the early stillness. Scully hesitated. Crossing this threshold was committing once and for all to this marriage. He stepped inside, took off his hat and gazed around, willing his empty stomach to stop jigging.

A cross with Christ upon it hung on the wall behind the altar. A few candles flickered at the feet of a statue near the front. The church smelled a bit damp. He followed the señorita to the statue and stood watching as she lit another candle and knelt to pray.

He had rarely been in a church. There weren't many on the frontier where he'd lived his life. He gazed around and up toward the high ceiling, wishing there were more light so he could see better. Gold glinted in the shadows.

Soon he heard the sound of approaching footsteps, hasty ones. The señorita rose. A plump priest in brown robes and sandals,

124

followed by a servant, hurried inside. "What is it, Señor Veramendi?"

The older man consulted with the priest in heated whispers, while Alandra prayed and Scully stood guard. Finally, the priest looked up and gave instructions to his servant, "Come to the front." The man hurried through the small door behind the altar. Señor Veramendi went to Alandra, helped her up and walked up the aisle on his arm. Scully and Ash walked behind them.

At the front, the padre looked at Scully. "Though you are an Anglo, I'm sure you are a good son of the Church. Please join right hands." The man gave Scully no opportunity to reply, but went right on in a language he didn't recognize. Not Spanish. Was it Latin?

He glanced sideways at Ash, who shook his head, obviously telling him to say nothing. The Anglos who entered Texas were supposed to convert but few had done so. And the Mexicans ignored the issue of religion unless forced to do otherwise, especially since there were so few priests in all of Texas. Scully knew of only this priest here and the one north in Nacogdoches though there might have been more.

Finally, when Scully was about to ask if

the man was going to marry them or not, the priest turned to him and asked in English, "What is your full name?"

"Scully James Falconer." His tight throat made it hard to speak.

"Scully is your first name?"

"Yes."

Then the priest went on with the ceremony in English. "Do you Scully James Falconer take Alandra Maria Inez Sandoval to be your bride?"

"I do." Scully had to scrape the words up from the bottom of his throat.

Then the priest turned to Alandra and asked her the same question. "Do you Alandra Maria Inez Sandoval take Scully James Falconer to be your husband?"

There was a long pause while everyone waited. Señor Veramendi whispered to her and she shook her head. Finally, the señorita whispered, "I do."

Scully sucked in air. Nearly there. He had promised Quinn he'd protect the señorita, and he was. An odd tingling ran through his flesh, as if reminding him that this was real.

"Is there a ring? And do you have *las arras?*" the priest asked, holding out his hand.

Scully was taken aback by the questions. *Las arras?*

"I have it," Ash spoke up. He pulled out a

leather pouch and counted our thirteen gold reals. He handed the coins to Scully. "Drop these coins, which are for the poor, through the bride's fingers to show that you and Alandra will be generous to the poor always."

Scully took the coins and did as he was told. The coins dropped between Alandra's fingers into a collection basket that the priest's assistant held under her hands.

"The ring?" the priest prompted.

Scully looked down at his hand. He had a ring. The gold ring barely fit his little finger on his left hand anymore. He had never thought to take it off but now had a reason to. he grasped it and twisted it slowly, working it off. Then he put it in the priest's palm.

Alandra watched him, her head tilted to the side.

Scully took her hand again. Without the ring, his hand felt naked, and inside him something was shifting, changing. The priest blessed the ring and instructed Scully to slip it onto Alandra's finger. He did so. The small ring fit her finger as if it had been made for her.

This wisdom of this hasty marriage seemed like something that should be prayed about. Scully usually figured God had enough to take care of. So Scully took care of himself. But both his mothers had prayed. And so he added silently, *God, help me protect this woman. Help me keep her land. I hate that these people are trying to cheat her out of her home. Don't let them do it. Nobody should be robbed of their home.*

*Like I was.*

He glanced at the señorita, and she appeared ready to faint. He took her arm. She looked up at him, her face a pale oval in the dim light. *Beautiful.*

The priest took a large double string of beads and laid it around Alandra and Scully's necks, joining them with it as the sun was rising outside the open doors. Señor Veramendi looked grave, as if this were a funeral, not a wedding. Impelled by the feeling of the moment, Scully leaned down and brushed the señorita's lips with his. He ignored the rush of sensation that coursed down his neck to his heart. Alandra reacted with a widening of her eyes.

"What should I do now?" he whispered in her ear, tempted to brush it with his lips too.

"Thank the priest and pay him," she whispered back.

Scully reached into his pocket and pulled out a pouch. He gave the priest several gold reals. The priest thanked him, lifted the string of beads from around their necks and made the sign of the cross over them. *"Gracias, padre."* Scully took Alandra's arm and turned her, saying as a husband should, "I need to get you to the inn. You're done in."

The lady said nothing. But she walked beside him as stiff and straight as the long rifle looped with leather that he wore over his back. Leading their horses, they walked outside the church gates, ignoring the curious stares from the townspeople just coming to the church for morning prayers.

Outside, Señor Veramendi halted under an oak tree. "Señorita Sandoval . . . I mean Señora Falconer, I must warn you that this is not the time to be in San Antonio. Reports have come to me that are very unsettling. After the siege in December, my son-in-law Bowie with the man Travis are in charge at the old fort. Do not linger here. I am planning on closing my house and going to visit relatives in Chihuahua this very day."

*"Gracias, señor."* Alandra clasped his hand.

*"Sí, gracias."* Scully held out his hand and the man shook it.

"Before I leave, I will make official note of your marriage in my last dispatch to Mexico City today. *Vayan con Dios."* Veramendi hurried away with a wave.

Scully, at Alandra's side, began walking

down the dusty main street toward the open plaza along with the others. He couldn't keep himself from glancing at the señorita. Her face was frozen like the statue in the church. He didn't know what to do to help her. Or if he could do anything. But she was a good woman and so much trouble had come upon her.

The fresh pink dawn radiated, reflected, shining even on the cloudy western sky in front of them. But the rosy sky did not lift his spirits as it usually did. None of them spoke. They reached the inn and Ash finally said, "I've got family here in Bexar. I'll take Carson there with me and Antonio. You two check into one room and get some rest. Make sure you stay in one room together. We don't want this marriage to be in doubt." He looked to Scully. "We'll be back after the siesta and then we'll talk about what to do next."

*One room.* Scully felt as if he were caught within strong arms, which were crushing him. *Alone with the señorita.* Who didn't want to be married to him or anyone.

Ash nodded at the inn servant who ambled over to take Scully and Alandra's horses to the inn's livery. Scully watched Ash, Carson, and Antonio leave them. Then he led the lady on his arm into the adobe inn.

Within minutes the innkeeper, obviously curious, led them up the steps to their room.

# FIVE

Alandra was drowning in fatigue. But more than that, how had her life spun out of control like this? In the past at fiestas, she'd seen men who had drunk too much wine lose their way in the midst of dancing the fandango. They began to wobble and turn and nearly topple. Friends helped them from the dance floor, laughing at their antics. But here and now, though she wobbled and feared she'd fall, she didn't feel like laughing. *How can I turn my life back to the way it was?*

Her numb feet managed to carry her up the stairs and into the small room. Since the coming of the Anglos, San Antonio had grown to a city of over two thousand, but the innkeeper, of course, knew who they were. He lingered in the doorway, smiling but plainly bursting with curiosity. She stared at him, unable to speak and hoping she would not fall on her face.

Finally, it must have occurred to Scully that the man was waiting for a tip for walking them up to their room. He reached into his pocket, gave the innkeeper two pesos, and the man left. Scully closed the door behind him. And turned to her.

Feeling as boneless as a rag doll, she slid down to sit on the edge of the bed. Then the last fragments of her composure began crumbling. *I do not want to cry. Do not want this fear, or to let it show.* But humiliating tears began to leak from her eyes. She turned toward the shuttered window so Scully wouldn't see them.

"Señorita, you must be tired. You should lie down. Try to sleep."

His low sympathetic voice ripped away the last remaining thread of her self-control. Deep, loud sobs wrenched her. She felt as if a reckless force had plunged deep into her, ripping her apart. The tears shamed her. The sobs embarrassed her. Yet she could not stop them. Lying back, she turned away and wrapped her arms around herself as if she were coming undone.

A large hand touched her shoulder. The touch was uncertain and gentle, like a shy colt nudging her. Yet she couldn't turn toward Scully, let him see her like this.

"Señorita, don't cry. Please don't worry.

We'll get through this." The low voice came again, cutting away her mask and opening her to him.

She tried to stop weeping but couldn't. Tried to pull herself back to one piece. She couldn't.

"You don't think I would try and . . . hurt you?" Scully's question sounded hesitant. "You know you are safe with me. Don't you?"

She rolled back so she was facing him. She still could not stop crying enough to form words. So she took his hand and tried to squeeze it. *Yes, you would never hurt me.*

He knelt beside the bed so their eyes were level. His large hand covered hers. It was so heavy, yet his touch so soft. She resisted its pull. She could not give in, act the helpless female. She was not just any young woman.

*I am the* doña.

She tugged free of his touch, and he stepped back and folded his arms. She sensed that she had wounded him with this snub, but could not help that.

Slowly, slowly, she gained control again. The sobs waned and she began wiping away her tears with her fingertips. In the low early light, Scully's gold band now on her ring finger caught her eye. Who had worn this ring before she? Dare she ask this *distante* vaquero, her almost-husband? No. It was not for her to pry.

Scully pulled a red bandanna from his pocket and handed it to her. "Use this," he ordered gruffly. "It's clean."

For some reason, this made her smile. She used the bandanna, which smelled of buckskin, to wipe away her tears. Finally she was able to sit up. "I am sorry I broke down like that. I am not a helpless weeping female."

His large eyes remained on her. "I don't think you're a helpless female. You've just been through a heck of a lot in one week. You were kidnapped by Comanche renegades. Relatives come and say they're going to take your land. And then you have to ride all night to marry someone you hardly know. And an Anglo to boot," he added, with an edge to his last words.

She did not know how to take back rebuffing his kindness, so she fastened on the only thing that mattered between them. "I know you. I know the kind of man you are. Tía Dorritt and Tío Quinn value you. They sent you to protect me. I know that I can trust you." Then she added his full name, "Scully James Falconer."

Scully looked embarrassed by her words. In the early morning light streaming from the window, his wavy hair was almost the same color as a polished gold real. Her fingers itched to delve into his hair. To warm her fingers there? "Why do you always cover your hair?" she asked, then blushed at her forwardness.

He too looked even more discomfited now. "I'm out under the sun all the time. I burn easy."

His modesty disarmed her. She sat very still gazing into his deep-set eyes. They were as vivid a green as a palm leaf. She rushed to end the sudden silence. "You are right, of course. About both matters. This week my life has . . ." She couldn't come up with a word or words to describe what had happened to her. She drew in a ragged breath and strengthened her voice. "But I will not give in. I will fight for what is mine."

Scully nodded solemnly. "Yes, miss."

"You must stop calling me that," she instructed him. "You must call me by my name, or *querida*."

"What does *querida* mean?" he asked.

"Dearest or dear one."

"I couldn't call you that. Wouldn't be right."

His shyness eased her qualms. "Then you must call me by my first name. You would not call your wife 'miss,' would you?"

"Guess not." He closed his mouth and

looked stern. "Alandra, you must rest now."

She nodded, knowing she could do nothing else. "Would you pull off my riding boots?" She hated to ask him but the boots were made to fit tight. And once more her fatigue was numbing her, as if her body were falling asleep bit by bit before her mind gave in.

"Sure." He moved to the bed. Brushing her ankles with his fingers, he quickly slipped her boots off and set them on the floor. "Now you rest. I'll just bunk here on the floor."

She was already almost asleep, but picked up the other pillow and tossed it to him. "Good night," she whispered, lying down, closing her eyes and hearing him moving around, fading into sleep. *Bless us. Keep us safe . . .*

Upon hearing a quiet tap on the door, Scully rose from the floor beside the bed. The señorita . . . or he should say, Alandra, was sleeping soundly. When he opened the door, he found Carson in the hall. Scully held a finger to his mouth, stepped out, and shut the door behind him, murmuring, "What is it, Carson?"

"We slept the morning and then had dinner at Ash's family's place. I decided to come here and see how you two are doing."

"The . . . Alandra's sleeping still. I don't want to disturb her."

Carson looked at Scully with brows drawn together, reminding him strongly of Quinn. "Things are happening here in town. Rumor has it the Mexican Army is on its way to the Alamo."

Scully shoved his hands through his hair. "Think it's true?"

"Don't know. But Señor Veramendi isn't the only Tejano packing up and leaving town. I talked to a few I've met in the past and they say it's true. They don't want to be here if there's another battle or siege. No matter which side wins."

Scully glanced toward the closed door behind him. "Carson, will you stay here with my . . . with Alandra while I go take a look at the Alamo?"

Carson took a moment and then nodded.

"Go inside and sit in the chair by the window. When she fell asleep, she was plenty upset, and I don't want her to wake up without someone she knows here."

Carson nodded. "You coming right back?"

"Yes." He let Carson in and picked up his hat, which had been discarded by the pillow on the rug where he was napping. Then he left silently, hurried down the stairs and outside. It was raining. He realized that he had been aware of this in some part of his mind. He just hadn't put the sound of the rain on the roof together with actual rainfall. *I must be as tired as the señorita . . . as Alandra.*

Scully went to the inn's livery and, from his saddle bag, removed his many colored poncho, made of such tightly woven wool that it shed water like oilcloth. He slipped his head through the hole in the middle and then walked as fast as he could toward the old mission fort, the Alamo. As he proceeded up Commerce Street, he saw that Carson was right. Even in the drenching rain, Tejanos were packing up and leaving. His gut tightened. *I need to get Alandra home safe and soon.*

He reached the Alamo, and the old colonial fort and mission looked dismal in the rain. This would be where it would happen. This is what the Mexicans would want to take back after General de Cos had lost San Antonio de Bexar in December. What were the Texians doing here to prepare for that?

The unpleasant answer came quickly. Nothing much was going on within the walls. Scully walked into the old fort without any challenge. He gazed around. Some men lounged near a long building. One of them looked up and hailed him.

Since the man was under the protection of an overhanging roof, Scully walked over and ducked under the cover. He recognized the Anglo, though he didn't recall the man's name.

"Aren't you Quinn's man?" the stranger asked.

Scully nodded and held out his hand. "I'm Scully. What's going on?"

"I'm Allen." The man shook his hand and shrugged. "We're just waiting to see if the Mexicans are going to try to take the fort back."

"Rumors are that the Mexican Army's on its way." The rain poured off the wood shake roof, splashing up on Scully's boots.

"Let 'em come," Allen retorted. "One Texian with a rifle is worth a hundred Mexicans."

Scully didn't like this man, but what did that mean? Nothing. He had worked alongside vaqueros long enough to know that skin color meant little. What was inside a man's heart counted. Just like his boss had proved that what most people thought about half-breeds was false.

Scully scanned the fort and was glad he wasn't going to be defending it. Though the stone walls were thick, they weren't all that high. With a boost from below, a man could climb over them. There was a gap too.

Two other Anglos had been listening in. One asked, "You come to join up?"

Scully shook his head. "No, I'm just taking a look around."

"What? Are you a coward?" the same one sneered. "You afraid of some Mexicans?"

Under his poncho, Scully's hand automatically drifted down to his side where his pistol sat in his belt.

"Hey," Allen warned, holding up a hand, "this is Scully, a top hand for one of the biggest ranchers in these parts, Quinn."

Scully stared at the two strangers.

"Well, then why isn't this Quinn and Scully joining up to fight the Mexicans?" the same Anglos jibed, his hands on his hips.

"We got other things to do," Scully said. "You're not from around here." He kept his hand on his pistol though he doubted he would need to use it.

The talkative stranger pointed a thumb at himself and then at the man beside him. "I'm from Louisiana and my friend's from Tennessee. We were in Natchitoches and heard Davy Crocket was here and decided to come too. We fight the Mexicans and we get this land, this Texas, for the U.S. and us." The man grinned.

Scully had heard of Davy Crockett. Who hadn't? "Well, I wish you all luck. But I have to get back." He lifted a hand in farewell and sauntered away into the rain.

Then he was hailed again. He turned and saw a familiar tall man with light brown hair, who asked, "Aren't you Scully, Quinn's top hand?"

Scully halted. "I'm Scully."

"I'm Bowie." The man held out his hand.

Scully shook with him. "What can I do for you, sir?"

"I was just saying farewell to Veramendi and he told me you married Don Carlos Sandoval's sister this morning."

"I did."

Bowie chewed on this awhile, and Scully waited, rain pouring down on them. Some of the chill rain was soaking Scully's neck bandanna and leaking down his back. Then Bowie continued, "I'm glad you're watching out for her. We're in for troubled times. I think you best get her home as soon as possible. I wouldn't want my wife here."

"That's my intention."

"Good. Give my regards to the Quinns, will you?"

"Of course, sir. I will." They shook hands again and Scully headed out onto the street. On the way back to the inn the rain streamed over his poncho and his boots got soaked. The feeling that a dark cloud was above his head about to dump more cold wet trouble on him grew within. If he was in charge like Bowie and Travis and expecting the Mexican Army, he'd have been doing something about getting the Alamo ready for a fight. But he wasn't in on that.

His job was to protect the señori — to protect Alandra. And getting her out of Bexar appeared to be the best way to do it. Just before ducking under the overhanging inn's porch, he looked up and studied the lead-gray clouds. This rain wasn't going to stop anytime soon. If they had been traveling by coach or wagon, mud would have kept them from heading home. On horseback, they'd still be able to make it, just slower.

He ducked under the porch, took off his hat and poncho and shook them both, flinging rain around him. Then he entered the inn, nodded to the innkeeper and hurried up the steps. His need to see Alandra safe and sound unexpectedly caught him around the heart. He knocked on the door and heard her, his wife — *Stop. I have to stop thinking of her as my wife. She's not my wife. I am only protecting her.* He heard Alandra say, "Who is it?"

143

"Scully." *Your husband. Stop thinking that.* Hearing the door lock click, he opened it and walked in. She was alone. "Where's Carson?"

"I sent him back to Ash. With this door locked and all the people in the inn, I am safe." She sat down on the side of the bed, as she had earlier. She still looked worn-out. Her hair had come loose and flowed like darkest chocolate over her shoulders.

"There aren't as many people in Bexar as you think," he told her. "The Tejanos are leaving town. Rats leaving a sinking ship."

"Are Tejanos rats?" she asked, challenging him.

He hung his hat and poncho on a peg by the door. "That's not what I meant." He shoved his fingers back through his damp hair.

"What did you mean?"

"I mean to say that everyone decent is clearing out of town. There are rumors that the Mexican Army is coming. And I talked to Jim Bowie at the Alamo. He told me to get you out of town soon."

Alandra covered her face with her hands. "Then we must leave."

Her voice was low and muffled. And the way she bent her head and covered her face made him guess that she was crying again.

And didn't want him to see. Again he moved near her. She'd snubbed his comfort this morning, but he still needed to offer it. He felt clumsy and out of his depth, yet he patted her back. She didn't shrug his hand away.

"I am feeling trampled down," she whispered, "as if my strength has been forced out. Stolen from me."

He didn't know how to help her, but he'd try. "You are a strong woman. You have stood up against Comanches and —" What were the terms Ash had explained? "— those Creole *ricos* who are trying to take your land, your rancho. They can't make you marry Fernando now. And Quinn, Ash, and I will not let them take your land."

She sat back, her legs folded under her long black riding-habit skirt. He followed her lead and moved away to the bedside chair.

"Thank you, Scully." She drew in a long breath. "It's just so many things have been hurled against me in such a short span of days. I have not been given any real time to recover. My sleep has been restless." She pressed her hand over her forehead, smoothing back stray hair. Then, sighing, she looked him in the eye. "You think we need to leave right away? Today?"

He gazed at her. She looked pale, starved and exhausted. She'd ridden all night. Still, she was ready to get up and go if he said so. Maybe they should leave now. But he couldn't bring himself to ask her to saddle up and ride for another night, and through a chilling downpour at that. Everyone had their limit. He didn't want her to get sick. "No. I think we should have a warm meal. You should have a hot bath. Then a good night's rest."

"Are you certain? If we must go now to avoid the Mexican Army and perhaps another siege, I can go. I can ride back to Rancho Sandoval if we —"

"We have time. Trust me."

She gazed into his eyes for a long while, as if trying to read his mind. His neck warmed at her attention.

He broke their connection, rising. "I'm going to go and get us food, and after we eat, you'll have that bath. That'll help you revive. We'll plan to leave in the morning. First light."

She nodded. "Will you ask the innkeeper to have someone press my riding habit while I sleep and have it ready for our departure?"

He picked up his hat. "I'll do that." He turned toward the door.

She stopped him with a hand on his

elbow. *"Gracias."*

He clasped his hand over hers for just a moment, then headed out of the room. Just as he closed the door behind him, he heard her whisper, *". . . esposo valiente . . . fuerte."*

The next afternoon, they were nearly home. The day was cloudy, but yesterday's rain had ended. Alandra rode between Ash and Scully. Carson and Antonio had ridden directly to the Quinn rancho to explain everything about the wedding and the state of the war. "We need to decide what we will say to my dear loving relatives."

Ash chuckled and said, "That's up to you and your husband. I just came along for the ride."

Scully glanced her way. "What do you want to do . . . Alandra? It's your rancho, your relatives."

She heard the slight hesitance in his voice when he used her name. That wouldn't do. She looked into his green eyes. "Well, first of all, Scully, you are a man of few words. But today you must behave very much as my husband, Spanish men are very . . . forceful, very much in charge in a loud way, not a quiet way." She fisted her hand and raised it to emphasize her point. "Not quiet like Tío Quinn with Tía Dorritt. More like her stepfather." She had accompanied Dorritt to visit her mother a few times over the years. "I never liked Señor Kilbride."

Ash chuckled again. "I never did either, but then the feeling was mutual."

Scully did not respond, just rode on, looking down.

She waited, realizing now that he was not a man who disliked talking, but a man who did not speak without thinking first.

Finally, he looked into her eyes. "You want me to do the talking?"

She grinned. How like him. "*Sí,* you must not stand back and let me do the talking. You must act as an *esposo* or as *they* expect a husband to act, do you see?"

He nodded. "That means I get to tell them to leave." He smiled suddenly.

She smiled back. "*Sí.*"

And then the rancho was spread out ahead of them. Alandra's horse broke into a trot, creating a welcome breeze, and she did not restrain him. As they rode up to the hacienda, her cousin Fernando stood in the doorway.

Scully slid from his horse. Coming to her, he put his hands at her waist and lifted her down like a bride. "Very good," she whispered, and he grinned.

Then turning toward the hacienda, he offered her his arm and led her to the doorway where Fernando waited. The man looked as if he were spoiling for a fight. Ash dismounted and gave their horses over to the vaqueros who'd come running. A few more vaqueros lingered in front of the hacienda as if waiting for orders.

Scully walked up to Fernando, who blocked his path. "Please let us by, señor."

Alandra heard the challenge in Scully's voice. She merely looked into Fernando's eyes with all the contempt she felt for him, a man who was trying to take what didn't belong to him.

Fernando lifted his eyes as if looking at Scully pained him and glared at her. "Cousin, *mi prima,* where have you been? And traveling with these low companions and without a chaperone? When will you learn how a true *doña* behaves? Didn't we tell you to have nothing further to do with these inferiors?"

*That does it.* "Your opinions don't matter here, señor," Scully said, put one hand to Fernando's thin chest and shoved. Hard. The dandy staggered backward, nearly falling. While he sputtered with outrage, Scully led Alandra past him, with Ash close behind. He was proud of how she looked, her face rosy and her chin high.

Benito and Isabella rose from their seats in the courtyard, their expressions shocked. "What is this?" Benito demanded. Flushed, Fernando moved to stand by Isabella as if she might be in danger from Scully. *Or maybe he thinks I won't knock that sneer off his face when he's standing by a lady.*

Scully removed his hat. "Yesterday Alandra and I were married in Bexar. I am the man here now."

Alandra tightened her hand around his elbow, and he pressed a hand over hers, acting like a husband.

Benito, Fernando, and Isabella all started speaking at once in Spanish. "Quiet," Scully ordered, raising his voice. Alandra whispered the Spanish word to him. And he repeated it, *"Quieten."*

All three Mexicans glared at Alandra. All three ignored him. "What have you done, you foolish girl?" Benito demanded, breathing hard.

"She married me," Scully replied with a show of indifference. "And you people are leaving our land. Tomorrow." For emphasis, he said the word in Spanish, *"Mañana."*

Fernando glared at Alandra, still refusing to look at Scully. "I do not believe it. But if you have married this vaquero, that only means that you, *mi prima,* are foolish beyond

150

measure. Your marrying this . . . this Anglo means that I will have the land and you will be dispossessed completely."

Scully tried to ignore the possibility that the Mexican might be speaking the truth. With the way things stood in Texas now, an Anglo husband might be more of a hurt than a help in this situation. But he couldn't let this stop him from doing what he had married Alandra to accomplish.

"You're going to have to prove that in court," he said, staring into Fernando's sneering face. "My wife and I don't believe that the document you have shown is legitimate. Now, get packing. I expect you to leave here tomorrow morning. If you're not packed by then, our vaqueros will pack you and escort you off our land. Is that clear?"

Fernando drew himself up and smiled. "You think you know everything. But you don't. We will leave tomorrow and go to San Antonio de Bexar and submit the will to the magistrate there. After that, it is I who will be ordering you both off *my* land." Fernando turned to Isabella. "Come. I will take you to your room. You should not be expected to endure such low company."

As they swept away toward the other side of the courtyard, Benito drew himself up and glared into Alandra's face. "To lower yourself to marry a common Anglo cowboy. By this action, you have proven that you are unworthy of the name Sandoval. You are your mother's daughter. She was just a low, conniving —"

Alandra slapped the man's face. It rang in the shocked silence. "You dare speak against my mother? To me?"

Scully sucked in air, ready to defend her.

Looking about to explode, the sputtering older man turned and marched after the other two.

Alandra started to pursue him, then halted. "I see why my father broke with his family."

Scully grinned. "Me too."

Ash spoke up. "Yes, looks like your father was a smart man. But we knew that." He gestured at the black wrought-iron chairs and table. "Let's talk."

Sitting down next to Alandra, Scully seethed at the strangers for hurting her. No one had the right to do that. He clenched his fists, looking forward to running them off the next morning.

In a lowered voice, Ash said, "I think they know something we don't."

# Six

A lighted candlestick in hand, Scully closed the door to Alandra's large bedroom. She walked ahead of him to the window. Her head was bent forward. Was she hiding hurt feelings? The coming of night had been a relief. He'd had about all of her relatives that he could stand. They had come to the table for the evening meal, only to sit in icy silence and ignore Alandra and him. He knew he wasn't anything near a gentleman and he didn't care what these people thought of him. But Alandra didn't deserve such scorn.

A few times he'd had to grip his hands tight together under the table to keep from shoving a fist into "fancy" Fernando's sneering face. He had even imagined how satisfying his bruised knuckles would feel. How was he going to get rid of them, not just from Rancho Sandoval, but from Alandra's life? For good?

He lit the candle in the iron sconce near the door and then set the candlestick he held on the bedside table. Trying not to stare at her, he gazed around at the gleam of the polished wood of the four poster bed with its white mosquito net pulled back and tied. He'd never seen a fine bedroom like this till he hired on with Quinn.

Her back to him, she murmured, "Do you think Ash is right? Fernando and Benito might already have bribed judges?"

"He might be." Scully mulled over Ash's words.

Standing here made him very aware that he did not belong in such a grand room. Much less to be here alone with this beautiful woman, the woman who owned this hacienda, the woman he had married yesterday. For a split second he wished that he were different, that he wore fine clothes like that Fernando, and knew fancy manners.

But no, he was who he was, a man born to wear buckskin. And that was God's will. His second ma had explained that to him. And she'd warned him not to question God. That never went well. She'd said, *Just be an honest man, a good man and let God take care of the rest.*

He looked to Alandra and wished he had fine words to say to a fine lady. She was staring out the window, her head down. A cool moist wind blew inside. Just the kind of unhealthy air that could sicken a person. That wouldn't do. He approached her and touched her shoulder.

She started and blurted out what she must have been thinking. "What will happen if the Mexican Army does come to take back the Alamo?"

"I don't know what will happen other than people are going to die." Then he regretted saying this. Her eyes had widened and her full lips parted. A man wasn't supposed to talk like that to womenfolk. But being forced to sit in silence while Fernando had insulted Alandra with his icy silence and lifted nose had grated Scully's nerves raw. He had wanted to take the Mexican by the collar, drag him outside, and beat the sneer off his face. But Alandra wouldn't have wanted that.

He sucked this scalding vexation down and rested his hand gently on her slender shoulder. "I'm going to close these shutters. That wind isn't good for you. And you're tired. You should get into bed."

She turned to him, and looked as if she was having trouble understanding.

*She's done in. Too much saddle time, too much bad in too short a time.* And more bad coming with Mexican generals fighting Texians for forts.

He snapped down the shutter openings, then swung the wood panels inward and fastened them closed. The lady still hadn't moved. So he took her hand and led her to the side of her bed. He tried to ignore how just touching her hand went through him, made him feel things he had no right to feel.

Finally she looked up, her large eyes sad. "Please open the door. My maid will be there waiting to undress me."

That kind of surprised him. She needed someone to help her undress? But she was a lady, and that must be the way ladies did things. He nodded and went to the door. As the girl entered, she smiled at him and giggled. He stepped into the hall. A few minutes passed and then the girl came out, giggled at him again, and vanished down the dark hallway.

Scully hesitated. He opened the door and murmured, "Can I come in?"

"*Sí,*" Alandra said.

He entered and paused. In a white high-necked nightgown, she was sitting in bed with the white mosquito curtains draped around it. A lovely picture. For a moment he had trouble drawing a breath. Then he noted her sober expression. That stopped him.

He didn't know what to say to her to try to make her feel better. Her beauty and her troubles tugged him in different directions. He wanted to go toward her, find a way to comfort her. But he was a husband in name only, an Anglo to boot. He made himself look toward the flickering bedside candle.

*"Estoy bastante bien,"* she murmured. "I am all right, Scully," she went on in English. "Do not worry." She sighed, tried to smile, and teased him, "I have not been helping you to learn to speak Spanish better. And that is the reason we gave for why you came with me, isn't it?"

He forced himself to grin. "Yeah, I mean, *sí.*"

She opened the white gauzy bed curtain and slipped out, making him take a hasty step back. Padding on bare feet, she brought out a pillow and blankets from a chest at the end of the bed. Then she slipped through the curtain and into bed. He couldn't stop himself from watching her small white feet disappear under the quilt.

As Scully watched her, he realized that here, in this room alone with him, Alandra wasn't only the proud señorita who had slapped Benito for insulting her mother. She was an innocent young woman. Only nineteen. It moved him to want to protect her more than ever. Especially at the troubling idea that the three unwelcome guests knew something about this blasted will and the courts they didn't.

Drawn against his will, he sat on the end of the bed, the sheer mosquito curtain like a veil separating them. Then he recalled Carson's opinion that it might be better all around if the Texians won this war.

He knew, at least, that here he could protect Alandra with his fists and gun. His hands clenched and he glanced at his rifle propped against the door where he'd stowed it earlier. He thought about seeing Jim Bowie at the Alamo. That man Allen too. What did it matter if he didn't like some of the Texians? What if the Alamo fell and Mexicans like these three took charge of things? Did they think that the court would side with them against Alandra simply because of who they were?

Her voice brought him back to the present. She was leaning toward the glow from the bedside candle, reading from an open Bible.

"Fret not thyself because of him who prospereth in his way, because of the man who bringeth wicked devices to pass."

The sound of her voice was like music to him, and her slight Spanish accent charmed him.

She looked up at him. And smiled. Her beauty blazed in the candlelit shadows. He was captivated. And suddenly he realized that he was here not only out of duty, but because this woman was special — to him. "That sounds familiar." He managed to squeeze out the words, shock at the sudden realization rippling through him.

She nodded, still smiling. "It is from Tía Dorritt's favorite psalm, Thirty-seven. She believes its promises and she taught me that I could trust them too. Do you believe that?"

Sitting at the very foot of the bed on only a corner of the mattress, he leaned back against the bedpost. He savored looking at her in the candlelight. Her long dark hair had been braided for the night and the long tail fell forward over her shoulder. Her pale olive skin and her ruffled collar glowed against the dark wood headboard. Beauty — unadorned, natural, heady.

What had she asked him about? The psalm. "Mrs. Quinn's an honest woman. I can believe anything she said."

"Then we must not despair." She looked

down again: My 'family' has brought wicked devices to pass. But we are not to fret."

"That's hard." *Especially since I'm the one who must protect you. And this might be a fight I can't win with a rifle or my fists.* That goaded him. He took a deep breath, holding back his tinder-ready anger.

"*Sí*, it is hard not to worry. I wish I could banish these three from my land and set guards to keep them out. But this isn't just about me. All of Texas is in turmoil. I do not know if this revolution is from God, and I do not know who will win it."

She moved onto her knees and slid down toward him, the quilt bunching up between them. "But I know that God knows what the outcome will be. I also believe that He loves me and that He will keep the promises He has made in this psalm, just as he kept His promises to Tía Dorritt. He brought her safely from Louisiana and gave her the strength to defy her family and marry Quinn, a half-breed. Will God do less for me?"

Scully had stayed where he was. But his neck warmed as she moved forward. From this drawing nearer — what was she trying to show him? "It's hard," he repeated, turning over in his mind what she had just said she believed. Keeping his thoughts from

160

straying where they didn't belong, he cleared his thick throat. "I want to do more than let God take care of everything. I want to do my part." *Take care of you.*

"*Sí,* we have work to do."

He suddenly realized that this woman was as lovely in her heart as she was to his eye. Her bent head was only inches from him, veiled by the mosquito net. *"Sí."*

She smiled at him in a way that made his heart jump. Still on her knees, she looked into his eyes. "Will we believe the Lord?"

"Yes, but we need to sleep now." *To have the strength to face what will come tomorrow.* He left the bed and did not look at her, but heard her sliding back, rustling the bed linens, making him think of her little white feet.

Trying to forget that, he blew out the candle in the sconce and settled on the rug beside her bed with the blanket and pillow there. The room seemed to have shrunk in size. She was so close that he found himself listening to her draw breath.

He forced his mind back to the words she'd read. *I will believe and I will do whatever it takes to protect you.*

After breakfast the next morning, Alandra sat in her office off the courtyard. In the turmoil of the past week, she hadn't had time to go over her accounts. And she needed to get ready for the planting season, which was upon them. She could not allow her three unwelcome guests to delay the early crop of corn.

Alandra studied a rough drawing of her acres and the plots that had grown corn last year. Dorritt had taught her about land management and how to rotate crops and which crops enriched the soil and which ones depleted it. She stared at the paper, but saw instead Scully's face as she'd seen it by candlelight alone in her bedroom last night. His golden hair and white skin had glimmered in the low light.

There was a quiet knock at the office door. "Who is it?" she asked, sliding the papers out of sight. She didn't want either Fernando or Benito sticking his nose into her business.

"It is I, Doña Isabella."

Alandra, tasting sour acid, made a face, but said politely, "Please come in." This woman's intrusion reminded her that just this morning her housekeeper had informed her that while she had been at San Antonio, the housekeeper and Ramirez had taken the precaution of hiding all the easily carried off valuables in the house. The hidden wall

162

safe had been emptied and Ramirez buried her store of gold in an agreed upon location. Her people were loyal. She would not let them down.

The black-garbed widow entered. "I would like to have a few words with you, Doña Alandra."

Alandra nodded curtly at the chair across from her on the other side of the desk. The woman's haughty manner triggered a marked reaction in her. She lifted her chin. She would let the woman say what she'd come to say and then usher her out. "How may I help you?"

The widow examined the chair for dust and then sat. "I do not think you will welcome what I have to say, but I feel compelled to speak. I am older and have seen more of the world than you." The widow looked down her nose, her expression sour and her tone pompous.

"I do not welcome advice from you." Alandra lifted her chin, higher and firmer. "You may say what you wish, but I know that I am the Sandoval. And I will keep my land."

Isabella shook her head, sneering. "Land? What is land? It is merely a source of wealth. You have behaved foolishly in the extreme by marrying that Anglo — if you have indeed married that cowboy."

Alandra rippled with outrage at the slur cast upon Scully, who had stood as her friend, more than her friend, in all this. "Scully is twice the man Fernando Sandoval is."

"You speak as a girl without experience in the world," the widow flared. "Fernando Sandoval commands respect wherever he goes in Mexico. Do you think your lands are all that important? He merely wanted to take possession of what is his. He has thousands of acres around Mexico City and he has silver mines too. To him, this rancho is just another source of wealth and power. And he graciously decided to marry you so that you would not be left destitute when your father's land is transferred to him."

"That was good of him." But Alandra knew she was wasting her irony on this woman.

Scully had halted outside the door of Alandra's office. About to knock, he had realized that she was not alone and froze. Now he pulled his hand down. The widow's speech had started his insides buzzing like angry wasps. And Alandra's tone was dangerous, alerting him of her anger. Should he stay or go?

The widow went on speaking in the tone

a teacher might use to an ignorant student. "Offering you marriage was good of Fernando. Many prominent families in Mexico City have offered marriage contracts to Benito for his son. But Fernando realized that he must do his duty to his blood and marry you."

Scully gritted his teeth. Didn't the widow have any sense?

"It is so gracious of him to overlook my Indian blood." Alandra's voice dripped with acid sarcasm.

"*Sí,* it is, and it tells you the kind of man — the proud man — you have spurned. And he will not forget it. If you have any sense at all, you would beg forgiveness, renounce your unfortunate and hasty marriage to a man far beneath —"

Scully laid a hand on the door.

"*Mi esposo* Scully is far above Fernando in my eyes. I do not weigh men by their possessions and position in society. I weigh a man by his character and his courage. I have seen little of Fernando's and much of his disdain."

*She is defending me.* It took him a moment to take in her words about him.

"Fernando has a fine character and great courage," the Mexican lady insisted, sounding personally insulted.

"Then you should marry him," his wife declared. "You will be able to console him over losing my land. Oh, and also losing me. My marriage may have wounded his pride, but I doubt it has nicked his heart."

Scully heard a chair being pushed back, scraping the tile floor. He'd heard that sound in cantinas when men rose in anger.

"You are a foolish, heedless little girl." The widow's tone blazed and her words rushed one after another. "Marriage is not about love. You are your parents' daughter. Your father gave up everything for that half-breed —"

Before his spitfire wife slapped the starched-up widow, Scully decided to halt this conversation. He knocked as he opened the door. "Alandra." Looking across the small room, he did indeed see his wife poised and ready to spit fire. He couldn't help himself. He beamed at her, with her eyes snapping and her dusky cheeks rosy.

He tried to straighten his face, but his smile widened. He swallowed a chuckle.

The red-faced widow swung around, pushed past him and left without a word or nod. Scully stepped inside and closed the door behind him.

"What are you smiling at?" Alandra snapped, obviously irritated that he had

166

scared away her prey before she'd been able to move in for the kill.

"You." He loved how she looked now, fire still crackling in her eye. "You are quite a woman —"

"Señorita! Señorita!" Ramirez's voice interrupted them.

Instant dread doused Scully's high spirits. He turned and opened the door. "What is it?"

"They're nearly here!"

Alandra moved forward to stand in front of Scully. "Who?"

"Mexican Army!" Ramirez stood, panting, forcing out the words. "They are within sight and heading this way."

# SEVEN

With eyes dry and gritty from lack of sleep, Alandra found herself walking through a waking nightmare. Ahead of her strutted General Santa Anna, dictator of Mexico. In full military uniform of dark blue and white with lavish gold trim, he was thin, sallow, and had piercing blue eyes. She didn't like him. For so many reasons.

But most of all he filled her with a fear that froze her to her marrow. From what she had overheard — after Santa Anna, along with his army of six thousand, had crossed the Rio Grande in mid-February, they had been divided into columns of around two thousand. These columns had marched north one at a time ahead of him toward the Alamo.

Hanging back with the final column, Santa Anna had decided to spend time here with his friends, the Sandovals, until the bulk of his army reached San Antonio. Then he would decide the right moment to go to there himself. And retake the Alamo.

His blatant arrogance lodged in her throat. She despised him. She feared him.

In addition to suffering Santa Anna as a guest, she was being forced to endure having two thousand soldiers, camped around her rancho and hacienda, butchering her longhorns, hogs, and chickens, tearing down her fences for firewood, digging a latrine behind her barn. She was not personally afraid of the troops camping all around Rancho Sandoval, but the rest of the women on her ranch were hiding in either the hacienda or in their shuttered and bolted adobe houses. Soldiers were not to be trusted.

Her vaqueros lounged around the hacienda and other houses, their rifles looped over their backs, a warning to the soldiers to keep their distance. The fear that some soldier might be foolish or reckless enough to try to break into one of the houses kept Alandra's stomach twisted and knotted. How could she keep her people safe?

Her dear cousin Fernando walked beside Santa Anna, preening. He was pointing out all the wonders of his new holding, Rancho Sandoval. "As you can see, we have many fine mixed breed horses."

"Those are from Quinn, who ranches about ten miles west of here," Scully said, his low voice conversational. "He breeds mustangs with thoroughbreds. Makes stronger stock."

Her eyes widening, Alandra turned to look at him. So did Santa Anna and Fernando. Then they turned their backs to them and behaved as if they had heard nothing. She did not know how to react. Scully speaking without being asked a question? And to General Santa Anna, of all people? *Please, Scully, no.*

Then the general and her cousin proceeded toward the spring fountain at the far end of the paddock. Water trickled steadily over the brick fountain. "You see this rancho has many artesian springs and wells," Fernando bragged.

"Alandra's father and then her brother took the time to find them and corral the water so it wouldn't be wasted," Scully said without expression. "Quinn told me."

Alandra's lips parted. What was Scully doing? Did he not know how powerful and how cruel a man Santa Anna was? Her heart was beginning to hop and skip as if trying to warn Scully to tread lightly.

Fernando turned to Scully. "I do not know why you have come along, Anglo. You were not invited. Please go."

"A man doesn't have to be invited to his own rancho," Scully said coolly. "What I want to know is why you're acting like you own Rancho Sandoval when you don't."

Fear hissed through Alandra's nerves.

Fernando made a derisive sound and said to Santa Anna, "Anglos think they own Texas."

"They own parts of Texas," Scully went on, ignoring the rebuff. "The parts they paid for with U.S. dollars and honest gold. But my wife isn't an Anglo, and this is her rancho until proven otherwise in a court of law."

Fernando swung toward Scully. "Leave us now or suffer the consequences."

Scully chuckled. "You're mighty cocky. I'll give you that. If you want me to leave, why don't you try and make me."

Alandra watched her cousin turn brick red. She laid a restraining hand on Scully's arm.

Fernando looked down his long nose at Scully. "Gentlemen do not lower themselves to fisticuffs."

"All right, then. How about pistols or rifles or tomahawks?" Scully offered nonchalantly. "You pick."

Alandra clutched Scully's arm. He had

just issued a challenge. *No, Scully, not now. Not in front of the dictator of Mexico.*

Fernando laughed with scorn. "You see the *angloamericanos* don't know their place," he said to the general. "They think land makes them gentlemen."

"Oh, I know I'm not a gentleman," Scully said in a cool, easy tone. "But what has that got to with this? I just said, pick your weapon. Or is 'gentleman' another word for coward?"

Alandra suppressed a moan, digging her fingernails into Scully's arm.

Santa Anna laughed. "This is why I have come to Texas. Thank you, Anglo. You have reminded me of what I've come to put an end to. Riffraff that thinks to be in charge."

Scully folded his arms. "Is that why you came? I been wondering for a while why the Mexican Army is here."

Alandra clutched Scully's arm as tightly as she could.

"Shall I have you shot for being a rebel?" Santa Anna asked, still grinning at Scully.

"Oh, I'm no rebel. If I were, I'd be at the Alamo or farther east with Sam Houston. But since I have the chance here and now, I got to ask you, why not just leave the Texians alone? What is it that has you going to all this trouble?"

172

The smile slid from the general's face. "I do not have to answer to you."

"That's true, you don't. Just asking." Scully patted her hand on his arm, looking as though they were discussing everyday matters.

Alandra found she was having trouble breathing. Fernando spoke up, "*Angloamericanos* think they can stand against Mexico. They must be taught that they answer to Mexico. They are not a state unto themselves."

"Is that why?" Scully rubbed the side of his nose. "Everything has its price, though. If you teach the Texians this lesson, the ones who survive will probably leave Texas."

"That would be no great loss," Fernando said, sneering. And Santa Anna grinned.

"Well, if they leave, who's going to grow the cotton? Who is going to plant the corn? Who's going to pay taxes to Mexico City?"

"This is not about taxes," Santa Anna insisted, his face tightening. "It is about who will govern Texas."

"And Texas belongs to the Mexicans, and Mexico City governs Texas," Fernando snapped. "This is a lesson that the *angloamericanos* must learn as well as my dear cousin."

Scully shrugged. "Well, some lesson will

be learned by this war. But why did Spain let the Americans into Texas in the first place? They did it because they couldn't get anybody else to live up here with the Comanches and Karankawas and Apaches. Or that's what Mrs. Quinn told me. So who's going to live here when the Anglos are driven out?" he asked.

Santa Anna and Fernando stared at Scully as if they couldn't believe their ears.

Alandra's heart beat so strongly that her whole body pulsed with warning. She felt a bit faint. "*Mi esposo,* I am fatigued. Will you walk me inside for some coffee?"

Scully patted her hand on his arm again. "Well, since your cousin won't let me challenge him, I guess so. Good day, gentlemen." He turned and led her toward the hacienda.

Alandra trembled from head to toe and had to force herself not to run toward the courtyard. Just as they entered, she whispered, "Don't do that again — I beg you."

"You told me to speak up like a Spanish husband."

"That was before I knew the Mexican Army was coming to stay." She leaned closer to his maddeningly calm face. "Santa Anna is not like anyone you've ever met. He is a dictator. He answers to no one."

"That's not true."

She clutched his elbow tighter. How could she make him take this danger seriously? "*Sí,* it is."

"No, every man answers to God."

Scully's reply silenced her. His words could have been spoken by Quinn or Dorritt. His words strengthened her and terrified her — both. Scully was not the same *distante* vaquero he had always been. The change was unmistakable, and it made matters here more precarious than they already were. She started to speak but Benito and Isabella entered the courtyard too, their presence silencing her. How could she make Scully realize the danger Santa Anna posed? How could she stop him from getting himself killed?

Night had finally come. Scully ushered his wife into their room and shut the door on their unwelcome guests. He had thought the three relatives from Mexico City were enough to contend with, but the addition of the big-headed general was testing the limit of his patience. He stretched his neck muscles, loosening the knots Fernando Sandoval and the fancy general had tied there. "How long do you think that general is going to stay?"

Alandra turned to him and gripped his upper arms. "Scully, how could you?"

He liked the feel of her small hands on him. He resisted the urge to encircle her small waist. "What are you talking about?"

"Speak to Santa Anna that way? He could have had you shot."

He looked into her large dark eyes and realized how worried she was. "I just asked the man a few honest questions."

"One does not question a man who holds the power of life and death over a nation."

He didn't like worrying her, but truth was truth. "I don't hold with dictators. Americans don't."

"This isn't America. It is Texas, a state of Mexico."

Alandra sounded more than worried now. And she looked scared, her lower lip trembling. He touched her sleeve. "Don't worry about me. I haven't done anything wrong. I didn't challenge Santa Anna to a fight, just that cousin of yours."

She pulled away from him and began pacing. "How can I make you understand? Santa Anna doesn't have to follow the law. He is the law. He can do what he wants. To anyone."

Scully came up behind her. He couldn't bear to see her upset. "I see what you mean.

But acting weak doesn't ever stop men like Santa Anna or Fernando. If a man shows weakness, they just get ornerier and act worse. I was letting them both know what they were in for — if they think they can take what belongs to others . . . take what belongs to you."

Letting out a long sigh, Alandra rested her head against the bedpost. "You do not understand the kind of men those two are. They aren't honest like you are."

Her words were good to hear. And her nearness worked through him, bringing him fully alive. "Well, maybe I don't know their kind. Maybe I don't want to. And if I don't, maybe I'm not the kind of man who should have married you." The final words cost him.

"That is not the issue." She turned and faced him. "No one could do better than you have. You are a strong man and a loyal one. I just do not want anything to happen to you."

He looked over her head, not wanting to let her see how her approval, her coming face-to-face, her concern for his saftey affected him. "I'm here to protect you. That's what the Quinns sent me here to do, and I'm doing it."

"I know. But you must promise me that

you won't challenge either Santa Anna or Fernando again as you did today. You could be killed, Scully." The way she said this left him off-kilter. She sounded genuinely worried about him, more worried than he'd guessed.

He plunged on, keeping his mind on the question at hand, not the lovely woman standing so close to him. "It seems to me a lot of people could be killed — will be killed. We're in the middle of a war. I didn't like some of the men at the Alamo, but they won't back down. And if Santa Anna thinks he'll have an easy time beating them, he's wrong."

Scully felt Alandra's warm breath against his face. He resisted the attraction to her and went on. "Every time the Mexicans took on the Anglos last year, they lost way more men. Anglos are armed and know how to fight. And they won't back down. Did you take a look at some of the Mexican troops that are camping around us? Most of them don't look like they know which end of their sad muskets to point."

"What does that matter to us?" Alandra went to the window, head down.

Didn't she understand he was just stating the plain truth? "It matters because we're in the middle of this war. And whether we like it or not, we may have to choose sides. I didn't think that would happen. I mean, I'm not here as a settler." He followed her, wanting her close again, but careful not to crowd her. "I'm just working for Quinn. But now the Mexican Army has marched right up to us. How am I supposed to ignore that?"

She touched the latch that held shutters tight and turned to him. "Won't they just march away soon?"

"Yes, they will. But the outcome of the revolt could affect your title to this land. And Quinn's title to his land. You see that, don't you?"

She sat down on the edge of the large carved bed, staring down at the woven wool rug. "How did everything get so complicated?"

He went to the nearest bedpost and leaned a hand on it. Her dark hair gleamed in the low light. The room smelled of her, smelled of spicy sweet flowers. "I'm sorry if I worried you earlier, but I know men. I know how they think. It's best I let them know right up front that taking Texas, taking Rancho Sandoval — neither is going to be easy."

"I understand what you did, but it was dangerous. I . . . I am frightened."

He heard in her voice how much it cost her to admit her fear — even in private here with him. He made a bold move and sat down beside her. "You'd be stupid if you weren't worried. We got worry all around us. We can't change that."

She touched his arm. "I know. Your words are true. We cannot run. We must face this and see it through."

"*Sí.*" He wanted to put his arm around her but didn't. And he couldn't help wondering what tomorrow would drop on their doorstep. Could anything worse come than a Mexican general and two thousand troops camped outside?

Six days later Santa Anna and his troops were only a distasteful memory at Rancho Sandoval. Under the roof at the front of Ramirez's house, Alandra stood speaking to him about the early planting that should start soon. War or no, the crops had to go in or her people would go hungry. The sky was gloomy and matched her lowering mood. Movement in the distance caught her eye. "Someone's coming."

Ramirez turned and muttered an oath under his breath. "Sorry, señora," he apologized.

Alandra thought she understood. The last thing they needed was more company. Then she smiled. Some of the vaqueros she had ordered to keep watch on the most common approaches to the hacienda were escorting Quinn, Dorritt, Carson, Antonio, and a few of their vaqueros.

Alandra beamed. Now she could discuss Santa Anna, her relatives, her wedding, everything, with Dorritt and Quinn, and then it would all make sense. She hurried forward to greet them. Just as Quinn and Dorritt reached the hacienda, Scully walked out, hailing Quinn and waving.

Alandra rushed to Dorritt, who was riding sidesaddle. Joy — the first free feeling Alandra had experienced in days — bubbled up like spring water in the desert. "Tía Dorritt, I did not hope to see you! But are you well enough to ride here?"

Quinn swung down and went to help his lady from her horse. "You might well ask that. But you know your aunt when she's made up her mind."

Alandra was not fooled by Quinn's scolding tone. His pride in his wife shone through his words. Alandra almost danced on her toes, as she had as a child. *Tía Dorritt!*

"I am quite well, or I would not have come," Dorritt said as Quinn set her on her feet. "I decided I would be less jounced if I came on horseback. We rode at a slow pace and I was comfortable on my mount." She turned to stroke her palomino.

Scully came up and shook hands with Quinn. "Glad to see you, sir."

"*Felicitaciones* on your marriage," Quinn said.

Alandra threw her arms around Dorritt, squeezing her to let her know how much she was welcome. "I have longed to see you."

Dorritt hugged her close and whispered, "I'm sorry I couldn't come earlier." Then she said, looking toward the doorway, "When Carson told me that you and Scully were wed, I knew I must come."

Alandra tried to think what to say to this and could not come up with anything. Her emotions about her wedding were beyond her understanding, as if shrouded by a mist. She had not given much thought of what her "family" would think of her marriage. Surely they accepted that it had been necessary, but only an expedient to protect her.

"Who are these people?" Benito stood in the doorway.

Alandra turned, an instant rage blistering her, making one thing clear. *I don't want you there any longer.* She had hoped the three would leave with Santa Anna, but they had not wanted to go to San Antonio until the battle was won. "If it is any of your business, these are my Tía Dorritt and Tío Quinn."

Dorritt laid a restraining hand on her arm. "Alandra, please remember your manners," she murmured, swishing forward with her gloved hand held out. "How do you do?" She curtsied. "I am Señora Desmond Quinn, Alandra's former guardian. May I make known to you my husband, Quinn?"

Benito looked disgruntled, but evidently could not be rude even to an Anglo who was so patently a lady with the whitest of skin. He bowed over Dorritt's hand. "Good day, I am Benito Sandoval."

Alandra noticed then that Quinn was wearing his black tight-fitting dress suit. In her joy at seeing her family, she had missed this very important fact. She chewed her lower lip, quelling a grin. Quinn approached Benito, his gloved hand out. "Desmond Quinn, your servant, sir."

Alandra looked away to hide her amusement. Evidently, Dorritt had taken pains to show that she and Quinn knew how to dress and behave in society so that her Mexican relatives would be unable to dismiss them as inferiors. Carson followed his father, and he too was dressed for this visit in his finest dark suit, with a snowy white shirt and folded neck cloth. "We've met before, señor.

I'm Carson Quinn." And he bowed.

Benito looked even more disgruntled, but after bowing over Dorritt's hand and shaking Quinn's, he couldn't very well dismiss Carson, so he shook his hand too.

"Why don't we all go inside?" Dorritt said. "Carson told me that you have a lady with you from Mexico City. I would dearly love to discuss what the latest European fashions are in the capital."

Again, Alandra hid a grin. Dorritt knew just how to act as gentry and thus put everyone else in their proper place.

And with that, Dorritt took charge of the situation. Both Fernando and Isabella also fell before Dorritt's commanding presence. It was obvious to Alandra that this irked her Mexican relatives, but they were powerless to resist Dorritt's sway. Their responses were polite but terse. And Dorritt behaved as if they were merely being courteous.

Only when Dorritt tried to detach Alandra from the group by suggesting a stroll did Isabella rise to the challenge.

"But I also would love to take a stroll around the rancho," she said, standing along with them. "The rainy and chill weather and entertaining General Santa Anna here has kept me inside much too much."

Dorritt could not refuse Isabella's company, so the three ladies ventured out into the weak afternoon sun. "You say that you had the honor of entertaining the general?" Dorritt inquired politely.

Alandra had caught a sidelong glance Dorritt sent her upon hearing this news. What would her aunt say? Alandra looked down, hiding her expression.

"*Sí.*" Isabella preened just like Fernando had. "We are old friends and had traveled from Mexico City with him. When we were told we were near Rancho Sandoval, we left his company."

"I wondered how it was possible for you three to venture from the capital with only four armed men," Alandra said truthfully.

"Yes," Dorritt agreed, "the Comanches are a danger to travelers, especially those from Mexico."

Isabella shuddered at this. "I do not know how you bear living here in the wilderness. And the climate is so cold."

"It is an acquired taste," Dorritt replied with serenity. "Though I grew up in New Orleans, I find cities confining and unhealthy now. This land has a wild beauty that I find irresistible."

In the midst of this stilted conversation they saw a lone rider, calling and waving his arm. As he approached the hacienda, Alandra recognized him as one of her own vaqueros whom she'd dispatched to San Antonio a day after the general and troops left, going north. She had asked him to watch from a distance and return with news about what happened in Bexar. Her heart began beating faster as she watched him gallop toward them.

The man drew up in front of her. *"Doña,"* he gasped, "the Alamo has fallen and the *generale* had everyone in the old fort slaughtered except for a woman and child and a few servants."

Horror flowed through Alandra, nearly taking the breath from her. "No."

Isabella laughed. "So that is that for the rebellion. The *generale* would teach the *angloamericanos* who was in control in Texas."

Alandra could not speak. The idea that many men had been killed, slaughtered like cattle, left her speechless.

Dorritt stared at Isabella. "You rejoice when men are killed? What kind of woman are you? Have you no heart?"

Isabella flushed. And turned and marched away.

Dorritt put her arm around Alandra. "Be strong," she said, and then recited familiar verses: " 'The wicked have drawn out the sword, and have bent their bow . . . Their

186

sword shall enter into their own heart, and their bows shall be broken.' "

Alandra pressed her face into Dorritt's shoulder, her heart pounding in her ears. "I can't believe it. What will happen now?"

Alandra, Scully, Dorritt, Quinn, and Carson stood by the carriage the following day as her relatives prepared to leave for San Antonio, now in Mexican hands again. Alandra's hand itched to slap the smug expressions from their faces.

"We will bid you Godspeed then," Dorritt said, not concealing her desire for them to leave and now.

Fernando ignored her. "*Mi prima,* we will present your father's will to the magistrate in San Antonio and then return to Mexico City with Santa Anna. It should not take long to get a favorable ruling on the will and a favorable end to this Anglo rebellion." Wearing a scornful expression, he bowed, helped Isabella into the carriage, and then followed his father inside. He closed the door, still smirking at them.

Alandra watched the carriage turn and move out of their sight. She had never been happier to see guests leave.

And now what was to be said, to be done? She was aware that all her servants had gathered in the doorway behind her and that her vaqueros and peons were standing nearby. All looked as if they were waiting for something. She glanced up into Scully's face, which was in shadow under the brim of his hat. Who would speak first?

"We need to talk over what we're going to do," Quinn said, opening the discussion, but then he began walking away. Alandra and the others followed him toward the barn.

"Are we going to fight, Pa?" Carson asked. His voice cracked, embarrassing him.

Quinn looked back. "I never thought I'd say this, but I think I need to go and take part in this rebellion."

Dorritt placed a hand on his arm. "That's what I thought you'd say."

"How do you figure that?" Scully directed his question to Quinn as he walked alongside Alandra.

Alandra looked at him in surprise. Was this the same man who had challenged Santa Anna to his face? Did he doubt what must be done?

Quinn drew in a long breath. "I don't like most of the *angloamericanos* who live near San Felipe — my father-in-law, for instance. I don't hold with their owning slaves. But that's another issue altogether."

He entered the barn and went directly to the stall where his mount was. "Right is right. There are laws in war. Indians have their laws, their ways, and Anglos have theirs. Anglos don't slaughter men they've defeated. Mexicans are different. They slaughter. They did that to American mustangers and to that Padre Hidalgo when he led a revolt before the *angloamericanos* came."

Alandra's people, having followed them, crowded around the wide-open barn doors. Quinn's calm voice was in sharp contrast to the tension in their expressions.

"So it comes down to this." Quinn turned and faced them all. "Do I want the Mexicans to win or the Anglos? I must side with the Anglos in this. Maybe that's because of all the years I've lived with this woman" — he squeezed Dorritt's hand — "or maybe it's from my father who was an American.

"I don't know. But I know what I must do. My honor demands I fight with the Anglos. Santa Anna and the government in Mexico City have violated the Constitution of 1824. Mexico was to have a president, not a dictator. I'm against tyranny. How can a free man submit to any one man having all the power?"

Quinn did not often give a long speech

like this. Alandra realized that she agreed with everything he had said — even though she was a Tejano. She looked to Scully. What would his stand be? And where would it lead them all?

# EIGHT

Scully looked at Alandra and then at Quinn.
A time for decision had come. Till now he'd
just been riding the rapid current, but now
he must dip his paddle into the water and
set his own course. He knew what he must
say. "You're right. I don't hold with having
men like that Santa Anna in charge. I don't
own any land here but that doesn't matter."
*Alandra does.*

"I don't hold with tyranny either," Scully
continued, and with each word, new
strength sparked within him. And the words
kept coming, as if without knowing it, he'd
been thinking about all of it and waiting for
this moment to declare himself. "I don't
want men like Santa Anna and Fernando
Sandoval having the say over me and others. It's not right."

But would Alandra agree? Would she see
that he had to go and do this for her? Leave
her?

Dorritt looked paler but resolute, her chin firm.

Alandra spoke, her voice low and urgent, "What will you do, Tío Quinn? And Scully?"

Scully stared at her in the chilly barn with sunlight filtering through the boards overhead. In that moment, she appeared to glow with her own light, as though Quinn's words about honor and liberty had fired her from within. Still, she didn't draw nearer to him. He felt the space between them. He wanted to move closer to her but hesitated.

"We better make our plans and saddle up," Quinn said. "We'll head to Sam Houston, who's commanding the Texas Army east of here. I don't think it will be hard to find an army." He grinned.

"You are going to go to war?" Alandra asked in a breathless voice. "Just like that?" Her eyes looked moist and she was blinking.

Scully couldn't stop himself. He leaned over and touched her cheek. "Don't worry." She looked down, but pressed her hand over his briefly, then drew back. What did that mean? Did she want him to go? Or stay?

"Before we go, Scully," Quinn said, "we have to figure out how to leave our wives well protected."

Scully had already thought of this snag.

"I don't see that as a problem," Dorritt said, her voice gritty. "Ash is nearly sixty and he won't be going to war."

Quinn snorted. "The Anglos wouldn't welcome him anyway. They don't want black men to fight alongside them."

Dorritt looked strained and nodded. "So he and Reva and our men will hold our ranch. Here, Alandra and I have Ramirez, Carson, Antonio, Emilio, and the vaqueros to hold Rancho Sandoval. We will manage to keep as safe as possible."

Quinn grinned, lifted his wife's hand and kissed it. "Forgive me. I forgot. My wife is strong."

Scully moved closer to Alandra, wanting to take her hand, feel it soft and small in his again. He wished she would say something to him. Just a word of how she was taking this.

"Pa," Carson spoke up, "I'm not staying here while you go fight."

His expression sobering, Quinn looked to his son. "Carson, you are not yet a man. If you were sixteen, I'd say you should choose. But you have to stay and hold the land."

"Ma just said that she and the vaqueros can hold the land. I want to go. I want to fight." Carson's face flushed to the roots of his hair.

Scully understood the boy wanting to go. And Quinn wanting him to stay safe.

Dorritt rested a hand on Carson's shoulder. "Son, I know you do, but I need you with me."

Carson looked mutinous.

Though still uncertain of his place with her, Scully moved to stand by Alandra. The five of them were grouped around Quinn beside the stall. And most of Alandra's people were still watching from the doorway.

"Son, it is a big thing to ask of you," Quinn said, "but I ask it too. I need to know that you're here with your mother guarding her and the baby. This is a lonely world when one is an orphan. What if we lose your mother in childbirth? If I am also taken, who will care for the baby?"

Scully was surprised by Quinn's bluntness. This was not the way men spoke in front of womenfolk. He cleared his throat. "Your pa's right, Carson. No one will think less of you if you stay behind to protect the womenfolk. It's hard being left alone." *All alone in the world like me.* He wished Alandra would look at him.

"*Sí,*" Alandra agreed, "where would I have been without your mother and father to raise me? Family must stick together. Not like my relatives who came only to take

194

whatever they could, but real family. That's what I'm talking about."

*Real family.* Suddenly, Scully felt choked, as if hands had tightened around his throat. *Real family.* He felt as close as family to these people. *But I'm not part of this family. Not really.* But he knew how to protect them, and he would.

The next hour raced past. Quinn and Scully packed as much lead and powder as they could into saddlebags. The housekeeper and cook quickly packed pemmican, tortillas, and three sacks, one of dried beans, one of coffee beans, and one of cornmeal, oil, and pans for campfire cooking.

Everyone was hurrying and helping, even Dorritt. Alandra felt completely useless. What could she do for Scully? He had already done so much for her. Would she let him go off to defend her and give him nothing? Then she remembered something of her brother's and hurried to her bedroom.

Lying prone on the cold tile floor, she reached under the bed and felt around until she found the box secured underneath the bed frame. Holding it with both hands, she hurried back into the courtyard and saw Scully at the door. He would leave for war. Perhaps death. That final word pushed her past the stiffness that had possessed her and kept her silent, until now. He was no longer just the Anglo cowboy. He had become her husband, her friend, her champion.

"Scully," she called, her throat trying to close. When he turned, she motioned for him to come to her so no one else would see this parting. He turned and moved toward her, looking as uncertain as she felt. That strengthened her, made her bolder.

When he reached her, she took his forearm and pulled him back into the shadows. "I want to give you something," she murmured. She opened the leather box to reveal two dueling pistols. "These were my father's and my brother's. I want you to take them with you."

He looked at them but made no move to accept them. "But they belong in your family."

"*Sí*, they do." She hoped he understood what she was trying to tell him. But then, what exactly did she mean by this offering? She wasn't sure. How were they supposed to feel about each other? He had acted on her behalf, maybe was that just loyalty to the Quinns? Maybe more.

*There isn't time.*

Closing her mind to this confusion, she took out each heavy, cold pistol and handed it to him. "In battle, I am sure it is best to have as many weapons as you can load and carry. And these are fine *pistolas*."

Looking grave, he hefted each pistol in turn. Lifting his poncho, he slipped one into the back of his belt and the other to the left side of his belt. He was about so say something when Alandra heard footsteps approaching.

For some reason she could not have explained, she did not want to be seen alone with Scully in this very private moment. She tugged him deeper into the shadows in the hallway that opened onto the courtyard. She glimpsed Quinn and Dorritt also halt before entering the courtyard, the two of them not far away.

"Stop," Dorritt said, turning to face her husband. "I'll say my good-bye to you here."

Alandra looked up into Scully's green eyes, holding her index finger to her lips, then tugged him farther back into the shadows. She did not want to eavesdrop on her aunt and uncle. She meant to retreat even farther, but could not as Dorritt spoke again.

"I don't know how I will bear to have you leave me," she said. "We have hardly ever been parted since you made me your wife."

Dorritt leaned her head against Quinn's chest. He stroked her face and kissed her hair. "I do not want to leave you, my sweet wife, my tall lady. You have made my life more than I ever imagined it could be."

Dorritt straightened and looked into his eyes. "I feel the same way. But we mustn't speak as if we'll never see one another again. I have faith that you will come home to me safe and sound." She rested a hand on her rounding abdomen. "And be with me for the birth of this child."

"I believe that too." Quinn took Dorritt into his arms and kissed her.

Alandra's emotions were so mixed and so many that she could not untangle them. All she knew for sure was that she did not want Scully to go to war. Turning, she wrapped her arms around his chest and clung to him. *Do not leave me. Do not go toward danger.* She thought the words but could not say them as she rubbed her face against the soft wool of his poncho. Would he push her away? Was she being too forward?

Then his arms came around her and his lips touched the top of her head. Though she was as close to him as one human being could be to another, she yearned to be closer still. She tilted up her chin. And Scully's mouth came down and claimed hers. Her response was instant and overwhelming. How could mere lips wield such power?

She clung to him, no longer feeling the floor beneath her feet. At that moment, Scully Falconer, her husband, was the only thing that existed for her. The smell of his skin, the feel of muscles under her palms, his strength pressing against her.

But most of all, the exquisite touch of his lips on hers. She answered his kiss with hers and another, then another. Irresistible sensation, mesmerizing experience. Then his breath blew against her cheek and he was whispering into her ear, "I'll be back. Just stay safe."

Tears tried to form in her eyes. She blinked and drew in air, refusing them. "I will stay safe. Be careful, Scully. I want you to come home." She took his hand and pressed it over her heart so he could feel how it raced because of him, because of his having to leave.

He stroked her cheek and gazed into her eyes. No man had ever looked at her this way. It was wonderful; it was overpowering.

Then Quinn, with Dorritt on his arm, stepped into the courtyard. "Scully!" he called. "Let's be going."

Scully dipped down once more and stole a quick kiss. It seemed that he wanted to speak, but then he shook his head and released her. "Go first," he whispered.

"No." She gripped his hand.

He resisted a moment but then allowed her to lead him by the hand through the courtyard and out the front doors. She wanted him to know how fine a man she knew he was, how much he had come to mean to her. Still, uncertainty over how he viewed their marriage kept her from using words. At this crucial moment she would do nothing to put a strain on the unexplored bond between them.

Dorritt stood beside Quinn, who was already in the saddle. Alandra went with Scully to his mount and waited while he checked the girth and then swung up. Just like Quinn, it hadn't taken very long for him to be ready to leave for war. His saddlebags were full and a blanket was rolled up behind him. Two canteens hung from his saddle horn. He wore his poncho, with his long rifle slung over his back. All this made it real. *He is leaving. He is going away to fight.*

Dorritt moved to Alandra, took her hand and led her back to the doorway. Then she stopped beside Carson, who looked as if he were swallowing tears.

Alandra made herself look toward Scully and Quinn. "*Vayas con Dios,* Tío Quinn.

*Vayas con Dios,* Scully."

And to herself she said the deep words she could not say aloud, *Mi esposo valiente y fuerte.*

Scully and Quinn followed the Camino Real as far north as they could and then headed northeast to avoid Bexar. Santa Anna was still there, no doubt gloating over his victory, his slaughter of the Anglos. They followed the high, rushing San Antonio River, then looked for a shallow place to ford so they could cross and continue to head north to the Guadalupe River at Gonzales. It was there that they'd heard Sam Houston was gathering troops.

At midday they came to an abandoned cabin. The door stood open and chickens squawked in the yard. Only the horses had been taken. A cow lowed in the yard where it grazed. They moved on and before nightfall had passed three more abandoned houses. Farms here were sparse. And it was eerie to see them standing empty, even their doors left open.

It looked like people had just left with the clothes on their backs. Dishes of spoiled food still sat on tables inside. The empty houses gave Scully a funny feeling in the pit of his stomach. He found himself keeping his voice low, as if someone were sick or had just passed away. At least, Alandra and Mrs. Quinn weren't in his path. But the empty houses drove deep the fact that this was not a normal time. This was war. People were running for their lives.

He and Quinn stopped and gathered eggs in one chicken yard, knowing they'd make a good easy meal, and that if they didn't, the eggs would go to waste anyway. Or would fall to the Mexican troopers, who Quinn thought would soon head eastward to engage Sam Houston. Santa Anna would go on killing until he succeeded in running the Anglos out of Texas, or until the Anglos ran him out.

Nightfall was nearly upon them and it was raining on and off when Quinn found a place for them to camp. A grove of oaks and poplar trees where they could take cover huddled around the sandstone riverbank. They hobbled their horses so they could graze and drink at will, then they built a small fire and made coffee and scrambled the eggs they'd gathered, wrapping them in warmed tortillas.

Scully held a tin cup of coffee in his hands and breathed in the fragrant steam. The night was damp and promised to grow chilly. "Where do you think we are?" he asked.

Before Quinn could reply, they heard the sound of voices and the hooves to the west, beyond the live oaks around them. Putting their coffee cups down, they drew their pistols.

"Anglos," Quinn whispered.

Scully nodded. There had been something strange about the voices.

They silently worked their way through the trees till they could see the strangers coming down the road on horseback. To their surprise, it was two women.

Scully glanced at Quinn, who nodded for him to move out of cover. "Ladies!" Scully called out, pulling off his hat, letting his blond hair show. "Where are you headed?"

Both women were startled, which disturbed their mounts. When they finally managed to get their horses under control, the older woman called out, "Who's there?"

"I'm Scully Falconer, a hand for Quinn, west of Bexar. And I'm here with Quinn. We're on our way to join Sam Houston."

"Quinn?" the woman repeated. "You mean Mrs. Dorritt Quinn's man?"

"Yes." Quinn stepped out from among the trees, "I'm Dorritt's husband, Quinn."

The woman pressed her hand to her heart.

"Thank the good Lord! I've heard of your wife, the New Orleans lady who married the half-breed Cherokee. I have a friend in San Antonio who knows her. My daughter and I are traveling alone. Our men are already with Houston and we're running from the Mexican Army."

Scully didn't like the way the woman talked about Quinn being a half-breed, but Quinn didn't look irritated. He was probably used to such rude comments by now.

Quinn went forward and took the older woman's reins. "We're camping here for the night. You women should come on and stay with us. We'll keep watch over you."

"Praise God," the younger woman said, slipping from her saddle. "We've been so afraid of staying on our own for the night without a man to protect us."

She swayed as her feet touched the ground, and Scully gave her his arm. Then he took her reins and walked her horse into the oak grove. A few dry leaves still clinging to branches rustled overhead. Soon they'd hobbled the women's horses and were all sitting around the fire, drinking coffee and eating tortillas and the rest of the eggs.

It was apparent that the women had left in haste. They hadn't brought anything but canteens and blankets. "Why didn't you stay on your land?" Scully asked.

"We're frightened, of course," the older woman replied, looking at him as if he lacked intelligence. "You can't trust Mexicans."

"You can trust some Mexicans and Tejanos," Quinn amended. "De Zavala and Navarre are just two of the Tejanos who are for freedom for Texas."

The woman sniffed. "You heard what that Santa Anna did to the men at the Alamo."

The younger woman began weeping. "It's all so horrible." And then she was leaning against Scully's shoulder.

He didn't want her crying on him. He had the urge to leap up, but that wouldn't be polite. "Miss," he said, "you're safe here with us. Don't cry."

She looked up, and in the light of their fire her eyes were swollen and red. She sniffled and wiped her nose with a handkerchief. "It's all so horrible," she repeated.

Scully didn't like the way she was looking at him as if he were a pie she wanted to eat. *No, thank you, lady.* "Why don't you turn in?" he suggested. "When my wife's upset, lying down helps her."

"Your wife?" the young woman said, abruptly looking as if she were mad at him, in the midst of her tears. "You're married?"

"Yes, Scully's married the *doña* of Rancho Sandoval just days before the Alamo fell," Quinn said, fighting a grin. "Now you ladies get your bedrolls out and lie down near the fire to keep warm. We'll stand guard tonight. Sleep, and tomorrow you'll feel better."

"Yes," Scully said, "we'll keep watch."

After finishing their coffee, the two women did what Quinn had suggested. Scully nodded to Quinn, letting him know that he would take the first watch.

"You married a Tejano?" the younger woman said, looking up at Scully before he moved off.

"Yes."

"Why?" the older woman asked. "I'm sure you could have found a decent white woman to marry you."

"I married a fine lady," Scully said, irritation digging into him like cactus needles.

The women rolled over and tossed, turned, and fidgeted until they finally settled down.

Scully found a stout tree trunk that would hide him from view, while Quinn picked up more fallen branches and boughs to keep the fire going against the creeping chill of the night.

When he passed by Scully, he whispered,

"Aren't you glad you're a married man? I am."

Scully managed a grin, but his mind was back at Rancho Sandoval with Alandra. He pictured her in her bed in her high-necked white nightgown. A yearning to be there on the floor beside her dragged at him like a physical pull westward toward home. He'd left her there in order to protect her from Santa Anna's tyranny, but had that been wise?

He wished he could have cut himself in two, been in two places at once. He bowed his head a moment. *God, I don't like bothering you, but keep my wife safe. Keep them all safe. Please.*

Alandra stared at the uniformed Mexican Army courier and then took the letter from him. She read the Spanish words twice. The black ink in the extravagant script danced in front of her eyes. Then she looked up. "Am I to send an answer?"

The man shrugged.

She called to Ramirez, who came out with her leather purse. She gave the man two pesos. He smiled and bowed, climbed back on his horse and was off.

Feeling mortally wounded, she walked inside, where Dorritt waited for her in the courtyard. "Who was it, Alandra?"

"A courier sent by Santa Anna with this." She handed Dorritt the document.

After reading it, Dorritt looked up. "Your relatives didn't waste any time in putting that will before a magistrate."

Alandra gave a brittle chuckle. "I didn't expect them to delay." She finally let herself sit down. "What am I to do? It says that I'm to appear in court tomorrow if I want to challenge the will."

Dorritt frowned. "The more that I see of what that Fernando and Benito do, the more I think that the will must be false. If it were valid, then why the hurry? And this ploy of Fernando's to marry you so quickly." She shook her head. "That tells me they wanted to make sure they'd get and keep the land whether they were entitled to it or not. No doubt they anticipated, hoped that a young impressionable girl would be over-awed by Fernando's elegance."

Alandra laughed without humor. "Well, they thought wrong then, didn't they?" She passed a hand over her creased brow. "None of what has happened feels real," she whispered, recalling Scully riding away with Quinn just two days ago.

"I know. The kidnapping, the arrival of your relatives, and then Santa Anna — of all people — and now Quinn and Scully having to leave us. The war. Everything."

"And now this," Alandra said, taking the letter back from Dorritt. "I must go."

"I'll send Carson with you," Dorritt said.

"No." Alandra rose, shaking her head. She didn't want anyone she loved along with her. This trip to San Antonio would not go well, and she would face it alone. "I will not take Carson."

*I do not want to hear comforting words or look into a face I love and see worry and pity.*

Alandra continued, "I want him here with Ramirez protecting you and the ranch. I'll take three of the best fighters of all my vaqueros. Santa Anna and his army are concentrating on battling the Anglos. I am important to Fernando and Benito, but not to Santa Anna. I won't be bothered."

Dorritt rose and took Alandra's free hand. "Be careful. There are always Comanches and stray Apaches and Mexican deserters. We can't forget that you were kidnapped just weeks ago. Maybe you should take more than three men."

"I think having an army march through here on the way to the Alamo will have scared off any *bandidos* or renegades. Rats hide when the cat prowls." She thought about Quinn and Scully again, heading toward a war. It left her feeling empty, as if her shoulders were floating in midair, unconnected to the rest of her.

Dorritt must have guessed what she was thinking because she put a comforting arm around her shoulders. "They'll be all right. Maybe you should stay here and ignore the summons to court. The war will decide who will win not only Texas, but also Rancho Sandoval."

"I will go." Alandra leaned her cheek briefly against Dorritt's cheek. "I must defend my land." They didn't know how the war would go, after all.

*Scully, please be careful. Stay safe. Lord, help me to believe your promises to foil the wicked. I know men die in wars. And many mothers and wives here and in Mexico are praying for the . . . ones they love.*

Walking beside the lawyer who always handled legal matters for her and the Quinns, Alandra entered the court in San Antonio. It was a small room, with the red, white, and green flag of Mexico at the front. The magistrate, all in black, sat behind an imposing desk. A secretary with ink, quill, and paper sat at a smaller desk in the corner. Two benches faced the magistrate.

Her relatives sat stiffly in a row on the front bench.

She had been relieved to find her lawyer in town. But some Tejanos residents had never left San Antonio, and others had already returned to town, no doubt thinking that the war was won for the government in Mexico City.

Still feeling very much alone, Alandra sat behind her relatives with her lawyer. Isabella turned and gave her a scathing look. Alandra forced herself to give a brave and gracious smile in return, hoping her low spirits didn't give her away. *God is with me here.*

The secretary rose and announced that the document, the will of the late Esteban Carlos Juan Sandoval, had been registered for probate. The magistrate finally looked up and addressed them. "I have the will in hand and am prepared to begin the probate proceedings. Are there any other petitions?"

Alandra's lawyer rose, and presented her petition to the secretary. It asserted that the alleged will was false or that her father had written the will under duress. The secretary took it to the magistrate, who read the petition and frowned. "This petition will be sent along with the will to the state court as soon as I have made my ruling. I will send both parties a reply through their attorneys."

The secretary finished noting what had been said, and then the magistrate left the room. Exiting, Alandra's relatives walked past her without looking in her direction. Since she didn't think she could be civil to them, she was glad to let them pass. Bitter but indistinct words swarmed in her mind, and if spoken, might have scalded her throat.

When she and her lawyer were alone in the small room, he told her, "I don't hold any hope for your case, Señora Falconer. I suggest that you send most of your cattle to another property and remove all your personal effects from the house. You will lose this case." With that, he bowed over her hand with obvious regret and left her.

She wandered out into the gloomy March day and thought of the bright summer sun. Her whole life had become as bleak as this day. Her lawyer's only advice was to take whatever valuables and cattle she could send and carry away from Rancho Sandoval. She wished she'd let Carson come with her. Maybe having some family here with her would have made her feel better.

She shook her head at this thought. No, it would have made it worse. Carson would have been outraged by the way the Spanish courts worked. More than once she'd heard Anglos complain about not being permitted to speak in court in their own behalf. And Anglos also deplored the lack of juries.

Today, she could not bear angry words even in defense of her. *I am so tired. I want to go home — while it is still my home.*

*Scully, where are you? Are you safe?*

She went to the inn where her three vaqueros waited inside. "I want to leave now. Will you get the horses saddled and ready?"

She paid the innkeeper and walked out to her horse, feeling stiff, like a wooden doll.

The cold wind sanded her cheeks until they felt raw. The gray sky wrapped around them like unbleached wool. The vaqueros rode around her, ready to protect her. But the miles stretched on. *What should I do? What can I do? Is there a way to keep my land? My inheritance?*

Numb with defeat, she missed the first warning that something bad was happening. Then rifleshot. The vaquero next to her fell from his horse. Terrified, she called out his name. The vaquero on her other side slapped his reins on the rump of her mount. More gunshots sounded as the vaqueros on each side of her kept pace with her horse as it raced ahead. She turned around but couldn't see the faces of the men chasing them.

Another gun shot. The vaquero beside her was blown off his saddle. He screamed, and she pulled up on her reins to go back to him.

"No, señorita! No!" the remaining vaquero shouted. "Ride! Escape!"

Another shot, and he fell too. She was surrounded, her mount danced on its hind feet, rearing and trumpeting, echoing her own panic. She was knocked from her saddle then, and lay winded. She looked up and couldn't believe her eyes.

# NINE

Scully and Quinn headed farther northeast, trying to find Sam Houston and the Texas Army. The mass of settlers fleeing before the Mexican Army clogged the muddy roads, slowing them. When the two talkative women who had traveled with them for the past two days met up with relatives also on the run, Scully and Quinn found themselves on their own again. How good to enjoy some peace. Alandra never chattered on as these two women had, barely taking a breath.

Coming around a bend in the timber, Scully and Quinn pulled up their horses. Ahead of them was a vast stirred-up sea of people, moving, talking, waving, shouting. The river had halted the exodus. Scully had heard the commotion but the timber blocked the view. He didn't think he'd seen this many people in one place since a fiesta day in San Antonio. His horse fidgeted beneath him, and the same restlessness vibrated through his flesh. He didn't like crowds.

And he didn't like the thought of going in the same direction all these strangers were headed. He was used to and liked living in the open, away from people. This swarm of humans pressed against him, making him feel as if he were being surrounded, corralled, trapped. Was everybody in Texas leaving?

He leaned toward Quinn and said, "What do you think? Around a thousand?"

Quinn shrugged and continued to stare at the frantic people, mobbing the lone ferryman. Fear of Santa Anna must be rousing them, Scully thought. "They all act as if they can't wait their turn to cross the Guadalupe River to the town of Gonzales," Quinn said. "They look like they might rush the ferry when it gets back on this side to load up again. Somebody could get killed."

Then the gray sky overhead opened and more rain sluiced down. Scully had made the mistake of looking skyward at just the wrong moment. And now he found himself gasping as if he were drowning. He sputtered, spitting rainwater from his mouth. Then he reached down and opened his canteen, letting the water from his hat brim pour into it.

The crowd around the ferryman screeched, shouted, and ran for cover. Did it have to rain like this on top of every of other misery? Even his wool poncho, though still shedding water, couldn't keep out the penetrating dampness. Why did this March have to be so unusually wet?

Quinn glanced over and shook his head. "Let's see if we can find somebody who looks like they know something."

Scully followed Quinn as he rode slowly around the edges of the crowd. Finally, Quinn halted, swung down from his horse and tossed his reins to Scully to hold, before striding away. Within minutes Quinn had detached an older man from the roiling crowd and hauled him back. Then Quinn led the man and Scully to stand under the shelter of a post oak surrounded by mud.

"You're Washburn from east of Bexar, aren't you?" Quinn asked when they were beneath the tree. Before the man could answer, he went on, "What's the news from east of here? Know anything? Where's the Texas Army? Who's in charge?"

Rain poured off the man's hat. "There's troops under Fannin at the La Bahia fort at Goliad, to the southeast. And Sam Houston is heading northeast of here gathering volunteers for the Texas Army. I heard somebody say he burned Gonzales to keep it from the Mexicans." The man sounded as if he had been waiting a long time for someone to ask his opinion of matters. "We were hoping to buy provisions when we crossed today. It's hard to know what is happening. I don't think anybody knows exactly. I mean, where's the Mexican Army? Where's Sam Houston going?"

Scully looked across the river. But because of the usually dry weather before this recent onslaught of rain, timber and canebrakes grew where there had once been water, crowding both sides of the riverbank. So he couldn't see ahead, to where Gonzales was said to be.

Quinn looked at the man, nodding his understanding. "Why are you here?"

"Santa Anna has ordered everything — every house, cabin, plantation — burned. He's driving us Anglos out of Texas. That's why everyone's running. I mean, after the slaughter at the Alamo . . ." The man shook his head. "I thought I could be happy living in Texas as a part of Mexico, but after that, I can't. That isn't the way things are done."

Scully understood. He couldn't live in a Texas squashed under the heel of Santa Anna either. If the dictator succeeded in

218

driving the Anglos out of Texas, how could he stay with Alandra? Then he remembered, his marriage to her was a sham. But how could Alandra stay in Texas if she lost her land?

"Where are you headed?" Quinn asked Washburn.

"I got family in Natchitoches. I guess I'll head there with my daughter-in-law. I'm an old man. I can't rebuild my place here. When we came to Texas, I had a son to help me . . ." The man swallowed and looked away.

"I'm sorry you must leave the graves of your family," Quinn said. "But do not give up hope. I have not. I intend that Santa Anna will be defeated. We will run him out of Texas."

Washburn clapped a hand on Quinn's shoulder. "Good man. Now I got to go and help my daughter-in-law with my grandsons. Godspeed and I hope you bring down that butcher Santa Anna."

Scully and Quinn wished the man well and then looked at one another as he walked off. "Which way should we go?" Quinn asked. "Should we cross over and see if Gonzales is indeed burned?"

Scully stood, watching the throng of people surging and cresting just like the river they wanted to cross, a river swollen and rolling fast with the spring rain. Miserable inside and out, he was restless. He looked to Quinn. "If I were Houston, I'd burn anything I thought the advancing enemy could use, and the old man said as much — that he burned Gonzales to keep it from the Mexicans. So I don't think we need cross this river just to see a burned-out town."

Quinn nodded. "Houston could be anywhere northeast of here. Fannin is at a fort. I say we go to Goliad and see if we can join up there."

Scully swung up onto his horse. "Let's go."

Quinn followed suit and the two of them rode away from the commotion at the ferry. Witnessing the widespread panic and riding through the constant rain pulled at Scully. These things were trying to drag him down like a calf surrounded by a pack of baying wolves.

"It seems like both armies are moving east," Quinn said. "I'm glad our women are west of Bexar. Out of this stampede."

Scully was struck by Quinn using the words "our women." Gritty determination fired him then, and he resolved to do whatever it took to keep Alandra safe. The image of her standing beside him, pale in the candlelit church, moved him, reminded him. When he went to Bexar to marry her, he'd taken a vow to protect her, and he'd do just that.

Still, he was only one man. Then the old memory, of being trapped in the dark and hearing screams, wrapped around his windpipe and nearly choked him. *God, keep Alandra safe.*

Just after dawn, Dorritt paced in the still dimly lit hallway off the courtyard at Rancho Sandoval. Her husband and Scully had been gone for days now. And Alandra had not returned from the court in Bexar, as expected yesterday. Dorritt knew she had to decide what to do.

As she paced, she whispered prayers. Prayer usually gave her confidence, peace. But today, in the dim morning light, after a sleepless night, she could not stop pacing and wringing her hands. Worry had dug in its poisoned talons and would not let her go.

Carson appeared behind her. "Ma, I know Pa left me here to guard you and Alandra's rancho, but I can't stay here. I have to go and find out what's keeping her in Bexar. Something's wrong. I feel it."

Dorritt wanted to argue with him, but she

couldn't. And he sounded so grown-up and sure of what he should do. Her son, who was nearly a man, was prepared to do what she had not wanted him or asked him to do. *This is hard, Father.* She turned and wrapped her arms around him. He was already dressed and ready to leave. *But he's too young,* an inner voice said, weakening her.

She closed her mind to it. His father had been orphaned at thirteen and explored Colorado with Pike. Carson was a year older than Quinn had been then. She drew in a deep breath. "I'm trying to have faith that Alandra has just been delayed, that your father and Scully are fine. I'm trying."

Carson hugged her back. "I'm holding the faith too. But I have to go. Alandra might be in trouble. I'll follow our usual route to Bexar. Maybe I'll find her on the way home, or find that she's been delayed in Bexar. Who knows what those relatives of hers have got going? She might have been forced to stay over. And may need help — family help."

Dorritt nodded, pursing her lips against fear-filled words that might flow out of their own accord.

"Ma, you'll be safe here with the vaqueros to guard you. Just don't leave the rancho,

222

all right?"

Two more figures came into the courtyard. "Carson," Antonio called, Emilio at his side.

Carson drew his mother along by the hand as he moved toward the other young man. "Antonio and Emilio are going with me," he told her. "You need to stay here, Ma, in case Pa or I send word," he repeated.

Dorritt couldn't speak, afraid that she might give in to tears. Tears that might drown all hope. So instead she mustered a smile and nodded, then spoke in Spanish, because it had just the phrase she wanted to use. *"Vayas con Dios, mi hijo."* She turned to Reva's son, Emilio. In turn, she stroked each of the darker, still boyishly smooth cheeks. *"Vayas con Dios, mi hijo."*

When Carson told Ramirez where he was going, Ramirez had insisted that he would join them on their way to find Alandra. They'd left while the sun was still low over the eastern horizon. Now it was high near its zenith — if a body could have seen it through the low thick clouds. Fortunately, they hadn't opened yet to pour more rain. When the four of them had left that morning, they'd been able to see their breath. But it was getting warmer in spite of the cloud cover.

But from back a long ways, they'd seen vultures circling ahead. A bad sign. One that made Carson's stomach slip lower. *It could just be what's left from an animal kill. Don't think that it might be Lonnie. Don't think that. She's probably in Bexar at the inn, drinking coffee and listening to gossip.*

But the vultures continued circling, and then the four of them came around a bend and halted. Carson's heart sped up, raced. He urged his mount forward. Men he recognized were under a tree, one lying and two slumped nearby. But no horses and no Alandra.

He reached the men and swung down from his horse. "What happened?"

The slumped man looked up. "Thank God you've come," he gasped. "I'm shot and they are dead."

Carson pulled his canteen from his saddle. Hurrying forward, he put an arm around the wounded vaquero's head and shoulders, held the canteen to his parched lips. The man drank thirstily and then, exhausted, laid his head back against Carson's arm. *"Bandidos,"* he said, wincing with pain. "They attacked us and carried away our lady. And took our horses."

"Which way did they go?" Carson asked.

"South, but that doesn't matter. One of

them left this with me." The vaquero tried to pull something from inside his shirt. Carson did it for him. It was a smudged piece of paper, and words had been scribbled on it in poor script. Scowling, Carson read it, then folded it and slipped it into his inside pocket.

The wounded man fumbled, trying to grip Carson's sleeve. "You must find her."

"I will." He looked around. *I will.* "Antonio and Emilio, first we'll cover the bodies of the two who died so they'll be safe from scavengers. Then we'll head back to the rancho and send some men with a wagon to pick up their bodies and take them back for decent burial. Now we'll take this man home. My mother will tend his wound and we'll get packed to head out and bring Alandra home again."

"What was the note?" Antonio asked.

"It's a ransom note. Let's get busy and get back as soon as we can."

The three of them acted quickly and didn't waste breath on words. Carson was sick inside as he piled rocks over the men who'd died trying to protect their lady, Alandra, his Lonnie. That's what he had called her since he was very little. Lonnie. He gritted his teeth and sucked in all the anger and worry. Thinking bad, sad thoughts that didn't help. *I have to find Lonnie. I will find Lonnie.*

A week or more since they'd left Rancho Sandoval, near the end of day, Scully and Quinn were in the midst of a stretch of timber when they caught the faint sound of rapid gunfire in the distance. And not just rifles or muskets, but what sounded like bigger explosions as well. Scully looked to Quinn. Had they found the army at last? But too late?

Quinn nodded, looking grim. "Sounds like we've finally found the army or maybe two armies."

"It can't be Santa Anna. We left before he did. He'd have been behind us."

Quinn looked ahead toward the sound. "There are other Mexican generals. General de Cos surrendered to Texians last year. Maybe he's back in this, and maybe there are a few more."

His heart flipping like a fish on a line, Scully moved up next to Quinn. "I kind of hoped we'd meet up and join an army before the fighting started."

"Me too. But we may not be too late. It depends on what's happening. We'll just have to go forward and see who is fighting."

Fear that they'd come too late jabbed

Scully in his gut. "I want to fight, but I want to win too."

"I'm in complete agreement with you. We'll go careful. I'm not going to go barreling in just to get slaughtered." Quinn grinned suddenly. "I am not a buffalo or longhorn. If I must die in battle, it has to make sense."

Scully didn't say anything, but with a rueful grin shook his head. Quinn was no man's fool. A man didn't mind fighting if he had a chance of winning. Scully's doubt that the Anglos could win bobbed up again. He pushed it back down. A man didn't go to war thinking that way. That way led to early death.

*And I got a wife to protect.* He knew that it was in name only. But having Alandra gave him an anchor, something he had lacked ever since he was four years old. It was a good feeling. Having something, someone, to fight for.

Moving through the close-grown trees, they listened to the sounds of battle. Until now, Scully had never heard big guns fire. "That must be cannon," he commented.

Quinn looked toward the sound. "Yeah, that would be my guess."

They moved forward, listening and looking. Then they glimpsed black smoke rising.

227

Quinn stopped and slid from his horse. He handed the reins to Scully. "Stay here. I will go forward on foot."

"No, I —" Scully started to object.

Quinn held up a hand. "You are not as good as I am in not being seen. That blond hair of yours," he joked. Then he moved off.

Scully remained where he was. Within minutes, Quinn was back and swung back up onto his horse. "I don't like it. Come."

They went forward at a walk to the edge of the timber. From the shelter of the trees, Scully saw it all laid out before him. Far ahead in the billowing black and white smoke, he glimpsed patches of blue and white, the uniform colors of Mexican troops. Just like the ones who'd camped around Rancho Sandoval so recently.

From Scully's vantage point on a rise near the Guadalupe River, they watched what must be a battle. It looked like a stormy sea of writhing men, clouds of black and white smoke, flashes of gunpowder, rearing horses. The pounding of big guns was louder now, and the reports of musket and rifles came fast and furious. And on and off they heard a Mexican bugle.

It was a sight Scully knew he would never forget. The knowledge that men in great numbers were fighting for their lives, some dying, washed over and through him in harsh, shivering waves of disbelief and horror. The gorge rose in his throat. He closed down before this immeasurable horror and looked to Quinn.

Quinn motioned to him, and they moved around, trying to get a better view. The Mexican troops in the distance had evidently surrounded what might be Fannin's troops. "The Mexicans must have come from near here toward the Texians," Quinn murmured. "Not good. No one ever wants to be caught out in the open and on low ground."

Scully couldn't argue. Quinn was right. Why had the Texians left the fort at La Bahia in Goliad?

Quinn must have been thinking the same thing because he said, "This doesn't make sense. But they might have been slowed down and cut off before they could reach the timber here."

"They might have been heading north toward the river and got caught before they could get across," Scully added.

Quinn nodded. "Those big guns we're hearing must be heavy to move, and the ground is —" He looked down and pushed his toe hard against the earth, and water squished up around his boot. "— saturated. They might have got bogged down, moved slower than they'd reckoned they could."

Scully felt ridiculous, pointless. They'd come all this way, traveled nearly two weeks, only to arrive too late to do any good. He glanced at Quinn. "We can't go there now."

"No, we can't. We're on the wrong side of the battlefield. We'd just get shot for no reason, and maybe by our own side."

Scully imagined that his own expression must mirror Quinn's grim expression. They'd come all this far — just to watch a battle? It was irritating, maddening. It could make a man crazy to watch yet be unable to do anything.

Quinn leaned against a tree and settled there. "We'll just have to wait and see what happens. Either way, we know Sam Houston and the main Texas army isn't down there. Everything we've heard says he's retreating northeast."

Holding the reins of his horse, Scully found himself a broad oak trunk to lean against. Did they know that? Would Houston ever turn and fight? Or would his army of volunteers fall apart? Were he and Quinn watching the end of the Texas rebellion or just another battle?

Alandra shivered with terror, a raw terror that had not left her since she had been taken against her will.

"You should be shivering," Eduardo Mendoza, snapped at her. "You refuse to talk? I am your cousin. You should be trying to please me."

She sent him as venomous as look as she could manage, though she was wet, cold, and hungry. And wanted to give in to despair.

"I could hold her close and warm her," one of the bandits riding with them said, riding closer to her, leering.

Alandra pretended she had not heard the disgusting innuendo in his voice. The other *bandidos* were all much younger than her cousin.

"You know better than to touch her. We have plans. Profitable plans for her," Eduardo Mendoza crowed, and then began coughing again.

The men all laughed in the most distasteful way possible. To her, they behaved like young savages. She closed her mind to the callous laughter. *Dear God, send help. Send . . . Scully.* She remembered the sun-

231

light gleaming on his golden hair. But he had gone to war. She knew from the sun that they had been heading northeast since she'd been captured within miles of home. Why was Mendoza heading toward the war? Didn't he know this?

"Aren't you curious, *mi prima,* about where we are taking you and why?" He had stopped coughing and began mocking her again. "Don't you think it odd that you were kidnapped twice?"

She glared at him, showing her anger, not her fear. "You were responsible for my being kidnapped by the Comanches?"

"Yes, it was me who went to that uncle of yours and told him you'd be ripe for the picking with your brother gone. I told him for five hundred gold reals I would kidnap you —"

"Renegade Comanches kidnapped me —" Alandra interrupted.

"And who offered to pay them to do that?" Eduardo grinned, leered at her. "I didn't want to have to do the dirty work. And if I had shown myself, you might have become suspicious of Fernando. It was safer for me to stand back till your cousin Fernando had married you and become the master of Rancho Sandoval. Then I was to be paid."

"I don't understand you."

Eduardo chuckled and then began coughing again. When he finally stopped, he said, "You being captured by savages was to soften you up. Fernando thought that you would be even more grateful for his proposal, which would protect your reputation. A lady must be so careful." He waggled a finger at her and the others laughed coarsely.

Alandra recalled Ash speaking to Señor Veramendi and alluding to the possibility of her being compromised to explain her hurried marriage to Scully. It still set her teeth on edge.

"And the kidnapping should also have made you, *mi prima,* realize how much you need a man to protect you."

Alandra forced herself to show no reaction, but outrage flooded her. Then, to insult him, she turned and declared, "You should have realized that Quinn would not rest until he found me."

"Quinn!" Mendoza snarled, then cursed the man.

"So why have you kidnapped me again?"

One of the *bandidos* answered first. "Because down in Laredo — when we found out you'd been rescued, your fine cousin Fernando told Mendoza, he didn't owe him a peso. It was in a cantina there. We over-heard them talking. And then we decided that there was money to be had in another way. We talked and Mendoza thought it was a wonderful new idea." The others laughed in that way that was supposed to fill her with fear.

She looked straight ahead, refusing to take the bait and ask the bandit what he meant. Mendoza acted as if he were the captain of this band of four *bandidos.* But she saw how the young savages looked at him with ill-concealed disdain. It was easy to see why. The years had not been kind to her cousin. He limped when he walked and his face was scarred. And yet he still talked big. All those years ago when he had attacked and tried to kill her brother and Quinn, why couldn't he have died?

Her brother, whom she'd loved more than anyone, had been wounded and never truly healed, and then died — all because of this man. She thought she had let the need for *venganza* go. But it rolled through her like the heat from a bonfire. *Lord, I know it's wrong to hate this man. But I do. Help me.*

Then far ahead on the plain they were riding over, she saw a line of black and squinted. Was it just a line of trees or buffalo, wild longhorns or mustangs? At this distance, it was impossible to tell.

Gazing in the same direction, Mendoza slowed and pulled out a battered eyeglass. Where had he gotten that? She was interested in spite of herself. She almost asked what the black line was when one of the bandits asked for her: "What is it?"

Mendoza handed the man the telescope.

He looked through it and said, "Buffalo."

Unexpected disappointment hit Alandra right between the eyes. Some part of her brain must have been hoping for . . . what? An army coming to rescue her? The Texas Rangers? Quinn and Scully and her vaqueros? *No one knows exactly where I am.* What had the note Mendoza left with her wounded vaqueros said? Would it lead rescuers to her? Or was she being taken to a completely different destination?

She grappled with renewed despair. *I can't think that way. Dorritt would send someone to find out why I didn't return from Bexar. I was kidnapped on the road we always use. Someone would come and find my vaqueros. Dorritt will read the note and know what to do.*

Scully was capable of finding her. He would not be stopped or turned from looking for her. Then she recalled the touch of Scully's lips on hers. It was a moment she would never forget. Yearning to see him again rushed through her like a deluge.

Now she did have to blink away tears. Three of her men may have died for her. *I must be strong. I must survive. Men gave their lives to protect me. And I know Scully will never stop looking for me. Never.*

But in reply came a nasty little voice in her mind, taunting her. *What if he dies in the rebellion? Who will come after you then?*

# TEN

In front of the hacienda, Dorritt took the ransom note from Carson. She hadn't expected him home this soon. Instant fear made her body stiffen. She read the note once, twice. And she had no doubt who had written it.

With Carson's help, Emilio and Antonio lifted the wounded vaquero down and carried him past her. She hurried along with them, directing them to take the man to the guest room, then ran forward to get her nursing supplies. In the courtyard, the housekeeper met her bringing the wooden chest.

Dorritt led her to the room. The vaquero had moaned once and then passed out. Dorritt worked quickly while he was unconscious. For the next few minutes she could think of nothing but cutting away the cloth over the injured leg, cleaning the injury, digging out the lead ball, and dressing the wound.

When she was done, she sat very still, gazing at the man's face. In the rush to doctor him, her worry for Alandra had taken a step away. Now it flashed back like a spark on dry grass. She held up the note and looked to the housekeeper. "Mendoza has taken our Alandra." Mendoza was Don Carlos's cousin. The scoundrel they'd all hoped they'd never see or hear from again.

The housekeeper gasped and crossed herself. "*Dios mio,* no, no."

Carson and Ramirez had gathered in the door to the room. With heated rage rising inside her, Dorritt stood and, holding herself on a tight rein, turned to the housekeeper. "You know the mixture of herbs I use to foment wounds."

The woman nodded.

"Do it three times a day until the infection is done. If red streaks start spreading up from the wound, summon the doctor to amputate. But only if blood poisoning starts. Otherwise, keep fomenting until the wound stops draining. Have one of the young girls stay with him constantly and feed him whenever he is conscious."

"But señora, why are you telling me this?" the woman objected.

"Because Carson and I are going after Alandra. To bring her home." Dorritt headed for the door, ignoring the objections everyone shouted at her in Spanish. She called to her maid to prepare her traveling outfit and then began giving orders to the staff about what should be done while she was gone. Ramirez hurried along beside her, listening and nodding, and still trying to stop her. *"Señora, por favor, señora —"*

"Ma!" Carson called over all the commotion, silencing everyone.

She turned and faced him, raising an eyebrow. Already knowing what he would say.

"Ma, Pa wouldn't want you to go. Think of your . . . delicate condition."

Everyone looked on in silence. The housekeeper was weeping softly.

The outrage still surged within her, but Dorritt willed herself to speak in a clear, sure voice. "Carson, I understand your concern. But I am well. The baby has started kicking, a good sign. And my mother had early trouble traveling from New Orleans to San Antonio and later safely delivered my brother. No more talk — we're going to leave within an hour."

Carson didn't take his eyes from hers. "You think we can trust the note? Just because it's signed Mendoza doesn't mean it is from him. Everyone in San Antonio knows what he did to his cousin Don Carlos."

"This stinks of Mendoza." Wrinkling her nose, she waved the grubby piece of paper. "He thinks he's so smart, and he's just as stupid as he was fifteen years ago. Kidnapping again! It didn't work for him then and it won't work for him this time."

The anger bubbling up inside her threatened to boil over. Fear swallowed it up, leaving her hollow. *I don't want this to be happening, dear Lord. Alandra is too precious to me. Quinn and I promised Don Carlos on his deathbed to protect her.* She looked at her son with narrowed eyes, hauling up her courage like a flag on a pole. *Don't fight me, son.* "We can't waste time arguing, Carson. We will —"

"But all the way to Matagorda? That's on the Gulf coast. Pa wouldn't want me to let you go to meet kidnappers —"

"We're not going directly to Matagorda. We're going to my family's home near San Felipe northwest of Matagorda. Your father was going to stop there on his way to find Sam Houston's army. Both of us figured that Houston will put as many rivers between Santa Anna and him as he can, and

San Felipe is right along that path. Your father will stop at Buena Vista, my family's plantation, and leave word for me that he's well and where he's going." Another flash of fear. *If nothing has happened to him before he gets there.*

"Ma —"

She hardened her will against this worry. "I know just why Mendoza has asked for a ransom and named Matagorda as the place to take Alandra. He wanted to get far enough away so we couldn't take our vaqueros with us. He thinks that will put us at a disadvantage. But no matter how many men he has with him, he's going to lose. Quinn can outsmart him without even breaking a sweat."

"But Ma, Matagorda puts Mendoza right where the war's moving," Carson said. "Santa Anna will head east to catch Sam Houston."

A sneer went through her like a cold wave. "Mendoza probably isn't even aware of the fact that there's a revolution on. Or if he's heard, he thinks that it won't affect his plan. Carson, we don't have time to argue. He's at least a day ahead of us. And we must find your father. Now get my horse saddled and packed with everything we'll need while I dress for travel."

"Ma —"

She whirled away and marched toward her room. "We don't have time, son. See that my horse is saddled and our bags packed. We leave as soon as I'm dressed!"

The gray of predawn glowed through the timber on the eastern horizon. For two days Scully and Quinn had lingered near the battle, waiting to see it to its end before heading to find the remainder of the Texian Army and Sam Houston. They wanted to be able to give a full and accurate account of what had happened to Fannin and his men. But waiting here where the battle had taken its course had been hard, desperately hard.

Scully didn't think he'd ever forget the awful night when darkness forced the two armies to stop fighting. The screams and moans of dying men had traveled through the foggy night air. The tortured voices in Spanish and English sounded looking-glass clear and appalling. Huddled under their ponchos and blankets, he and Quinn had leaned against their saddles on the wet ground all night, unable to light a fire, unable to sleep, unable to see the men they heard suffering from mortal wounds, suffering and dying.

Scully had found himself praying for those men, both Mexican and Anglo, praying that they would make peace with God and go to a better place. A place where men didn't die while still in their full strength and far from their loved ones. A few times he'd heard Quinn reciting the Lord's Prayer and the Twenty-third Psalm, and he joined him. Who could a man turn to at a time like that, but God?

The awful night had taken him back to the worst day of his life. He recalled those hours as a little child when he hunkered down under the well cover, hearing the screams of his family being slaughtered. He'd scrubbed his face with his hands over and over as if he could rub away the memories.

The screams of the men on the nearby battlefield ripped, shredded him, and made him think of the past, made him long for Alandra. In her arms, he could be at peace. In her arms, he could find a refuge from the past.

*Alandra.* She had moved through his mind in a kind of waking dream. A dozen, a thousand, different images of her that he'd never guessed were imprinted on his mind. He saw her laughing at a rodeo, dancing in San Antonio at a festival before Lent began.

Then, closer to his heart, he recalled her kneeling in the church lit with flickering candlelight in the early dawn when they had wed. These images were so sharp they cut him, peeled away uncertainty and awakened the truth of his feelings.

He wanted to see Alandra again, just look at her. But, no, he realized he didn't want to just look at her. He wanted to hold her in his arms, feel her softness against him and kiss her full lips. He had rubbed his hand, feeling the old scars where she stitched his skin that day. And then he had touched the *pistolas* she had given him to take to war. The longing made what he wanted come clear. *I want her to be my real wife.*

The dreadful night he would never forget had finally ended. On the second morning after the battle, he and Quinn, bleary-eyed and drowsy, knew it was time to move. The day before, the Texian army, surrounded on all sides, had surrendered in the morning and were marched back to the fort at La Bahia near Goliad, which sat upon a rise in the distance. Now, drawn by curiosity, they followed, keeping to the fringes of the timber that flanked both the San Antonio and Guadalupe Rivers, which came together like an arrowhead near Goliad.

Thin morning light trickled through the clouds. "We might as well leave," Quinn said, shivering. He stood near Scully, his voice low. "These men are out of this war. They'll march them the thirty or so miles to the coast probably at Matagorda and send them by some boat or other to Vera Cruz or another port as prisoners of war."

Then, in the distance, they saw Mexican soldiers marching out of the fort. In the midst of them marched the prisoners. Scully and Quinn exchanged puzzled glances. What was this? The Mexicans parted into three columns, with prisoners marching in close order within their ranks. Then the three columns turned, leading the Texian prisoners off in three different directions.

"What are they doing?" Quinn whispered.

Scully knew Quinn didn't expect an answer, and was as baffled as Quinn. He rubbed his stubbly chin, trying to make sense of what his eyes were telling him. One of the columns was coming straight for them.

"Saddle up," Quinn hissed.

The two men saddled and untied their horses. They stood shoulder-to-shoulder at the edge of the woods, their pistols in hand. Scully's heart hammered in step with the marching troops. And inside him, foreboding descended, enveloped him. *No, no, no* began beating.

Upon command, the Mexican troops halted, turned toward the prisoners and lifted their muskets. The mounted Spanish officer shouted an order in Spanish.

Scully turned to Quinn, who translated, "He's ordering them to kneel. Oh, no —"

Quinn's horrified voice was interrupted by an explosion of gunfire. The Mexicans had fired upon the defenseless prisoners. Scully felt himself screaming but could not hear his voice. He made to rush forward Quinn grabbed him by the shirt. "Fall back."

Still holding Scully's shirt, Quinn turned, pulling him along.

Scully resisted. "But —"

"We can't help them," Quinn bawled against the noise and the chaos behind them. "The ones that aren't shot dead will be running straight toward us. Fall back!"

Scully couldn't think straight, couldn't believe what he had just witnessed. He stumbled after Quinn, pulling his horse along. Another explosion of muskets. Another. One execution volley for each column of prisoners?

Almost to the river, Quinn halted and turned. Their horses were fidgeting, upset by the noise of battle. No, not battle. Cold-blooded slaughter.

Grim-faced, Quinn raised his pistol, ready to aim and fire. "We'll wait. I kind of hope some Mexican will try to come through here following any Texians who're able to flee."

Flushed with outrage, Scully echoed this. Breathing out invisible flame, he gripped his pistol at the ready too. In the distance, amidst clouds of black smoke, a frenzied brawl had broken out. Some Texians lay dying. Others were fighting off their attackers with their fists. But some were running for the Guadalupe River, just as Quinn had said. Running for their lives.

Scully tensed, waiting, hoping some Mexican would chase someone to them. *Come on. Come on.* Then two Texians ran straight into the timber, right at them.

"Get behind us!" Quinn barked.

The men leaped to obey, and three armed Mexicans barreled in after them. Scully and Quinn fired at almost the same moment. Two Mexicans fell and the other turned and fled.

Quinn shouted, "To the river!" And all four of them bolted for the thick canebrake. Unencumbered by mounts, the two Texians ran ahead. Quinn and Scully threaded their way to the thick canebrake that topped the steep riverbank. More screams and shouted curses. More gunshots.

Then Quinn halted, held up a hand and pointed to the water's edge below. From the high bank, Mexicans were shooting at Texians who'd made it into the river and were swimming for their lives.

Scully wanted to turn and start shooting. The desire was so strong he shook with it. He wanted to blot out men who would murder unarmed prisoners of war in cold blood.

Quinn put a hand on his shoulder. "This isn't the Mexican soldiers' fault. This is Santa Anna, the butcher. And we will pay him back. For the Alamo. And for this. When Americans hear of these two slaughters, they will pour into Texas. Santa Anna doesn't know what he has unleashed."

*But he'll find out.* Scully burned. *And I want to be there to see it. And to teach him how free men defend their rights.*

Champing at the bit, Scully waited beside Quinn, hidden in the thick brush and canebrake. Finally, the Mexicans must have decided enough killing had taken place. The sound of marching ceased. The Mexicans had returned to their fort. The prairie and riverbank became quiet again. Scully heard the call of a mockingbird.

"Let's go back upstream and find a place to ford," Quinn muttered. "Then we'll look for wounded on the other side of the river."

Soon they were riding their horses across the murky Guadalupe, thigh high in water. The horses didn't lose their footing. Scully and Quinn mounted the riverbank, found a steep trail other travelers had worn into the bank and used it to go through the canebrake.

When they finally reached the rear of the lush trees and shrubs along the river, they worked their way quietly eastward along the bank. Within minutes they found two injured survivors lying on the ground. Scully and Quinn dropped to their knees and examined the men's wounds. One was unconscious but breathing. The other stared at them as if too shocked to speak.

After treating and bandaging their shallow wounds, Quinn asked the conscious man, "Do you think you can ride?"

"Yes." He panted as if he were still running.

They helped the man onto Quinn's horse and together lifted the unconscious man to ride facedown over Scully's saddle. Then they moved farther east and picked up more men. Some were wounded, most were not. But all of them looked dazed. And all of them acted relieved to have someone to lead them.

Then on the breeze came the smell of burning flesh. Gagging, Scully closed his eyes, trying not to think, not to imagine the horror of the dead piled high and being burned to ash. Not even a decent burial. He was horrified, filled with the desire for justice. *Santa Anna, you will pay for this.*

Quinn looked at him. "I think we've found everyone that hasn't gone ahead already. Let's go on and find cover. Make camp for the night. Why don't you see if you can bring down a deer for us? They look like they could use a good meal."

Scully nodded, and as soon as they had found a small clearing within a grove of oaks, he headed away to hunt for their supper. Having something to do felt good. He glanced back and saw Quinn gathering wood for a fire. The survivors sat huddled together. The smell of burning human flesh still reached them and it sickened him, made his stomach roil with disgust and revulsion. He vowed Santa Anna would not leave Texas scot-free.

Dorritt had made good progress since leaving Rancho Sandoval in the hands of Ramirez, his son, and Antonio. She and Carson followed the San Antonio River east and managed to ford it that morning. They had reached the Guadalupe River but were still west of the main Austin settlements. Dorritt tried not to show her fatigue, but after almost two full days in the saddle, she was feeling worn thin.

The sun was lowering in the west. Dorritt straightened her spine. They had camped out last night, and Carson had caught two trout in a stream. She wished they'd come to a cabin so she didn't have to spend another night on the hard, damp ground. *I've been living too easy all these years.*

They slowed their horses to a walk as if winding down, preparing to rest for the night. There was timber along the river. It gave the shadows an eeriness that chilled Dorritt from the inside. She knew this route well since it was the one she'd traveled at least once a year to visit her mother at San Felipe de Austin on the Brazos River.

They came to a clearing, a cabin with no smoke rising out of the chimney. "Hello the house!" Carson shouted, calling out the customary frontier greeting. "Hello the house!"

No reply.

He swung down from his mount and handed her his reins. Dorritt held them and waited while he went to the door and knocked. Then he pushed the door open and went inside. He came out and said, "The owners have run off. Probably afraid of the Mexicans."

Dorritt couldn't help herself. With a loud sigh of relief, she slid from her horse, and hitting the ground, wobbled. Carson ran to her. She steadied herself by gripping her saddle. "I'm all right, son. I'm just tired."

Carson looked like he wanted to scold her again for coming along. She was grateful that he didn't. Soon she was inside lying on a rope bed in the corner of the cabin. Her son had built a fire and was out scavenging for food. Feeling as flat as a line drawn on paper, she closed her eyes.

Then her eyes flew open and she swam up from her nap. A face looked down at her, and she gasped.

It was deep in the cold night. Alandra had been waiting for her chance to escape her captors. She couldn't depend on being rescued. She was at least five days east and north of San Antonio. And what if Mendoza had been lying all along? What if he had no intention of collecting a ransom? What if he had something completely different and much worse planned for her?

The bandits were snoring around the fire that had nearly burnt out. She was accustomed to their routine. Only one bandit was keeping watch, and she was watching him. He was nodding off to sleep. She waited, waited. His chin was slumped against his chest and he had not moved. If she were very quiet, she might not wake him. Her hands were bound and her ankles hobbled, so she couldn't go fast.

Her terror welled up like an icy cold spring. She pushed it down and cautiously rolled away from Mendoza, rolled toward the trees around them. If she didn't wake the sentry, she might get far enough away to find something like a sharp rock with which to cut her bonds.

She stopped rolling and lay very still, listening. When no one called out, she got onto her knees and then her feet. She swayed in the chill night. Then, with mincing steps, she started forward, careful not to move so fast that she tripped and fell or broke any large branch. It was so dark. While her feet shuffled along, her heart raced.

And beat so loudly it felt as if the bandits could hear it. *Lord, help me get away. Lead me to shelter and freedom.* And in that moment, Scully's face — his clear green eyes and determined expression — came up before her. In that moment, she felt the touch of his rough hand upon hers, heard his low caring voice, making the hair on her nape prickle.

*He will never stop till he finds me. Never.*

# Eleven

Alandra had never been as terrified in her life. Though fear was making her tremble, she felt her feet moving forward inch by inch. Not faltering. Not tripping. *Dear Father, help me. I have never needed your help more than I do now.* The image of Dorritt kneeling beside her when she was just a little girl came back. Dorritt had set the example of prayer, of believing God was a God worthy of trust. For a moment it was almost as if Dorritt were there, embracing her and kissing her hair and telling her how much she loved her.

A bird swooped close. Alandra stifled a squeak. She was moving as fast as she could, expecting every moment to hear shouts and someone coming after her. Then she recalled sitting up in bed, reading Psalm Thirty-seven to Scully, such an intimate sharing. She saw him there beside her bed — so tall and strong and fair. He had listened, and she'd felt so safe, so sure that everything would work out.

A small creature ran across her path. She sucked in air and kept moving. Ever since the night when the Comanche renegades had dragged her from her room, nothing in her life had gone the way it should.

But then why was that to be wondered at? Texas was in the midst of a rebellion. Nothing was going right anywhere in Texas now.

She ignored the stitch in her side and kept moving. Her heart beat hard and loud inside her, making her breathless. On and on she shuffled, while the gray light of dawn began to lighten the eastern horizon. If only she could find someplace to hide before daylight. *Please, Lord, please.*

Then what she feared happened — a shout! *"Déjete!"*

Screaming silently, She tried to find a place to hide. And then he was there, the *bandido* who'd been on watch. From behind her, he grabbed her elbows and squeezed until she screamed aloud.

As they headed toward the rising sun and Buena Vista, Dorritt followed Carson's horse. Riding up behind Carson was the little towheaded girl they'd found in the cabin the other night. She looked to be around seven years old and hadn't yet spoken a word. She followed Carson around like a puppy. She might have come from the house where she'd appeared looking over Dorritt as she napped. Or she might have just wandered in. Yet who would leave a child behind in the mad rush to escape an invading army? Then again, who knew what might have happened to the child's family?

Dorritt wouldn't admit it to Carson or anyone else, but she was tiring more quickly than usual. She knew it was the child she was carrying. She rubbed her hand over the spot where it was kicking. She could only wonder at the energy making a child cost her. Sadness swept through her like a wintry wind. *Quinn, I want you. I need to be with you.*

She ignored the sudden weepiness this brought as best she could. She was happy to be given one more chance to receive another child to love. But why did her emotions have to be so volatile on top of everything else?

She called to Carson, "Today we should be at Buena Vista before dark." She recognized the countryside and knew that Carson did too. On this trip, he had become more sure of himself, and she was proud of him. He was his father's son.

After passing so many empty farms, she wondered if they'd find anyone at Buena Vista. Hearing voices in the distance, Carson slowed his horse and she came up alongside him. They exchanged glances. The little girl tightened her hold around Carson's waist. Farther ahead, Dorritt glimpsed a line of men walking within the shelter of the trees along the road ahead of them.

"It might be others running from the Mexicans," Carson murmured to her.

She nodded. "It might." *Or it might be a dangerous band of looters.* She pressed her finger to her lips, praying they would pass on.

Two days of steady travel had brought Quinn and Scully to San Felipe, another deserted town. Two of the wounded survivors of the slaughter at Goliad had been too weak to walk or fend for themselves, so they had brought them along. Each of them had a wounded man mounted behind him now, leaning against his back.

As they rode, the two had become more feverish. He and Scully had been unable to find the men any safe shelter near Goliad, and they couldn't leave them defenseless anywhere with Mexican troops roaming around. Quinn had hoped they would find a family to leave the wounded with on the way, but all the houses they came to were deserted.

The morning after the massacre those survivors of Goliad who could walk, headed north to find and join Sam Houston, while Quinn led Scully farther northwest toward Buena Vista. There, they planned to leave the two wounded men to be nursed before moving on toward Sam Houston's army. Quinn would also leave word with his wife's relations there that he and Scully had gotten that far safely.

Now, Quinn scanned the short muddy street of San Felipe. The emptiness gave him an eerie feeling, as if he were visiting a place of burial. Scully slowed his horse and turned to Quinn. "How far to your in-law's place?"

"Not far," Quinn said, nudging his horse with his heels.

Scully did the same, and they trotted down the road. "Buena Vista is a pretty fancy name for a farm."

Quinn snorted. "My father-in-law thinks he's pretty fancy."

Though the grassy prairie still drenched from the March rain rolled before them, the breeze was warm. Spring was budding the trees and greening the coarse grasses. In the distance, Quinn saw the familiar two-story frame house. He turned his horse to travel the grass border of the muddy dirt lane that led to it. Flanking the big house to the rear were a line of rough jacales where the slaves lived.

Quinn had traveled here about once a year since marrying Dorritt in 1821. He had never been welcome. But he continued to visit because Dorritt wanted to see her mother and baby brother Scott, who was a bit older than Carson.

There was no smoke from the chimney of the main house, which was ominous. But why should his in-laws be here? Everyone in Texas was fleeing east toward the Gulf shore or the Sabine River, which separated Texas from Louisiana.

They stopped before the wide double doors. Quinn called out, "Hello the house!"

No reply.

Quinn held his fidgeting horse.

"Is this your place?" the wounded man behind him asked.

"My wife's family," Quinn replied shortly.

"Mr. Quinn! Mr. Quinn!" A tall black man, approaching from behind the house, hailed them with an upraised hand.

With care for the man behind him, Quinn slid from his saddle. He helped the wounded man down, supporting him as he staggered on the ground. Quinn greeted the young black man. "Amos!"

The two shook hands as Scully helped his wounded companion down.

"Everybody's gone, Mr. Quinn." Amos held his hat in his hands. "I didn't expect to see you. Anybody, really. Everybody's run off. Afraid of that Santa Anna."

"Amos, this is my top hand, Scully," Quinn said, introducing them with a nod. "Can you let us into the house? These men need nursing."

"The house ain't locked, Mr. Quinn. Me and my wife were left to take care of the place, keep trespassers off. But you are family. Come on." Slapping his shapeless leather hat on, Amos slid under the wounded man's arm and helped Quinn half drag, half carry him up the steps and into the house. Scully followed with his wounded companion. A young pretty black woman had come running with a wooden chest.

Soon they all were on the second floor in the guest bedroom. Both men were laid upon the large four-poster bed with mosquito netting tied back. Amos introduced his wife, Nancy, who tended the wounds quickly and efficiently. Finally, she dosed the wounded men with strong home-brewed corn liquor and they fell into a deep sleep.

In the detached kitchen at the back of the house, Quinn was quick to agree when Nancy offered to fix them a meal. The three men sat around the table.

"Amos, how did Kilbride come to let you remain here?" Quinn asked. This question that had been niggling at him.

"He didn't want to," Amos replied with a grin. "But they took off so fast. His lady said that somebody had to stay behind and keep looters from the house. And she wanted someone to bury all the valuables too. So she told me, 'Amos, you and Nancy stay behind and do that. And when we come back, I'll give you your freedom for being loyal and staying in time of danger.' "

"Really?" Quinn couldn't mask his surprise.

"Yes, sir, that's just what she said," Nancy chimed in.

Amos picked up the story. "And she told us if the Mexicans burn the house, to wait and when they were gone to dig up the valuables and bring them to your rancho. And they'd send for them."

Dorritt's mother was not one to lose her head in a crisis. Quinn nodded. "Scully and I are headed to join up with Sam Houston. Dorritt asked me to stop here and leave word for her that we made it this far. What day is it, Scully?"

"I think it's March twenty-fourth."

Suddenly homesick, Quinn looked over Amos's head. Thinking of Dorritt being so far from him lowered his spirits. Hiding this, he continued, "Then if you end up at my rancho, you can tell her you saw us safe and well on March twenty-fourth."

"I will surely do that, Mr. Quinn," Amos said, nodding. "But I hope it don't come to that. I helped build this house, one of the grandest in Texas, and I don't want to see it burn."

Scully gave him a grim look. "Santa Anna is capable of anything. Just make sure you and your wife don't get in his way."

Quinn and Scully made short work of the meal of biscuits, beans, and sausage gravy, then rose to leave. "You'll nurse the men, then?" Quinn asked.

"Yes, sir," Nancy replied with a curtsy.

"And if the Mexicans come, we'll carry them into the woods and hide them," Amos promised.

"Good man," Quinn said, clapping a hand on Amos's shoulder. "We'll be off, then."

Quinn promised himself to make sure Kilbride kept his vow to Amos and Nancy. As he and Scully rode northeast to find Sam

Houston and his army, he was feeling all of his forty-some years. Wars were for young men. But he couldn't forget the bloody slaughter he'd witnessed in Goliad. Santa Anna would regret it. To his very soul.

Just as the sun was setting, Dorritt and Carson trotted up the dirt lane to the Kilbride house. Carson didn't think they'd find word of his father and Scully here. It looked deserted. But then Amos and Nancy came running toward them. "Miss Dorritt! Miss Dorritt!" they both called.

Carson stayed in the saddle as his mother slid from hers. He didn't like how worn her expression was. Everyone they'd met had mentioned this.

She embraced Nancy. "I'm so glad to see someone here. Have you seen my husband?"

"You just missed him," Amos said, smiling and taking Dorritt's hand. "He and that Scully stopped here mid-afternoon. Nancy cooked them a meal."

His mother gasped and looked up at Carson.

"They brought us two wounded men to tend," Nancy said. "They said the Mexicans slaughtered all the Texas soldiers at Goliad." She looked and sounded horrified. "Can you believe such wickedness?"

"Yes, I can," Carson answered, his stomach clenched. "Which way did they ride, Amos? I'm going after them."

Dorritt tried to object, but Carson ignored her. "The moon will be nearly full and the sky's clear, no rain clouds. I'm going after them, Ma. They're not trying to cover their tracks, so I can follow them pretty easy. We have to have their help to get Alandra back." He turned to the girl. "Little one, you have to stay here with my ma and these good people. Do what you're told and I'll be back with my pa."

The little girl clung to him for a moment, then slid silently from the saddle. Carson turned his horse and galloped off in the direction of the road northeast.

His mother called after him, "Godspeed!" And Carson heard the urgency and longing in her voice. The need to see his father expanded inside him, too. Godspeed was what he needed. Now.

Alandra was punished for trying to run away. She ached from being beaten, and had been given no food. The bandits had been riding hard due east all day, and she hadn't been allowed down from the saddle. She could not recall ever feeling this miserable and desolate. *Scully,* her mind chanted, *where are you? I need you.*

"We are almost there, *mi prima,*" her cousin said with a harsh laugh that sent him into a gale of coughing. The old man could barely stay in the saddle.

Alandra didn't feel sorry for him, but she was concerned about his becoming too ill to travel. He was evil, but it seemed to her that the others were worse. It was becoming oddly clear that her relative safety depended on Mendoza. She must keep him alive until Scully came for her.

Dorritt had taught her the sound of the distinctive rattle in a cough that signaled that a person had pneumonia. And riding for days in pouring rain and sleeping on the damp ground could give anyone pneumonia, even someone young and in good health. And Mendoza was neither.

She had to clench her jaw against the hysteria, to keep herself from screaming. She'd just been told they were almost "there." But where? And what if her cousin died? What would happen to her then?

They rode over the flat grassy plain toward the Gulf of Mexico. Near a creek was a thick grove of poplars. "This is it," Mendoza rasped, then coughed for nearly a minute.

The band dismounted and dragged her into the trees. There was an abandoned jacale that they had evidently known about. They threw her inside, and she rolled on the packed earth floor, trying not to cry out in pain.

Her upper arms throbbed where the sentry had squeezed her until she'd collapsed. And she knew her lip was bleeding, blood trickling down her chin and into her mouth. Tears seeped from her eyes. She couldn't help it. *Scully, come and get me. Please. Soon. Lord, help him find me.*

Over the next hours into night and then into morning, Mendoza's health declined. When the increasingly restless *bandidos* came inside, as they did now and then, she tried to act as if Mendoza was napping, not lapsing into unconsciousness. She stayed close to him in the small jacale, swabbing away sweat on his face with an old rag she'd found in his pocket.

Outside, the bandits played cards, some game of chance, and argued about what was dealt to them. She hadn't had anything to eat for nearly a day, and the thirst finally moved her to the door. She called out, "I'm thirsty."

One of them shouted a vulgar insult in response and they all laughed. She turned away. She wouldn't beg. Then the door opened and one of the bandits shoved a canteen toward her. She hated to think of putting her lips onto anything this man's lips had touched, so she poured a bit of water into her hand before drinking from her cupped palm. She turned, then, to give some to her cousin, who lay, gasping for breath on the floor. But before she could move in his direction, the man was suddenly beside her. He raised his pistol and shot Mendoza.

She screamed and dropped the canteen. The gunshot echoed through her and shock made her stagger.

The *bandido* grabbed her sore arm. "The old man was dying. And we don't have any more time to waste here. We can do better without him. And we have a ship to catch." He dragged her from the jacale and shouted to the rest, "I took care of the old man. Let's get out of here!"

Scully shook Quinn awake, and nearby Carson woke up on his own. "Let's get going. It will be light soon." They'd only stopped to rest for a few hours. Ever since Carson had found them, they'd ridden fast, south for Matagorda on the coast. Now the three of them swallowed water from their canteens and then mounted. They had been riding hard and would until they found Alandra.

In a few more hours they'd reach Matagorda.

Scully had memorized the ransom note:

Bring 500 US dollars. Meet me at El Golfo Cantina in Matagorda before the end of March.

Scully had thought he'd left Alandra safe in her home with Dorritt, Carson, and all her people to protect her. When he thought of her being carried off by bandits, her light olive skin pawed by rough hands, waves of cold sick terror slicked through him. Followed by a seething rage. He felt capable of murder.

Later that morning, they saw the town of Matagorda ahead. The masts of ships on the eastern horizon and the smell of salt air made them pick up the pace.

Carson turned to his father. "What's the plan, Pa?"

Scully slowed his horse. Quinn gazed ahead. "I've only been to Matagorda a few times, and that was years ago. But it's one of the biggest towns in Texas now. It's a busy harbor, from what I hear. I would think that it will not be deserted, since a lot of people will flee here to board ships to New Orleans. I've been trying to come up with a plan, but all I want to do is barrel into the El Golfo Cantina, grab Mendoza by the collar and start pounding in his face." He demonstrated by pounding one fist into the other.

Scully's own anger still surged like a wild mustang when first roped. "We don't have five hundred U.S. dollars with us," he said, voicing the problem that had been vexing him over the miles.

Quinn nodded. "We don't have the money, and that might not be Mendoza's only reason for this. He was crazy hateful toward Don Carlos — Alandra's brother. That could still be mixed into this mess too."

Scully willed his heart to beat at the normal pace. "You said this Mendoza is a real snake, so we can't trust him anyway. Is Alandra even in Matagorda?"

"What are you getting at?" Quinn watched him, looking like he was sizing him up.

The thought that this might all be a hoax froze Scully in the saddle. He forced himself to go on. "Mendoza asked for money. If he had just wanted to kill Alandra, what would have stopped him from doing that on her way home from San Antonio instead of kidnapping her? Nothing. There's more to this than just another kidnapping. There's a reason — another reason — he specified

Matagorda."

Quinn and Carson watched him as if waiting for him to give the orders.

Scully wasn't used to holding forth to his boss, he was used to taking orders. But this was different. Alandra was his legal wife, his responsibility. "You also said he wasn't very smart, so we'll go in and see what he has planned. And then we'll outsmart him." He looked at Quinn. "Mendoza knows you, but I doubt he would recognize either Carson or me. We can use that to our advantage."

"What do you mean?" Quinn asked.

"Let's roll into town separately and look things over. It's best that they think you have come alone. Then they won't be watching me and Carson. We'll just be a couple of Anglo strangers in town. And before any of us go into the cantina, I want to look around. It could be a trap. We'll ride in and you two get set near the cantina while I look everything over. When I'm ready, I'll ride down the main street in front of the cantina, whistling. That will be your signal to go into the cantina separately, as if you don't know each other."

Quinn and Carson nodded in agreement. Though he wasn't used to giving orders, it seemed that Quinn thought his plan was a good one.

The three of them separated then, and each headed from a different direction into Matagorda. Scully dawdled over the sandy, shell-encrusted main street of the busy harbor town. He pretended not to notice Quinn coming from the opposite direction and riding past. A few storefronts down from the cantina, Scully tied his horse at the rail then leaned against it, gazing up and down the street as if in awe of the bustling crowds.

After Carson rode past without looking at him, Scully mounted again, wandered to the wharf, then dismounted and walked his horse along the quay. It had been a long time since he had been near the Gulf or large sailing ships. At around Carson's age he'd left his second family and traveled down the Mississippi on the deck of a steamboat to New Orleans.

One point kept niggling at him. Why Matagorda? Why not Laredo, on the Rio Grande? Or Chihuahua? Either one would have taken them deeper into the heart of Mexico. Surely that would be the better route, since so few people lived west of San Antonio. It would have been easier to keep anyone from seeing them while they waited for the ransom to be paid. So why had Mendoza chosen this busy seaport?

*Because seaports have ships that sail far away.*

Scully's heart stopped and then roared back, pounding in his chest and nearly deafening in his ears. Where would they send Alandra, a beautiful young woman, by ship? And to what advantage? How would that serve bandits?

Scully didn't want to wrap his mind around all the possible horrible answers to these questions. The world was a wicked, dangerous place for young unprotected innocents. He concealed his rage, which billowed with heat. Mounting again, he rode back to the main street. It was hard, but he made himself just amble along, whistling as if he didn't have a care in the wicked world, gawking like the stranger to Matagorda that he was.

After seeing Quinn enter the cantina, he waited a good ten minutes, then wandered inside too. He paused in the doorway, letting his eyes grow accustomed to the shadowy interior. He saw Quinn sitting in a chair, leaning it against the rear wall, and Carson leaning against the wall near the front door.

This was the kind of establishment that sold only tequila, whiskey, and ale. And he needed a very clear head to plan how to find out if Alandra were here in town, and worse, if she was aboard one of the two ships in the harbor today. So he went to the bar and ordered ale.

The barkeep drew him a glass from a keg and took two pesos from him. While Scully held his glass, a couple of nasty looking hombres pushed up from their chairs and sauntered toward Quinn.

"Amigo, you look familiar," one of them said. "Aren't you a long way from home? I think I've seen you in San Antonio."

Scully leaned his elbow on the bar and watched Quinn lower his chair to the floor.

"I'm from west of here, *sí*," Quinn replied.

"We might have a friend in common," the hombre continued. "Do you know Mendoza?"

"I did a long time ago," Quinn replied in an even tone, "but we weren't friends."

The hombre and his companion laughed. "Mendoza talked to us about you. We might have something you want. Perhaps we can make a deal."

At the sound of their dark, mocking laughter, Scully wanted to grab them from behind and crack their heads together.

"Perhaps," Quinn said, without revealing any particular interest.

"It is crowded here, amigo," the outlaw

drawled with a grin. "Let's go where we can talk in privacy."

Scully stared at Quinn and winked once.

"Why not?" Quinn rose. "Let's step outside."

The two hombres and Quinn sauntered out the rear entrance. Carson looked over at Scully. With a slight motion of his head, Scully told Carson to go outside and enter the alley from the right side. Then Scully drained his glass and with a wave to the barkeep sauntered outside as well. Then he hurried cautiously around the building along the other side, heading to the rear.

Pulling his pistol from his belt, he remained hidden at the side of the cantina and listened to the voices in the alley.

Another of the bandits said, "Mendoza told us to collect the money and then we'll tell you where what you've come for is."

Scully heard a noise behind him and turned. He saw a man who also held a drawn pistol. They stared at each other for a moment, each of their pistols pointed at the other's heart. Then the man motioned with his pistol for Scully to go toward the voices. Scully nodded and backed toward the alley. When he reached the corner of the building, he edged around, keeping his back to the cantina wall, his pistol covering the other man. When the two of them entered the alley, Quinn looked up.

The man Scully was facing said, "Look what I found when I made a sweep around the cantina. I didn't think our man would come alone."

Scully smiled, his eyes flicking over each man in the alley. He wondered where Carson was. "Of course not. Now if you have what we want, where is she?"

"Where is the money?" the bandit asked.

Scully said, "We're not giving you any money."

"Then you do not get the señorita," the man who'd approached Quinn inside sneered.

Scully gripped his pistol, ready. "I think we can —"

The man with Scully jumped sideways and fired at Quinn. And then pistols barked, sending lead flying everywhere. Using his pistol, Scully took down another man who charged into the alley, and then dropped one more with his tomahawk.

When the smoke cleared, Quinn was kneeling beside the man who'd been doing the talking. Four others were lying dead around them.

Carson dropped down from a nearby roof. "I made every shot count." And he had.

He'd brought down more than one.

People peered into the alley and then hurried away. Scully wondered if there was any real law in Matagorda. He had expected no help from Mexican law officers if they were in town, but whoever was the law here couldn't avoid gunshots. "We should get away. Fast. There are probably a few Mexican troopers in town to keep the peace. Bring the one that's still breathing along. We need to question him if we can and find out where Alandra is."

Quinn rose and dragged the wounded but unconscious man with him. "Right. Let's move. Now."

A man dressed in a blue and white uniform, aiming a musket, entered the alley farther down and called in Spanish, "What's going on down there?"

Quinn nodded toward the man he was supporting. "There's been a shooting. This one's still alive. Where's a doctor?"

Scully was impressed with Quinn's cool voice. He hadn't said anything that wasn't true, but managed to sound like merely a witness.

The soldier looked confused. He obviously didn't know what to do in the face of Quinn's calm manner.

"Where's the doctor?" Quinn repeated.

"At the end of this street," the soldier said. "Do you know these men?"

"Never saw them before in my life." Quinn dragged the limp man past the soldier, who started toward the dead men. When Quinn turned the corner at the end of the alley and was out of the soldier's sight, he said, "Quick. Empty the man's pockets. Something's not right here. This one looked and acted like he'd already pulled a trick on me, and that's a bad sign. What does he know about Alandra or Mendoza that we should know?"

Scully and Carson made quick work of searching the man and found a pouch, bulging with gold coins. Scully shoved it inside his buckskin jacket. Where had the man gotten all this?

Still dragging the man, Quinn proceeded down the length of the alley and onto the street, heading for the doctor's office. Meanwhile, Scully and Carson returned to their horses, picked up Quinn's horse, and led them to the doctor's office.

After a moment Quinn came out and climbed into his saddle. "Have you figured out where Alandra is — if she's here? Or should we hang around till he gains consciousness? And question him?"

Scully sensed that Quinn had already

come up with the same guess he had, but was letting him make the call. "Let's go to the two ships in the harbor. He's not going to wake up anytime soon, or maybe at all. We can always come back here if we don't find anything. But I'd just as soon not be connected with the likes of him."

Quinn nodded.

Scully kept his eyes moving, looking around at the people walking by. "Anyway, the bandits must have come here to deliver her to a ship. Otherwise, there was no reason for coming to Matagorda. And I don't think the hombre that approached you worked hard for years to earn this gold. He might have already —" Scully stopped. He couldn't bring himself to say that he might have already sold her.

Quinn agreed. "That's what I'd decided while I sat there waiting for Mendoza. Matagorda is the best harbor on the coast. They didn't head here for the Gulf breezes."

"Was Mendoza in the alley?" Carson asked.

"No, he wasn't. But this bunch looked capable of killing him if they wanted all the gold." Quinn fell in behind Scully, and the three of them turned their horses toward the narrow street to the quay.

Once there, while they reloaded their

weapons and looked over the two ships, Scully debated what course to take. The ships looked about the same, except that one had a slightly disreputable air. The battered and shady appearance of the crew, but more than that, how they eyed passersby, made him think they had something to hide.

He hefted the soiled leather bag of gold lifted from the bandit. Had they gotten this gold from one of these two captains in exchange for — His mind shut down again, unwilling to think of Alandra in such peril. He made his decision then. Why not just take the straight course?

In a low voice, he said, "Quinn, you come with me. Carson, you remain ashore. If you hear gunfire or one of us shouts, come in ready to fight. You seem to be good at that."

Scully walked to the closest ship and up its gangplank with Quinn at his back. On board, he was directed to the captain in the fore of the deck. Scully frowned, holding back his first inclination, a direct challenge to the captain. But when a man went looking for a fight, he'd surely find one. If he gave the man a way out and money too, it might get him what he wanted — Alandra's freedom and safety — without shedding blood.

The deck rocked underfoot. Scully tossed

the bag of gold in one hand, playing with it. He spoke to the captain, an unpleasant looking man with greasy hair. "You speak English?"

The captain shook his head, and Scully switched to Spanish. "I'm looking for my wife. I'm afraid that we had an argument and she decided to run home to Vera Cruz. Her name's Alandra Falconer." Scully lightly tossed and caught the pouch of gold, making the coins rattle and clink. At the same time, he readied himself to grab his pistol and put it to the man's head.

The captain watched him toss and catch the gold once, twice, three times. And he looked over Scully and Quinn and made an obvious inventory of their long rifles, pistols, tomahawks, and Bowie knives. And it didn't hurt that they smelled of fresh gunpowder smoke. And maybe the gunshots in the alley had been heard here, down at the quay.

The captain finished weighing and measuring them and gave a bark of a laugh. "I wondered why a lovely young woman would be traveling alone. You should keep better control of your wife." He turned to a sailor and ordered him to bring the woman onto the deck.

And there was Alandra, coming up from below deck. She looked terrified, starved and beautiful. Scully had to wrestle down his spiking anger. Seeing her like this made him want to mow down every man on the ship. He even felt capable of taking their scalps. They didn't deserve to live. But sanity and the pull toward her, the urge to protect her, won out.

Without a word, he dropped the pouch into the man's hand and went to her. Lifting her into his arms, he carried her off the ship. Quinn, with pistol drawn, followed in their wake.

# TWELVE

With Alandra up behind him, Scully led Quinn and Carson out of Matagorda. He held his horse back, keeping them all moving at a normal pace to avoid attracting any attention. But in truth, he craved nothing more than to urge his horse into a dead run, heedless of the roiling dust. He wanted to stretch and widen the distance between them and what had happened in Matagorda.

He glanced over his shoulder at Alandra, grown so precious to him. She had rested her smudged cheek on his back and encircled him with her arms. But she had yet to meet his gaze. Now that she was here with him, he couldn't grasp the fact that he had actually found her. How had it happened? How had they found her in the chaos that now was Texas?

After putting Matagorda several miles behind them, his concern for Alandra made him slow his horse. "Do you need anything?" he asked her.

She glanced up but not into his eyes and muttered, "I'm thirsty."

He drew up his canteen and opened it for her. She drank long and finally handed it back, still avoiding his gaze.

Then she asked, "How did you find me?"

Scully's mind only brought up images of Matagorda, the bandits, the ship captain. Then the battle and slaughter at Goliad jumped in too. But he couldn't put any of it into words. "I don't really know. It all happened so fast."

"Where are the bandits? Did you see them?" She clutched his chest and peered around him as if afraid they might be pursued.

He pressed her hands clasped in front of him. He noticed her wrists chafed red and raw from being bound and simmered with anger. "We killed all but one, and he's probably dead by now."

She shuddered against him as if he had just poured cold water over her, and he wished he knew how to comfort a lady. "I'm going to keep you safe," was all he could whisper to her.

Quinn and Carson had ridden up and now flanked Scully's horse on both sides.

Quinn leaned forward and spoke gently. "Alandra, Mendoza was in on this, right?"

"They shot him." She covered her face with her trembling, dirty hands. "He got sick. They shot him."

She'd seen more murder done. Scully murmured soothing sounds to her, worry bubbling up in him.

"Where was this?" Quinn asked.

She raised her head and looked around. "It was not far from Matagorda . . . in a grove of poplars . . . an abandoned jacale . . . near a creek . . ." Then she slumped against Scully's back, burying her face in his shirt.

He looked at Quinn and shook his head, telling him without words that there would be no more questioning. He felt her gasping against him. She was crying and trying not to show it. He folded one hand over hers.

Along with Quinn and Carson, Scully scanned the area, looking for the grove of poplars near a creek that Alandra had mentioned. He would have liked to find Mendoza alive so he could smash his fist into the man's face. But what did that matter if the man was dead?

"In my experience, it takes a lot to kill Mendoza," Quinn commented. "Let's go on a ways, find a creek to camp by and refill our canteens. And if we find the jacale and him, so much the better."

A few miles later they found a clearing by a stream in the canebrake near the Colorado River that had led them to Matagorda. They made camp early. Alandra was obviously done in and needed attention. Scully chewed his lower lip, wondering what he could do to help her.

She looked like a different person, and not just because she was so soiled and unkempt. She looked caved in, somehow, as if a fearful silent stranger had come to live in her body. That worried him. He knew how to provide food and water and rest for her, but she needed more than that. He wished Mrs. Quinn was there with them. They were going to head back to the plantation at Buena Vista, but it would take them two days, and Alandra needed tending now. *I'm her husband. It's up to me to help her. But how do I do that?*

Carson had waded into the creek and caught several plump bass. Now, he sat on the bank and cleaned the fish. Scully had unsaddled his horse and set his saddle on the coarse grass. He stood near Alandra, who sat on the ground, leaning against it, resting. He gave her some pemmican to chew while Carson went on preparing supper.

"I can't remember when I ate last," Alandra muttered, watching Carson.

Scully slid down and sat beside her. Her pitiful condition cut him. He had never seen her so beaten down. "It won't be long till we eat. That pemmican is all I have left from our provisions. I'm surprised I had anything."

"What day or date is it?" she asked, sounding lifeless.

"Around March twenty-fifth, I think. We've been all over East Texas, and I'm losing track of time."

"Where's Santa Anna?"

Scully didn't want to give her more bad news, but he wouldn't lie. "We don't know, but he's said to be coming east."

She nodded.

It felt funny, sitting there trying to catch up on things when so much had happened. He didn't want to, but considered the possibility that Alandra had been . . . He couldn't make himself even think the ugly word. He winced inside, thinking about what might have happened to her. Again, his lack of understanding of women and their emotions tangled up inside him. *I don't know what to say or do to make it better.*

■ ■ ■ ■

Quinn watched Scully and Alandra and felt bad as he could, actually worse than he thought possible. When Santa Anna crossed the Rio Grande, Quinn hadn't realized that his peaceful existence and those of the people he loved most would be shot to smithereens. Alandra might lose her land to relatives. Dorritt, pregnant, had ridden all the way to Buena Vista. Mendoza had come back to mess around in their lives again. And it was only by God's grace that they'd found Alandra. So much could have prevented them from saving her from that ship. He tried to shut out what might have happened to the girl they had raised, but failed to protect.

He had no doubt that when Scully handed the ship's captain the bag of coins, the man was merely getting back the gold he'd just paid the bandits for Alandra. There were brothels all over the Caribbean islands and Mexico. A beautiful and light-skinned young woman would have been worth a lot in gold. She might even have ended up in New Orleans. These thoughts made Quinn queasy. Thank God, they'd come in time, just in time. Who knew how many days it would have been before that ship sailed away?

That turned his mind to finding the jacale where Mendoza's body might be. Had Alandra seen aright? Had the bandits turned on Mendoza and killed him? *I have to make certain this time. I want to know for sure that he's done for. I don't want him creeping up behind me or my family again.*

Quinn quietly swung up onto his horse, bareback. He waved to Carson, and not wanting Scully and Alandra to know where he was going, told Carson in sign language that he'd be back before dark. Then he nudged his horse toward the sun low on the western horizon. He'd go up one side of the creek, then cross over and down the other until he found the jacale or it got dark.

A few miles along the river's canebrake, Quinn found a grove of poplars and a jacale. He drew his weapons and approached the hut cautiously. The sun was quite low now. He checked his powder and then swung down from his horse and crept forward. No sound came from the jacale. He read the ground around the derelict hut and saw that there had been horses and men there not long ago. Just outside the thin mesquite pole and mud wall, he waited, listening. Finally he pushed open the rude door and looked inside.

A body lay sprawled faceup on the dirt floor. Quinn edged inside and muttered, "Mendoza? Mendoza?"

The body didn't move. Bending low, he crept closer and nudged the man's boot. Nothing. Blood pooled around the body on the dirt floor. Quinn straightened up, moved to the man's head and looked down into Mendoza's dirty face. He knelt and lifted one eyelid. Dead. The man who tried to kill him years ago had finally come to his own violent end.

Quinn frowned. Mendoza would never do anyone any harm again. But the man's death didn't make him happy. He said a prayer in his mother's language and then one in Spanish, then stood and wondered how he would bury the body. He had no spade with him.

It occurred to him that he could set the jacale afire, with Mendoza in it. The weather had been so wet, there probably wasn't much danger of starting a wildfire. But the jacale was not that far from where they had camped, and he didn't want to call attention to them.

Quinn went outside and, with strips of leather he carried in his saddlebag, secured the door to the jacale shut. The hut would have to be Mendoza's tomb. A fitting end to a wasted life of a man no one would grieve. Then he mounted again and headed back to camp.

After dark, Alandra stared into the fire, sitting against Scully, still unable to meet his eyes. His solid presence was all that kept her from losing control and descending into hysteria. Carson had roasted the fish he caught on a hot rock in the fire and had salt for seasoning. She'd eaten two fish and then made herself stop. Though very hungry, she didn't want to eat too much on her still unsteady stomach.

In fact, not just her stomach was unsteady. When she walked, the ground felt as if it were moving underneath her. She fought this, and also could not crush the need to be within touching distance of Scully at all times. And she hated herself for this weakness. Where was the brave *doña* she had been?

The past fear-filled days hung like a string of heavy weights around her neck. She wanted to lie down and sleep, sleep for a very long time. She wanted to shut out the memories of being forced, carried away, touched by rough, rude hands. Tears came on and off and she couldn't stop them. She cried silently and tried to hide this from the men.

"I'm dirty," she said, surprising herself when she heard her voice in the silence around the fire.

Scully sat up straighter. "Come. I'll take you to the creek. You can wash up."

"Wait," Carson said. He dug into his saddlebag, pulled out a towel and then some clean cotton underclothing, a shirt, and trousers. He handed the bundle to Scully. "There's soap wrapped in the towel. Clean clothing might make her feel better."

Alandra noticed that Carson talked about her as if she was there but not conscious. That didn't surprise her either. She felt as if part of her had been left behind with her vaqueros when she was kidnapped. Only a shadow of herself was present here.

Scully started to lead her away from the fire.

"Lonnie," Carson said, "you'll be all right when we get to Ma. She always knows what to do."

Carson's use of his childhood nickname for her touched her deeply. It was as if he had wrapped his arms around her and kissed her cheek with soft baby lips, like when he was little. But she didn't feel like Lonnie. Somehow she felt as if she'd been stripped naked and dumped in the town plaza for all to see.

But why did she feel that way? She shuddered and tottered on her wobbly feet. Still, she did not wish to worry the men more than she already was. "Thanks, Carson. I'm going to be fine," she said, lying out of love.

She leaned against Scully, her steps unsure. He led her along the steep creek bank to a place thick with bushes and pines, then steered her down closer to the water. "I think this will give you some privacy," he told her. "I'll stay here while you undress behind those bushes. Don't worry. I'll be watching out for you."

She nodded and took the bundle that contained the towel and clothing from him. The idea of undressing out in the open, something she couldn't remember ever doing before, seemed as unreal as everything else. She went to the bushes Scully had pointed out and shed almost all her clothing. Then, wearing only her white cotton chemise, she took the bar of homemade soap from the towel and waded into the water.

The fact that Scully was watching her didn't seem to matter. On some level she felt that she did not need to hide herself from his honest gaze. He would never look at her as the leering *bandidos* and sailors had. Their lustful grins alone had made her feel dirty, tainted.

She inhaled deeply. The night was warmer than it had been for a long time. Spring had arrived while she'd been dragged across Texas. The creek water, however, was chilling. Barefoot, she walked carefully over pebbles and sand out into the stream, where it flowed deeper.

Her teeth chattering, she quickly scrubbed every inch of her skin and hair, then knelt and rinsed herself. She nearly lost the soap but managed to grab it back, slippery as it was. Staggering back to the sandy bank, she nearly fell, her feet numb and bruised. Gooseflesh had risen all over her skin.

"Are you all right?" Scully asked with concern, obviously trying to reassure her. In vain.

"Cold." She shivered violently and hurried into the cover of the bushes. Dancing from bare foot to foot, she shed her soaked chemise, dried herself, and donned Carson's clean underwear and clothing. It was too big for her in some places and tight in others. The washing and the drying had chilled her and warmed her at the same time. She felt whole, fresh, cleansed. But a sense of deep insecurity kept her hollow, on edge.

Alandra looked at her crumpled filthy riding habit and other clothing draped over the bush and couldn't bring herself to even claim it. She stood there refusing to touch the garments. "Scully," she finally called.

"What's wrong?" he said, coming closer.

"Can we just burn this dress?"

"Sure." He snatched up the clothing and gripped her hand. "Come. I'll throw it on the fire and then get you warmed up."

And he did. She watched the orange flames devour her discarded clothing. Scully took her to his saddle, which served as his pillow. Lying down, he wrapped a blanket around himself and opened his arms.

Lying in a man's arms was something she'd never done before. The filthy things the bandits had said to her, embarrassing her and demeaning her, washed over her like dirty water. *But this is Scully. He's sworn to protect me. He is my husband. He is not like them.*

She knelt down and, turning her back to him, eased up against him. She shivered once, violently, as she let him fold the blanket closed in front of her. On the other side of the fire, Carson had already turned in and was lying wrapped in his own blanket.

Then she heard Quinn's voice. He had

returned quietly, from wherever he'd gone, and it came from the darkness away from the fire. "Scully, Carson and I are going to split watch tonight. You just keep our girl warm."

*Our girl.* She recalled sitting at the table at Quinn's rancho just a little over a month ago and hearing him call her *our little Alandra.* She'd been upset with him that night, upset that he had called her "little." Tears streamed down her face. She hoped Scully wouldn't say anything about all her crying. She wanted to treat her tears as if they were like the rain — outside of her, beyond her.

He began to stroke her damp hair. He lifted it away from her toward the fire as if to help it dry and continued in a steady, mesmerizing rhythm, soothing her. The fire crackled and an owl hooted in the distance. So quiet.

*I'm safe here.*

But then she recalled what Quinn had said — that he and Carson would keep watch. That meant danger still lurked. She pressed herself closer to Scully's strength. After all, the Comanche renegades had stolen her from her own bed. Was anywhere in Texas safe? Would she ever feel safe again?

A low moan woke Scully. He sat up and

found Alandra whimpering in her sleep, "No, no, no." Should he wake her? She moaned again.

He shook her. "Wake up, Alandra. You're having a nightmare. Wake up —"

She was struggling with him. He took hold of her thin arms and she jerked. Her eyes flew open. "Help." She panted.

"Alandra —"

"Scully?" she said, looking at him, still struggling.

"Yes, I'm here. You're safe. You're safe."

She stopped trying to get away. "You're hurting me," she whimpered. "My arms are bruised. Please."

The note of stark entreaty in her voice hit him hard. He loosened his hold on her arms but did not release her. "I'm sorry," he said, making his voice low and gentle. "I didn't know I was hurting you. You were having a nightmare. But we found you and you're safe now." He tugged her close to him. "Let me warm you and then you can get back to sleep. I'm here. Don't worry."

She allowed him to draw her to lie down with her back tucked against him. He didn't know what else to do for her. But he felt that he should touch her again as he had when he tried to dry her wet hair earlier. That had seemed to calm her into sleep. He brushed her loose hair back from her face, letting himself savor the thicker texture of her hair and her smooth skin.

A memory came to him from long ago when he was very little. His second mother sat beside him, stroking his back and singing "Amazing Grace." He didn't sing much, but he began to hum that old hymn that his second ma had loved to sing. He whisper-sang into Alandra's ear:

"Through many dangers, toils and
    snares . . .
we have already come.
'Twas Grace that brought us safe thus
    far . . .
and Grace will lead us home."

*Father in heaven, make this so. My almost-wife is hurting and I don't know how to fix it.*

Standing in the yard behind Buena Vista, Dorritt looked up as a vast flock of crows screeched overhead, flying north as fast as they could. And then she glimpsed the white smoke in the direction of the town of San Felipe. A doe and two fawns hurtled past her, racing away from the town, followed by a stream of squirrels. Fire. The animals smelled fire. She recalled seeing this type of flight of birds and small animals and the sound of the fire bell in New Orleans. And then it rushed through her — the panic fire let loose.

Did this mean the Mexican Army had reached San Felipe? No time to think. They might be coming for them. Taking the hand of the silent little girl, she raced toward the house, calling, "Amos! Nancy!"

Amos came running from where he had been hoeing in his freshly planted garden patch, and Nancy looked out the upstairs window where she was tending the wounded men.

"The Mexicans must be burning the town!" Dorritt shouted to them. "Get the men downstairs and we've got to run, hide!"

The three of them managed to help the men down the stairs and outside. Amos ran to get her horse out of the barn. They loaded the men onto it and, as fast as they could, headed for the surrounding woods that lined the property on the west.

Dorritt remembered her trip long ago on to Texas, watching in horror as Mexican soldiers burned a Caddo village and chased down the men, women, and children. She'd hoped she would never see such terror again, or feel it, and realized she was praying out loud, "Lord, help us! Lord!"

Gasping, they entered the woods and had to slow down. "Follow me," Amos said, "I found a good place for us. They won't find us unless they come deep in here."

The afternoon shadows crowded around them as Amos led them to an area of dense fir trees. They slipped into a cocoon of branches thick with pine needles and peered back toward the columned house.

Dorritt stroked her mare and murmured to her, keeping her still. The little girl pressed herself into her skirts as if hiding there. The wounded men sat huddled together on the ground, holding their heads in their hands. Would the Mexicans pass by or follow the lane to Buena Vista?

# THIRTEEN

The next afternoon they rode up the lane of Buena Vista and Scully pulled on his reins in shock. The big house they'd been inside just days ago had been severely damaged by fire. Scully glimpsed Mrs. Quinn running toward them down the lane. Quinn swung down from his horse and gathered her into his arms. "Woman, I told you to stay home," he growled into her ear. "Why don't you ever mind?" And then he held her against him and kissed her over and over.

She chuckled, clinging to him.

A little towheaded girl Scully didn't recognize appeared and went directly to Carson, who bent down and reached a hand to her. "Hi, little lady. See, I came back."

"What happened here?" Scully asked with Alandra sitting up behind him, her arms encircling him. He had been hoping this could be a safe place for her, but saw that the roof had nearly burned away. The charred walls, though still standing, exposed the blackened interior in places. The telltale odor of burned wood drifted on the breeze.

The sight tightened his jaw. It was clear now that they couldn't leave the women here. But even more, it angered him to see the Mexicans burning what others had worked hard to build. He remembered how lovely the house had been, furnished with rich dark woods and shiny brocades.

The ruined house showed the same abuse his beautiful wife had suffered. He placed his arm over where her hands met at his belt buckle, trying to bolster her spirits. *You will be well again, Alandra. And have the life you deserve.*

Carson slid from his horse and, leading a little blond girl by the hand, moved toward his mother. Quinn stepped back from his wife and asked the question Scully had been waiting to voice, "What happened here?"

"I can't quite believe it still." Mrs. Quinn was hugging Carson. "We saw the smoke from San Felipe and we headed away into the woods to hide."

Scully clenched his reins tighter. The slave Amos and his wife Nancy came forward, with the two men Scully and Quinn had brought from Goliad limping along behind. Scully nodded to them. "Santa Anna has passed us, then," he said. Anger and disappointment like flint on rock sparked within him. Were they cursed? Would they always catch up with the armies just in time to sit and watch them fight?

Dorritt Quinn gave a dour look. "No, it wasn't Santa Anna. *Sam Houston* burned San Felipe. And the fire spread through the poplar trees to here. The only thing that saved the house from burning to the ground was a rain shower that put out the flames." She shivered and rubbed her arms.

Sam Hosuton had burned San Felipe just like Gonzales, Scully thought. And it put them in a bad position — between two armies. *We can't tarry here. We must get going. Fast.*

"There wasn't no way for us to fight the fire," Amos added. "We just got hid and then we were watching the Texas Army march by while the big house caught fire and burned." The man shook his head. "It's going to take a lot to rebuild it."

Mrs. Quinn approached Scully's horse. "Alandra, come down so I can hug you. I've been — we've all been — so worried about you. I'm so grateful to God to see you rescued safe."

Scully was surprised that Alandra hesitated. Dismounting, he helped her down.

Mrs. Quinn folded Alandra into a gentle embrace, kissing her forehead, then rocking her in her arms. But Alandra appeared stiff somehow.

"Houston burned Gonzales too," Quinn commented, not looking happy as he gazed around at the devastation. "I know why he's doing this. He doesn't want the invading army to profit from what they can loot. But it seems like Texas is losing a lot to the Mexicans and their own army to boot." He shook his head, looking disgusted.

Scully felt like snarling in agreement, but remained silent.

"That's war," Mrs. Quinn said, drawing away from Alandra but sending a decided nod over Alandra's head to Scully. Then from behind Alandra, she added a beckoning motion with her hands. What was she trying to tell him? She cleared her throat. "I was in New Orleans when Andrew Jackson routed the British in 1815. I heard the musket fire and the cannon. And saw the fires burning in the swamps." She shuddered but gave Scully another decided nod.

He realized that she must be signaling him to draw Alandra closer to himself. He did so. Alandra came without reluctance but kept her eyes lowered. He put an arm around her. She leaned against him but gave no hint of what she was feeling. He knew that she'd had another restless night. He had comforted her through more than one nightmare.

He thought back to the February night when he'd shot the Comanche who'd kidnapped her. She'd been hysterical then and jumpy for the next few days. But on that occasion she'd only been held against her will for one day. This time was worse. For over a week she had been at the mercy of lawless men. Now she seemed flattened somehow. He was at a loss over how to comfort her, to help her.

"The kitchen didn't catch fire," Amos went on. "We've been sleeping there while I build another jacal. All the slave jacales went up like tinder. And I'm trying to salvage what I can from the house. For the mistress. I'm going to build a shed to protect what's left." The man exhaled long and loud in disgust, shaking his head.

"If Sam Houston went through burning, then Santa Anna can't be far behind," Quinn said. "Amos, you will need to hide whatever you manage to salvage deep in that wooded area. And hope the Mexican Army is going too fast to loot and finish burning the house."

Scully felt Alandra press closer to him. He

put both arms around her. "What are we going to do with the women? I thought we could leave Alandra here with Mrs. Quinn —"

"You're not leaving me anywhere!" Alandra reared back and struck his chest with her fist. "You're not leaving me behind again, Scully Falconer!"

Her sudden burst of anger caught him by surprise. He encircled her small wrist with his hand to calm her.

"Alandra is right," Mrs. Quinn said in a tone that threatened battle. "We are not staying here while you two —"

"Three or four," Carson interrupted. He patted the little girl who was still clinging to him. "I'm not staying here. I've come this far and I'm fighting. I showed what I could do in Matagorda."

At the word "Matagorda," Alandra collapsed against Scully's chest as if she'd just run completely out of energy. He closed his arms around her, feeling her trembling against him. He hated how frail she felt in his arms. He hated everything about the situation they faced, but what good did that do?

Quinn looked put-out and propped his hands on his belt. "War is no place for women."

"That's nonsense," Mrs. Quinn said. "My grandmother accompanied her husband and son as they fought in the American Revolution. She told me that George Washington usually had around three thousand women and children in family camp. They followed the Continental Army throughout the Revolution. Who do you think did the cooking, laundry, and tended the sick? Even the British and German officers brought their wives and children from Europe."

Scully couldn't mistake the fire in Mrs. Quinn's fine eyes. Quinn kicked the dirt road with the toe of his boot. The sound of a mockingbird and a few crows filled the human silence.

Scully scanned the burned-out mansion. He and Quinn had no choice. "I can't leave Alandra here. The Mexican Army is sure to be coming this way. Our women wouldn't be safe, Quinn."

"Pa —" Carson began.

"I know." Quinn didn't sound happy. "Even when I was thinking that we could leave our wives here in Carson's care, I knew the Mexican Army was prowling around. And unfortunately, there are always bandits and looters, unscrupulous men who will take advantage of disordered times like these."

Quinn looked into Scully's eyes. Scully wondered if the men they were forced to shoot in Matagorda were weighing on Quinn's mind, as they were on his. The worry was that there were probably more lawless men like them swarming over Texas like birds of carrion, scavenging. Neither he nor Quinn could risk letting their wives fall into such hands. Scully pressed Alandra closer.

"A battle doesn't happen in a minute," he said, anger at being forced into this dreadful position leaping to life inside. "The women would have time to take cover away from the shooting. I'm not leaving my wife here unprotected." He was surprised that the word "wife" had issued from his lips without any qualms.

Alandra rubbed her face against his shirt, and he pressed her closer still. Quinn nodded with obvious reluctance, accepting the inevitable. Mrs. Quinn motioned toward the kitchen behind the charred house. "Let's go eat. Then we'll get ready to leave for the war." She inhaled deeply and ran her hand over her rounded abdomen. Then she turned toward Quinn. "I thought our rough days were over."

He went to her and put his arm around her shoulder. "Well, we're still breathing.

And our life together has always been filled with the unexpected." He began walking with her on his arm toward the back of the house. Carson picked up his father's reins and Scully's and went off with Amos to get the horses some water and grain. The little girl ran to keep up with them.

Scully coaxed Alandra to go with him, to follow the Quinns. Before she would budge, she said fiercely to a point in the middle of his chest, "You're not leaving me. Anywhere."

"I'm not leaving you. We're staying together." *No matter what.*

After eating a hearty midday meal prepared by Nancy, they refilled their canteens from the bucket at the well. Quinn decided that it would be best to leave Dorritt's horse with Amos and Nancy in case they needed to escape either the Mexicans or bandits. So after they bid those remaining at Buena Vista farewell, Scully and the others headed northeast on the road toward San Jacinto. The Quinns rode point, then Scully with Alandra in the middle, and Carson with the little girl sitting in front of him, bringing up the rear.

Once they had decided to stay together, they moved swiftly. They needed to cover ground before camping at dark. They were traveling between two armies, theirs retreating and the enemy advancing. They couldn't afford to delay. Who knew how close behind them Santa Anna or another of the Mexican generals rattling around Texas were?

Scully had Alandra up behind him again. She had donned a skirt that smelled of smoke, borrowed from Dorritt's younger half sister's armoire. She had put it on over the heavy cotton trousers Carson had loaned her. Scully had insisted on this. Going toward an army and perhaps battle, he didn't want anyone mistaking Alandra for a man. He didn't want her shot.

Since she didn't have a riding habit, the trousers ensured her modesty as she rode astride behind Scully. And the dress ensured her relative safety as a woman. No decent man, Mexican or Texian, would shoot a woman.

Scully watched the miles go by and the sun lowering in the sky. He finally decided that he must talk to Mrs. Quinn and get her help on how to comfort Alandra. But first the everyday tasks of being on the trail — finding a sheltered place near a free-flowing creek and setting up camp — kept them all busy. Finally, they were sitting around the crackling fire. They had all filled up on smoked ham and corn bread Nancy had sent along. And Scully and the rest were drinking hot coffee, feeling full and weary.

Scully filled his cup again and then did the same for Alandra. He had tried to think of a way to get a moment for a private word with Mrs. Quinn but had come up empty.

Then Mrs. Quinn spoke up, "Alandra, I'm so happy that God led our men to you. No matter what happened to you, we still love you. And we'll do whatever we can to make you feel safe again." The lady paused then, staring across the flickering fire into Alandra's eyes.

Scully didn't move, waiting for Alandra's response.

Finally, Alandra nodded.

"I'm sorry we can't just go home and let you rest and recuperate. But Mexicans have come with muskets and cannon, destroying our peace. Where we will all end up, I don't know." Dorritt reached out and took her husband's hand.

Quinn pulled his wife close to him. "But we are together. And God has not forgotten us."

Scully didn't know what he could add to this. So he just said, "Amen." Carson echoed him. Then everyone was quiet again. The little girl was already asleep beside Carson. The mosquitoes had not hatched for the season. The wind became warmer each day, but still the dampness came up from the earth at dusk.

Scully touched Alandra's shoulder. She leaned against him, closing the inches that had separated them. He wished he knew what had happened to her. But he dreaded knowing. He wished he could help her to forget any hurt that had been done to her. But he knew that would not be. What happened to a person stayed with them forever.

But what came to him was that while the Lord had allowed Alandra to be taken, He had brought Quinn and Carson and him to rescue her. Trials came to make us stronger. That was what his second ma had taught him.

He rubbed Alandra's arms, feeling how thin she was under the cotton and buckskin jacket. Then her head was resting against him. All he wanted was for her to be safe, whole. Everything had become so mixed up.

Quinn cleared his throat. "Carson, you and I will take watch again tonight."

Scully tried to object, offer to take his turn.

"No," Quinn cut him off, "your wife needs you. We'll keep watch."

Grimacing, Scully nodded. "Very well."

Then it smacked him. Quinn was telling him that they considered him, in fact, to be Alandra's real husband. Of course, he was her husband, but that had been just to protect her land. And though here and now the land and her Mexican relatives were so removed from them, the marriage had come to serve a different purpose. He was her husband. He was to provide for her and protect her. And he would.

"Come on, Alandra," Scully murmured, "let's get you settled for the night." He wrapped the blanket around him and drew her against him as he had the night before. She came to him and nestled close — though he felt her reluctance, her hurt, her fear. How could a life be changed so much in just a little over a month?

Scully recalled Mrs. Quinn's words. "You're safe here," he whispered into Alandra's ear just beneath his mouth. "I'll protect you."

"How can you," she whispered back, her words chilling him, "if you're killed in this war?"

Scully heard his own shout. He jerked up and gazed around. He tried to remember where he was. The nightmare was an old one, taking him back to the faraway past.

Across the low fire he saw Mrs. Quinn sleeping and her blond hair catching the moonlight. Then he glimpsed motion and recognized Carson, standing with his long rifle at the ready. "Bad dream," he muttered to Carson, who moved away then and everything was quiet.

A soft hand touched Scully's cheek and he looked down into his wife's open eyes. He pressed his hand over hers. "I'm sorry I woke you," he whispered. "Let's try to go back to sleep."

"What was happening in your bad dream?" she asked, holding onto his hand, not letting him release hers. Her large eyes glistened in the night.

The vivid sensations from his nightmare rushed back, making him a little boy again. He shuddered and closed his eyes, not wanting to tell her.

"I've been having nightmares too." She shifted and turned her body full against his.

He ignored the way he reacted to her pressing against him, or tried to. He thought about her nightmares, had hoped she would tell him more about them, give him a clue about what had happened. But she hadn't. So he didn't know if telling her about his own nightmare would help her or hurt.

He gazed down at her. And though he

could see little of her face and form, he knew she was beautiful. Even when he was just a cowboy and she was a young girl, he had always thought she was eye-catching. He recalled so many images of her that dreadful night after the battle at Goliad, listening to other men, many men, die.

And he was the man — her man — who had to help her. If he wanted her to tell him about her nightmares, maybe he should tell her about his.

He cleared his throat and whispered so no one else would hear. "I think it's because of what happened after we got to Goliad. We were going to meet up with Fannin and join up with the Texas troops, but we got there too late. The Mexicans had surrounded Fannin's men and we watched from the canebrake. There was no sense trying to get into the battle. But it was hard watching and not be able to do anything. At night it was worse. It became too dark to fight anymore. The two armies had to just stay put there. And the wounded — Mexican and Texian — were screaming in pain and dying."

Alandra snuggled closer to him. He could feel her breath against his neck just below his left ear.

"This is a bad time, Alandra. It's not just

us. Texas is bleeding. Texas is on its knees. And we have to help Texas get up and start fighting again. I'll do my best to protect you, but if something does happen to me — maybe to all of us — you still have yourself, a beautiful and brave woman, and you still have God. When I was a very little boy, I found out that you can lose everyone, but you still have God."

"Were you dreaming about Goliad, then? About the wounded?" she asked.

"No," he said, forcing himself to go on, "I was dreaming about what happened to me a long time ago." He had to make her understand, so that she could go on even if the rest of them were lost to her. "When I was just a very little boy, hardly more than a baby, we — my family — were attacked by Indians. My mother heard them coming. She was drawing water so she shoved me down onto the lip of the well. She hid me, hid me with the wood cover. She told me to be quiet and not to come out." Even after all these years, his heart was beating fast, just remembering. But he had to make her understand. "I heard them all die. My ma, pa, and big sister. They were screaming. And then it was silent."

"What did you do then?"

"I stayed in the well. I didn't know what

316

to do. But then a day or two later, people came. I didn't know them. They were on their way west. When they tried to draw water, they found me in the well. They became my second family. The ring I gave you came from my mother's hand. When they buried my family, my second ma took it off and hung it around my neck. It was all that was left of value."

"Scully . . ." she whispered.

Feelings crowded in on him, he kept on, telling the story, "I could only say my first name. I didn't remember my family name so I just took their name — Falconer. Sometimes I wish I could remember my family name so that maybe I could find some blood kin. But that would be hard. Everyone moves around so much."

"I'm sorry. I didn't know."

"Don't be sorry. That wasn't why I told you. A lot of people die in Indian wars on both sides. People live, and people die. That's out of our control. But you see, I was saved and I got a second family. They raised me just like their other three boys. I stayed with my second ma until she died. Then my brothers decided to settle in Illinois. But I wanted to see some more of this country. So I got on a riverboat and traveled down to New Orleans."

"I don't want you to die."

Hearing her say these lonely words moistened his eyes. "I don't want to die, and I don't think either of us will. But I have to fight this war. I can't let someone like Santa Anna go on being in charge of the whole country. We have rights. We are free men. And Texas has to be free or we can't have a life here."

She clutched him. "Don't leave me. I don't want you to die."

"I'll do my best to stay alive. But if I do die, I believe God will take care of you." For so many years he had taken care of himself, not needing to depend on God. But now he admitted he couldn't handle all this alone, all of it — Alandra's relatives trying to take her land, Alandra being kidnapped and hurt, this rebellion and Santa Anna slaughtering free men.

His first ma had given him life and saved his life. But his second ma had taught him about the God who'd saved his soul, and she'd given him the strength he needed now. The strength and hope to get Alandra and himself through this war. "God will never leave you. Even if I die, you won't be left alone. Do you believe that, Alandra?"

She didn't answer in words, merely rested her head on his chest, clutching his shirt and trembling.

He had no more words to say. He had said it all. Had it been enough? He thought back to his second ma and remembered her song. So he whisper-sang "Amazing Grace" to Alandra.

"Through many dangers, toils and
   snares . . .
we have already come.
'Twas Grace that brought us safe thus
   far . . .
and Grace will lead us home."

It was the song his second ma had sung to him many times when he had a hard time as a boy with nightmares. Now he stroked Alandra's hair and prayed that he wouldn't die. That grace would lead them home again to Rancho Sandoval.

Two days later, when they crossed the Brazos River, they finally caught up with Sam Houston. Stunned by what an army looked like, Alandra stared open-mouthed. Hundreds of men were busy on the prairie before them. They appeared to be training and marching in groups. Officers were shouting orders.

Quinn led the six of them to the nearest

man who appeared to be giving orders. "Where do we sign up?" he asked. The man motioned toward a large canvas tent in the midst of the troops. Quinn led them on to the tent and then slid from his saddle. He gave Dorritt his reins.

A man of medium height with wavy brown hair wearing a uniform of blue stepped outside the tent. He was still talking to two other men who had followed him. He stopped then and looked into Quinn's face.

"We've come to join up for the fight," Quinn said, studying the man in return. Then he added, "Oh-see-*yoh*. Quinn, dah-wah-*doh*."

The man grinned and clapped a hand on Quinn's shoulder. "Oh-see-*yoh*. Sam Houston, dah-wah-*doh*. It's good to find someone who talks Cherokee."

Alandra gazed at the man. Everyone in Texas knew that Sam Houston had lived with the Cherokee for many years before he entered politics.

"I thought you must be Houston," Quinn said. "My mother was Cherokee. My father an American exploring with Pike. This is my family." He indicated his wife and son. "My wife's family are the Kilbrides who settled near San Felipe. And these are our friends, Scully Falconer and his wife, the former Alandra Sandoval. We own ranches southwest of San Antonio."

"You've come a long way." Houston's attention lingered on the women and little girl. "We don't have many women in camp. Most wives and daughters have fled to Louisiana." Then he sent another look toward Alandra. "Did you say Sandoval?"

Alandra looked away. Of course, people would recognize her name. Her ranch was one of the largest in all of Texas. But she didn't want anyone to know that Doña Alandra Maria Inez Sandoval had come to this. The feeling of being shamed, of being stained, riddled her. She just wanted to get away.

"Yes," Scully spoke up, "my wife is the *doña* of Rancho Sandoval. We were forced to entertain Santa Anna there while he waited to go to the Alamo and slaughter the men there. And Quinn and I witnessed the massacre at Goliad."

Houston's face hardened. "Don't worry. We'll make the butcher Santa Anna pay for those lives."

Alandra recalled Scully's words about God the night before, the promise that God would stick with her no matter what. She had heard them with her mind, but they didn't seem to sink in. Dorritt had told her the same thing. But now, paralyzing fear was all she could feel or know. And suddenly she longed for sleep, deep dreamless sleep, the end of remembering, shivering, and weeping. Her eyelids became heavy, drooping lower.

Houston went on, "Make a camp for your women near the physicians' tent. They can help the doctors prepare bandages and such for the wounded. Then you three men go over that way." He motioned to the tents and campfires, the men lingering around them, with horses grazing in the vicinity. "You look like you know how to fight on horseback. Attach yourselves to the Texas Cavalry."

Quinn and Houston shook hands and then they moved in the direction he'd indicated. As they rode away, Alandra glanced back at Houston. Why did a man become a general? How did a man decide to lead an army?

She understood why Santa Anna became the dictator of Mexico and the general of its large army. He wanted power, to take the best of everything for himself, to order the lives of others to his satisfaction, for his benefit. To make everyone bow to him. But why did a man like this Houston want to lead a rebel army that looked held together with what seemed like nothing more than spit?

Then she glanced at Scully and changed her mind. No, this army was not held together with spit. It was held together by spirit, by free men who wouldn't knuckle under to a dictator, a man who would delight in slaughtering them if he could.

It made her think, take stock of herself.

Last year, at eighteen, she had been so proud to become the *doña* of Rancho Sandoval. And show men that a woman could run a rancho as well as any male. When her "relatives" had come, she had stood up to them and would not let them take her land.

Where had all her *confianza* — her confidence — run off to? Even though Mendoza had ended up being murdered, had he succeeded in stealing something so precious from her? Had all her pluck fled across the Sabine with most of the women and children from Texas? And left her body here completely empty, spiritless?

# Fourteen

Alandra and Dorritt watched their men ride off to join the cavalry, which was practicing charges. As the little girl watched Carson ride off, she looked terror-stricken. Dorritt knelt down and took her hand. "Sugar, couldn't you tell us your name? We'd like to be able to call you by your right name."

The little girl did not even look at Dorritt, just stared at Carson riding away. Alandra understood. The little girl reminded her of the time when her brother had become ill and the Quinns had become a part of her life. And now, as she watched Scully leave, a feeling of being abandoned swept over her, through her, leaking into every fiber of her body. This she believed is what the child must be feeling as well. The little girl needed help, so she wouldn't tumble into the depths of fear.

As if swimming in a rushing current, Alandra reared up to fight being swept away by the surging, rolling fear. "That's a good name for you. We'll call you Sugar, then," she said, "because your hair is as light as white sugar. Now let's go pick flowers." Where these words or ideas had come from, Alandra could not say.

The little girl looked up.

"You can call me Lonnie, like Carson did when we were children, and you can call Carson's mother Tía Dorritt, like I do. *Tía* means aunt in Spanish. Sugar, we can walk right over there in the meadow by the timber. There might be some dandelions or maybe a bluebonnet or two. Bluebonnets are my favorite." Alandra quivered but pushed down her own panic.

"I recall one year going to San Antonio with Tía Dorritt . . ." She paused to nod at Dorritt. ". . . when I was a little girl, and the whole prairie was a quilt of green grass and bluebonnets."

The words flowed on their own from Alandra's mouth, leaving her exhausted. But they stirred up the memory of her early journeys with the Quinns — after the death of her beloved brother. The brother whom Mendoza had wounded, and in the end who had died from the long-term effects of that wound. Now sorrow swirled in and around her *miedo* — her fear.

325

Dorritt smiled at Alandra. "I remember that visit. The prairie was blue with them, and you wanted to just stop and play in the flowers."

With these simple memories, the deep well of sorrow over losing her brother opened wide again. Alandra tried to hide that the old sadness was trying to suck her under. She forced herself to keep smiling.

According to what Carson had told them on the way to Buena Vista, this little girl might have lost everyone. At the very least, she had been left behind, left alone. As Dorritt had done for her years ago, Alandra took pity on the innocent child and held out her hand. "Carson likes flowers too. I used to pick them with him when we were children."

Like a wary dog approaching a stranger, the little girl inched toward her. Alandra kept smiling and holding out her hand. The little girl didn't take her hand, but nodded toward the meadow. Closing the gap between them, Alandra finally took the little hand in hers with a gentle but firm touch.

If she could not banish her own lingering dread, she could at least try to help this little innocent. "Come. We will make a chain of wildflowers and show them to Carson when he comes back for the next meal."

Dorritt sighed. "I think I'll rest for a bit. Take a short siesta."

"We will not leave your sight," Alandra promised. Then she led the child through and around the many individual camps where soldiers grouped together. And then they were in the open, luxurious green meadow, dotted by the spring flowers. The little girl began to pick the first brave daisies of the spring and the unabashed golden dandelions.

Alandra showed her the low-growing blue dayflowers, flourishing between the tree roots. And then they examined white antelope horns, a kind of milkweed plant on which little white blossoms grew out like the spokes of a wheel, creating airy balls about two inches in diameter. And there were foxgloves, tall and lavender.

As Alandra touched the delicate flowers, stroked their leaves, and sniffed their wild, fresh fragrances, her spirits lifted. The two of them roamed from clump to clump, picking flowers at will. Then Alandra sank to the ground, leaned back on her palms, and stretched her legs before her and leaned her head back. Closing her eyes, she let the sun warm her face.

But in an instant she heard the sound of the pistol shot that killed her cousin exploding in her head. She saw the bullet plow into his chest and his body jerk. Her eyes flew open, her heart pounding as if she'd just sprinted across the meadow. *I must not let the child see I am upset.*

The little girl had dropped down beside her. And just as every child did, she began plucking the petals of the daisies one by one. Alandra picked up one of the dandelions and held it to the child's skin. The golden flower glowed next to the pale cheek. "You are pretty," she said, dragging the soft flower down the side of the child's face.

The little girl shook her head and turned her back to Alandra.

"I think you are *muy linda,* very pretty," Alandra insisted.

Another wave of terror slashed through her like a knife slicing into her flesh. She was being dragged aboard the ship, and then watched the captain pay the *bandidos* gold for her. She gulped air and held herself still, though her blood pounded and she wanted to spring to her feet and run.

"Which flower do you like best?" she asked the girl, forcing herself to speak in as normal a voice as she could.

The little girl looked over her shoulder at Alandra, then stroked a bluebonnet with one tiny finger.

Alandra sighed. "Yes, it is hard to have a favorite, though. I like them all."

Another memory attacked her then. She was manhandled down the steps into a ship's hold, which stank so vilely that she retched again and again. She was sure she was lost. For good. Scully would never find her.

Alandra blinked back tears but couldn't keep herself from stroking her wrists, which were still raw from all those days of being bound. She forced a smile for the little girl. What had the child seen or lived through that she kept her from talking, from even telling them her name?

Alandra continued tracing the dandelion along the curve of the little girl's ear. "You are going to be all right. We will take care of you."

Then, staring into Alandra's eyes, the little girl began to cry, tears trickling down her smudged cheeks.

Alandra pulled her close and rocked her in her arms just as Dorritt had held and comforted her when they had reached Buena Vista after the kidnapping. Alandra stroked the soft hair and sang the words that Scully had sung to her the night before. And as she did, the beautiful words flowed over her like water yet seemed unable to soak into her heart. She held her feelings in. No tears rained down her face.

She starred up at the limitless blue sky above the endless rolling prairie. How could she shield this child from what might come? She had not been able to protect herself from her relatives stealing her parents' land. Or from the bandits Mendoza had prompted to kidnap her. She kissed the child's fine, silky hair. How could she shelter this little child in the midst of a war? How could everything or anything ever be all right again?

As the shades of golden twilight were claiming the sky, even Scully was saddle sore. And worn thin as thread with the waiting. Days, weeks, nearly a month spent training had passed. Sam Houston's troops, still avoiding the Mexican Army, were now retreating northeast to Harrisburg to protect the provisional Texas government, which had fled there.

In all this time, Houston's grumbling, frustrated army had seen no Mexicans. But knowing that Santa Anna's army was out there, marching through Texas looting and burning, kept Scully's nerves on edge. And the worst part was, he had to hide it. Alandra was still jumpy and withdrawn. He could not add to her worry.

As he had for weeks, he had ridden all day with Alandra behind him. While nearby Dorritt rode on Carson's horse with the little girl they now called Sugar. Her son walked beside them.

Quinn had been away most of the day scouting. His reputation as a scout had reached Sam Houston's ears, and Quinn had become one of the lead scouts, along with "Deaf" Smith. What would he find while scouting? Where was Santa Anna?

Now, nearly dark, the order finally came down the line to stop for the night and make camp. Breathing a sigh of relief, Scully swung down away from Alandra's soft form, which had moved against him with the horse's gait — pure torture. Each night had been a similar torture for him. And another long night of it loomed ahead.

The final glow from the sun radiated burnished rays like polished bronze over the horizon. Alandra looked over at him in the low light. He tried to read her expression, but as usual, her face was closed to him. Over the past weeks, she always looked pinched and tired. Her nightly bad dreams disturbed both of them, and they both suffered the same fatigue from broken sleep. But he had another reason for sleeplessness.

Could he bear another night of having Alandra lying soft against him and not being able to touch her the way a man touched his wife? But she had been through a horrible ordeal, and they were in the midst of an army. This was not the time to ask her to consummate their marriage.

"Something's happening ahead," Alandra said, sounding exhausted. "Some commotion. I see Tío Quinn."

Scully motioned that he'd heard her. Knowing that he might be needed as a scout, he swung up into the saddle. He leaned down, squeezed her hand, then galloped toward the front of the assembled army.

Had they finally found a way to face Santa Anna and his much larger force? *Lord, let it be so.* But he tried not to let his hopes rise as he rode past the forward troops, the infantry, who had stopped marching and had thrown themselves onto the ground, exhausted. Soon they too would light fires and begin preparing suppers.

General Sam Houston stood amidst the scouts. Scully swung down from his horse and drew near enough to hear what was happening.

Among the buckskin and homespun-clad scouts stood three unhappy-looking men, two in blue and white Mexican uniforms. Many pistols were aimed at them. Houston, holding a slim leather pouch and a document, looked around. "Anyone read in Spanish?"

Quinn raised a hand, and Houston gave him the document. Quinn took a moment to read, then looked up. "We must have captured two Mexican couriers. It's a dispatch. Santa Anna is telling General de Cos and General Fisola that he has burned most of Harrisburg but didn't catch the Texas rebel government he intended to execute."

Execute. Scully had no trouble believing that. Images of the slaughter he had witnessed had been seared into his mind. He clenched his jaw to keep himself from interrupting.

Quinn paused to read silently again before resuming. "The rebel governor has fled, he thinks, to Galveston or New Washington. So Santa Anna headed southeast along the San Jacinto River toward the bay. But he's coming back to cross the river at Lynch's Ferry." Finished, Quinn handed the document back to Houston.

A few men made sounds of surprise. Houston said, "So Santa Anna's cut himself off from the main body of the army, then.

And he's only a day or so march ahead of us."

Scully's breathing quickened. This information must be what they had all been awaiting. His horse fidgeted, and he stroked its neck, soothing him.

Deaf Smith spoke up, "I done some nosing around up there, and Santa Anna will be taking his army onto a neck of wooded land that juts out between San Jacinto Bay and Buffalo Bayou. With a marsh to the east and another bayou to the south, it's a perfect trap."

A trap? Was it possible that the strutting general who Scully recalled all too clearly might make such a blunder? Might lead his column of troops into such a snare out on the open prairie? In a heavy silence, he waited for their general to speak.

Houston suddenly beamed. "So General Santa Anna has divided his army, weakened his advantage. And if he will be so obliging as to put himself into such an indefensible place then I think we better beat him to Lynch's Ferry. We will be waiting there to spring the trap when he marches his army into it. If we can catch this general, this butcher who is also the dictator of Mexico, we will have a bargaining chip that could force the Mexicans to make peace on our terms."

The excitement that was suddenly on every face burst inside Scully too. Was this the chance they'd been waiting for? Could they catch Santa Anna away from his superior numbers? They were only about nine hundred men, a small force compared to Santa Anna's thousands. But now that the Mexican general had evidently split his larger army into three parts, their numbers were about equal.

General Houston rolled the document into a scroll and tapped it against his chin as he thought. Every man watched him, waiting for what they'd all longed to hear.

Houston turned to his officers, who had gathered here too. "We won't bother going to Harrisburg. The government isn't there anyway. We'll cross the small bayou ahead of us and then Vince's Bridge, spanning the bayou of the same name, and head straight for Lynchburg and the ferry there. We'll head out in the morning and get there as fast as we can march."

Quinn asked, "What about our women and the sick?" Scully had the same question.

Houston's expression turned serious. "We'll leave them behind on this side of the bayou so they will be less easy to get to. And we'll meet the enemy farther ahead, away from them."

He turned to Colonels Burleson and Sherman. "Have three days' rations prepared, and be ready for me to address the troops in the morning. You scouts, don't reveal this to anyone. I suggest all of you get some sleep. Tomorrow we are finally on our way toward a battle. Providence has given us a golden opportunity to corner Santa Anna before he can be reinforced by his other generals. Good night, gentlemen. And well done, scouts."

Everyone walked away in silence. Quinn fell in beside Scully as they made their way back to their wives. He murmured, "I'm glad our women will be safe back here."

Scully nodded. Still, he wondered about leaving Alandra behind. Whenever he left her sight just to go scouting, she said nothing, but her eyes begged him not to leave. Worry over her blunted his relief at finally taking action. How would she take this news?

In the bright light of early morning, General Houston in a carrying voice had just announced the plan. A great shout went up from the troops — who had been muttering and sullen just the day before — "Remember the Alamo!" was shouted over and over.

"Remember Goliad!" Scully added, and was echoed by Quinn and others. Then everyone was hustling, preparing the rations and making sure nothing useful was left behind.

"You're leaving us?" Alandra asked, looking at Scully in a way he had anticipated but still hated to see.

"I'm sorry to have to leave you behind," he said, taking her hand. "But this could be the battle that wins the war, and then we can all go home. Get life back to normal."

"He's right," Mrs. Quinn agreed. "It's hard to let you men go to battle, but that's the only way to end this and keep our land, our homes. Santa Anna must be defeated or Texas will be lost to us."

Still, Scully noted that she rested a hand on her swollen abdomen as if comforting the infant hidden there. He had held Alandra close last night, knowing that his parting was coming in the morning. Her expression now was wrenching.

Carson was kneeling down in front of the little girl. "You must be brave and you must help your Tía Dorritt and Lonnie," he told her. "Will you do that for me, Sugar?" The child wrapped her arms around his neck and began crying silently. Carson kissed her forehead and then, pulling away, stood up. He mounted his horse. "I'll be back. Promise."

Scully couldn't help himself. He pulled Alandra close and kissed her, kissed her like a husband kissed a wife before going into battle. He let all he had been holding back play out as his lips moved over hers. Her sweet breath exhaled into his mouth, and he deepened the kiss. There were so many words he wanted to say. But in this crowded place, he couldn't voice them.

*Alandra, I want you to be my wife in every way for the rest of my life.* What would she say if he said that out loud — here and now? He didn't have a clue. When he could no longer delay, he murmured into her ear, "Keep safe. I'll be back. Promise." Then he turned and mounted his horse.

Quinn was already astride. Without looking back, the three of them fell in with the cavalry ranks in front of the infantry troops forming into files. The cavalry held their excited horses on tight reins, waiting for the order to start the march toward the nearby Buffalo Bayou, which they would ford or ferry across. The order came. The Texas Army started forward toward the bayou.

Her hands on Sugar's shoulders, Alandra

stood at Dorritt's side and watched the men they loved head off to battle. Still reacting to the feel of Scully's demanding lips on hers, she felt stirred and at the same time too weak to move a step. Sugar was weeping. Alandra felt the telltale shaking under her palms.

She sucked in her own tears. She could not give in to despair. Sugar and Dorritt were counting on her. But a door had burst open as she watched Scully turn away. Fear had jumped out and was trying to make her lose control, show her broken and scarred.

Major McNutt, who'd been left in charge of the baggage and wagons, two or three hundred sick men, and the women and children like herself, Dorritt, and Sugar, rode up. "I need you, ladies, to help with the sick. They'll need water, food, and tending."

"Of course, General," Dorritt said, moving toward the few tents that had been left behind for the sick. Measles had broken out in the camp, and one tent was quarantined for those suffering from the contagion. Since both Dorritt and Alandra had suffered the disease as children, they could safely take care of the sufferers. Alandra dreaded another day of endless nursing.

Watching such suffering lowered her spirits further.

At the tent entrance, Dorritt turned to Sugar. "Now, I need you to go and play with your doll under that oak tree just there, not too far away. Will you do that, Sugar?" Dorritt had managed to sew a rag doll from her petticoat cloth for the little girl.

The child stared up at them and then nodded. She walked over and sat down on the exposed gnarled roots of the ancient tree, hugging the doll to her. Alandra looked back once, smiled, then went into the tent. But her smile had only been for Sugar. It wasn't genuine. The burden of worry about the men who'd just left them behind settled over her like a weighty shawl. She began praying silently for their safety.

Underneath each word of concern for Scully, Quinn, and Carson, lurked her own desolation. Words from the psalm Dorritt had taught her from childhood bubbled up in her mind. *Cease from anger . . . For yet a little while, and the wicked shall not be . . .*

But how long was a "little while"? When would she have her life, her land, her place in the world back again?

No answers came to her as she began helping those too weak to sit up to drink water. In the midst of such high fever,

Dorritt insisted that the men needed water as often as they could sip it. As Alandra carried the tin cup and the wooden bucket of water from bed to bed, she began praying for these men too, thinking of the women they had left as they set out for war. Every time she recalled Scully riding away, the fact of his leaving stabbed her. And she resisted touching her lips where his kiss lingered.

She recalled the arrogant Santa Anna and her haughty cousins at Rancho Sandoval. She wanted men like them run out of Texas. But could Scully and others like him do that? And what would that cost her and Dorritt? And other nameless women?

After the noonday sun had passed over them, Dorritt turned to her. "I can't stand or walk another minute," she confessed. "We must lie down and then find some food for ourselves. And Sugar will need to eat too."

Alandra nodded, her eyes nearly shutting by themselves. The restless nights were taking their toll on her. She hoped that Scully wouldn't be hampered by the same weariness today. *I have been keeping him up nights too.* The thought of lying down alone tonight shook her, but she pushed it away. Scully was not a coward, and she could not give in to fear.

She followed Dorritt out of the tent. "Sugar!" Dorritt called. "Sugar! Time to eat!"

The child was not under the tree. Dorritt and Alandra went through the camp, much smaller now that the men had left, calling the child. When they didn't find her, Alandra stared ahead at Buffalo Bayou. "Where did she go?"

Dorritt put into words what Alandra feared. "I'm very much afraid she might have gone after Carson."

"She couldn't have gone far," Alandra said, fatigue making it difficult for her to speak.

"Yes," Dorritt agreed. "She can't walk fast enough to have gone that far yet."

Alandra nodded as if in agreement, but these bayous were not safe for a little child alone. There were Texas wildcats, bears, and even gators in the bayous.

"Maybe you should stay here," she said to Dorritt. "You look dead on your feet."

Dorritt sank to the ground. "I'm just so tired, Lonnie." Indeed, her aunt looked about to faint.

"You must stay here and rest, Tía. I'll go look for Sugar."

"I should go with you," Dorritt said, but Alandra heard the acquiescence in her aunt's voice.

"No, I won't go far. She could not cover much territory. And Carson and I used to play scouting games as a child. I know how to track as well as he does." Dorritt reached up, and Alandra bent to squeeze her hand. "Rest, Tía."

# Fifteen

After that long, hurry-up day, Scully rode beside Quinn as the sun sank close to the horizon. That morning, he and the rest of the cavalry had swum their horses across the bayou. His buckskin had taken hours to dry out. The day had been filled with the sound of marching. He had never heard anything like it, the sound of hundreds of men moving forward. He thought that the soft wet prairie would muffle them, but it had merely muted the noise. The tempo of the march gave him a feeling of urgency, as if he were a fresh horse pulling and rearing to start the race.

Earlier, when the army had headed east toward Buffalo Bayou, he hadn't looked back at the women, at Alandra. Deep inside, his instincts had clamored for him to stay and protect his woman. But, of course, by helping defeat Santa Anna, he was protecting Alandra.

He heard shouting and groaning from ahead and cantered forward. The wagon bearing the "Twin Sisters" — their two cannons — had bogged down in the mud. Tossing Quinn his reins, Scully slid from the saddle. He found himself shoulder-to-shoulder with Sam Houston, pushing against the wagon wheel, shoving it through the mire. He and Houston grunted with the effort. Inch by inch they forced the stuck wheels to turn. Finally, the wagon rolled onto firmer ground. Panting, Scully stepped back, better for this exertion. It had released some of his pent-up urgency.

"Well done," Houston said, and clapped a muddy hand on Scully's shoulder.

Scully nodded respectfully and then hurried to claim his reins from Quinn. The march resumed at the same slow pace. It still grated on him. But an army of nearly a thousand could not cover as much ground in a day as just he and Quinn alone.

"Who's that?" Quinn pointed to a figure coming at a run from the right of the troops.

The two of them rode out toward the man, and as they approached, saw that he was a Negro. When they reached him, he stopped running and bent over, resting his hands on his knees and panting, out of breath.

"What do you want?" asked Deaf Smith, who had caught up with Scully and Quinn.

The man looked up and swallowed. "I got a message for the general, for that Sam Houston."

"Climb up behind me," Quinn said. "We'll take you to him." The man did as he was told, and the scouts galloped toward the head of the troops.

"What is it?" the general asked when they dismounted, and the man they brought with them slid from his horse.

The black man swept off his hat. "I belong to a family near New Washington, sir. I was captured there, trying to protect my master's home. When the enemy let me go, that Santa Anna give me a message for Sam Houston. Are you that man, sir?"

"I am. What is the message?"

"I dearly hate to say this to you, sir. But he told me to tell you, Mr. Houston, that he knows you're up there in the bushes; and, as soon as he has whupped the land thieves down by New Washington out of the country, he will come up and smoke you out too."

Scully gripped his reins tighter. The butcher dared to taunt them.

Houston looked grim. "Thank you. Have you eaten?"

"No, sir."

Houston waved to one of the men near him. "Take this man and give him a ration. Then let him head home."

"Thank you, sir. And if you don't mind, I think I'll come along with you. I didn't take to that Santa Anna. I heard what he done to the men at the Alamo. And I'm a Texian too, sir."

Houston studied the man. "Can you shoot?"

"I can."

"I won't turn back any man who's willing to fight. Get this man food and a musket and shot." Houston turned to his officers. But not before Scully saw the shock on many faces. Arming a slave was not done.

It seemed that Houston didn't notice the reaction, or pretended not to. He said to the assembled men, "We'll not be stopping at sunset. We must march to Lynch's Ferry and get there before the Mexicans. I'll be darned if Santa Anna is going to beat us there. Smoke *us* out? We'll see about that."

Scully mounted and let the officers move ahead. The sound of marching started up again. His horse pawed the ground, wanting to be off, and he felt the same way. But he was caught between conflicting impulses. He wanted to take off for Lynch's Ferry to defeat the sneering Santa Anna. And he wanted to return and protect Alandra. How was she? Well?

"I am thinking of them too," Quinn commented beside him.

"What?" Scully turned to Quinn in the steadily lowering light.

"Our wives."

Scully looked down at his horse's mane, thinking of Alandra's thick raven hair. *Our wives.*

"You're in love with Alandra. Have been for a long time."

Scully's head jerked up.

"Don't try to tell me different." Quinn grinned. "Why do you think we asked *you* to go to Rancho Sandoval to protect her?"

Scully glanced away. "I don't understand. Why would you think she'd have anything to do with me? I'm just a cowboy."

"You're a great deal more than just a cowboy. I saw that a long time ago. So did Dorritt. So has Alandra."

Scully didn't know what to say. His horse danced, wanting to join the infantrymen marching by in file. He wanted to object that he didn't have feelings for Alandra, but now he realized that Quinn had seen things much more clearly than he had.

"Do you think Dorritt married me because of my wealth?" Quinn chuckled. "She married me after I got over thinking God couldn't do something wonderful for me. Stopped thinking that white New Orleans ladies didn't marry half-breed leatherstockings. To women like Dorritt — and also to Alandra, who was raised by my wife — it is the man himself, not his possessions or his skin color, that they marry. Don't get that wrong."

"I — I —" Scully stammered. Quinn had never said anything about how he and Mrs. Quinn had made their unusual match. He wanted to ask if him if he thought Alandra had feelings for him, but then Carson rode up beside them.

Quinn turned his attention to his son, reached out and gripped Carson's shoulder. "Son, you're young to be facing this. But you know how to fight. Ash and I have taught you, and you have learned well." Quinn looked to Scully, including him in his remarks. "You two just make sure to stay alive. I've fought Indians, and when you go into battle, just make up your mind before it starts that whatever it takes, you're going to come out on the other side, breathing."

Scully nodded and, while keeping up with the pace of the marching troops, slid from his tired horse to give the animal a breather. He thought over what Quinn had just said.

Was he more than a cowboy? Did thinking about what a man had to go home to, save him in a fight? Wasn't that what every man thought on the eve of battle? He pondered as he walked his horse. And the now familiar sounds of the marching went on, lulling him.

The march went on and on until deep into the night. In the moonlight, Scully had kept Houston within sight. Finally, the general gave the signal to halt. The infantrymen threw themselves on the ground where they stopped, exhausted from flattening miles and miles of prairie. They had reached the edge of a stretch of timber. According to the scouts, Lynch's Ferry was just a few miles ahead.

Scully glanced at Quinn, who nodded. Though bone-deep weary, the two of them, with Carson following, rode to the head of the army. There, they waited with the scouts who were ready to receive their orders for night reconnaissance. Fortunately, there was a healthy moon overhead.

They saw the other scouts gathered around Houston, who turned to Deaf Smith. "You better go back and take an ax to Vince's Bridge. I can't allow General de Cos with Mexican reinforcements to follow us here. Or leave Santa Anna any way out of this trap we're setting. I don't want him to be able to slip through our net and escape."

Scully digested these words, then added silently, Or give any Texian that turns coward a way to run. *We're in it now.*

At dawn on April 20, Scully was awakened by the tap of drums. Houston had forbidden the sound of reveille. Who knew how close the Mexican Army was? Scully's horse grazed nearby, hobbled. Reclining against his saddle, he rubbed his face, his eyes gritty from the short sleep. Houston had finally called a halt to the march well after midnight. After an all-day and most of the night march, the men and horses had been nearly ready to drop.

Now, the sound of men waking, yawning, and talking was all around him. Standing, he reached into his saddlebag to pull out a sea biscuit. Then the order called on and on down the line reached him. They were to assemble into their files and start forward. No time to lose in their move to reach Lynch's Ferry first. He snapped to attention and his whole body woke up. The dry biscuit in the side of his mouth like a cigar, he checked his gear and saddled his horse.

Soon the troops around him had assembled. When the drummers smartly tapped out the beat, the Texians started forward, every face grim, every man eager to meet the enemy at last.

Anticipation pulsing through his veins, Scully joined the scouts, along with Quinn and Carson. "Why aren't we taking time to eat breakfast?" he asked.

"We spotted the Mexican cavalry ahead," Quinn answered, "near that neck of land where Buffalo Bayou and the San Jacinto River meet near Lynch's Ferry. We rode back here as fast as we could to tell the general. We've got to beat the Mexicans to the timber nearest there."

Scully's gut tightened. *We're getting close.* He recalled the troops at Goliad caught out in the open and surrounded. He didn't want that to happen to this army today. They had to reach, take the timber near the ferry first. He urged his mount to keep up with Quinn.

They headed for the ferry to continue to reconnoiter ahead of the main body. From behind, he heard that mixture of noises that indicated men were marching. Their cadence had sped up to a double quick march.

The Texian Army marched on and on. In late morning Scully's stomach growled. He reached into his pocket and gnawed off another bite of sea biscuit. He let the dry tasteless bread melt into an unappetizing gritty lump in his mouth.

The timber they'd been aiming for all day was now within reach of the infantrymen. Marching over a rolling prairie made it hard not to feel exposed. The men marched even faster, seeking cover in the thick stand of timber within their sight. Quinn and Carson, who'd been out the night before scouting, cantered up to Scully.

"Is this it? Where we'll meet up with the Mexicans?" Scully asked.

Nodding, Quinn quieted his horse. "We reckon the ferry across to Lynchburg is due east just a short way. We scouts have just been ordered to head there and make sure no Mexican has crossed."

Scully, Quinn, Carson, and several other scouts galloped straight toward the river. At the end of the woods, a marsh opened up before what must be the San Jacinto River in the distance. The marsh was thick with dead cattails and dried milkweed from the summer before. As the horses picked their way through the mushy ground, Scully saw something he hadn't expected. Ahead of them at the river, and guarded by a few cavalrymen, Mexican foot soldiers were loading a substantial new flatboat with boxes. Of what? Provisions for the Mexican Army?

The enemy's mounted guard saw the approach of the Texians and bolted. They raced eastward, evidently back the way they had come. The Mexican foot soldiers in their fancy blue and white uniforms abandoned the goods and ran after their cavalry or jumped into the river and swam for it.

With shouts, Scully and Quinn chased the Mexicans on horse and foot and then turned back. After a brief conference, the barge with food, medicines, and ammunition was towed by lines lashed to saddle horns up the bayou to the Texian camp in the woods. A cheer went up when the hungry troops saw the boxes being unloaded by Carson and other scouts.

Scully swelled with the feeling of success. The Texian Army had achieved its goal. They had arrived near the ferry and taken the best position there. And in their first encounter with Mexicans, their enemies had run. If Santa Anna was interested in crossing at the ferry, he would have to deal with them first. And they had just captured fresh provisions for the troops.

Scully and Quinn left the other scouts and rode out of the timber, studying the layout of the future battle site. It felt odd to Scully to look over the prairie in front of them and know that the enemy was so close. Warm relief that Alandra and Mrs. Quinn had been safely left behind filled him. It made it easier to think of what must come. As he looked around, his spirits rose even higher. Houston had chosen the battlefield wisely. There was satisfaction in that. Now Scully was certain all the men who had talked against Houston had misjudged one smart man.

"We've got the advantage," Quinn said, voicing what Scully was thinking. Where Buffalo Bayou, at their back, met the San Jacinto River, the two bodies of water created an arrowhead of land. Timber covered that arrowhead to the north behind them. To their left, when they faced away from the timber, were a large marsh and the ferry. No army would choose to squish over the soggy swampy soil of the marsh and let their cannon get mired, stuck.

So the Mexicans would have to march over the prairie, straight into the line of fire from the timber the Texians had already claimed. Also, the gently rising prairie stretching in front of them created a natural defense. When the enemy advanced, they would have to mount the rise in plain sight of the Texians.

Scully looked over his shoulder, watching the infantry fan out behind the two Texian cannon, the Twin Sisters. On both flanks, riflemen were taking up their places. Had some order come down? Why were they moving into battle formation? His horse neighed and danced. He held it on a tight rein. "We better get with the cavalry or we'll be in trouble."

Quinn nodded, and they galloped back to join the rest of the cavalry, centering themselves behind the infantry. It took time for hundreds of men to be marched into place. Scully and Quinn's mounts, though tired, still fidgeted within the ranks of the cavalry. The troops had been downhearted from being on the run so long. Now, a jittery tension began running through the troops, which Scully felt as well.

The order came for the cavalry to charge. What? Had the main body of the Mexican Army been sighted? Along with about eighty-five cavalrymen, he started toward the enemy, his heart and horse doing an easy gallop.

When they were closer, he saw some enemy cavalry huddled in a thin line of trees near the large marsh. But just as the Texians were about to begin firing, they heard the signal to retreat. Their cavalry turned and galloped back. "That just tired our horses," Scully growled to Quinn, wondering why they'd been called upon to turn back.

Quinn shrugged. Then, when they were back in position behind the infantry, he leaned over, stroking his winded horse. "I don't think a lot of these men have ever been in a battle. They'll be restless. If we get more of these false starts, they'll just start charging without the order. I hope Houston knows what he is doing."

As Quinn's fear sank in, Scully heard the sound of marching and looked forward. It was not the Texas infantry; it was the Mexican Army. Scully pointed toward the south, where the Mexicans were visible beyond the rise in the prairie. The enemy was advancing in a column toward the Texian line. So, it had started. Excitement broke through him like Gulf waves. "I guess General Houston does know what he's doing."

All the troops, infantry in front of him and the cavalry around him, snapped to attention. The Mexican infantry was marching straight for the Twin Sisters. Did they think they could capture the cannon with the infantry? Was Santa Anna suffering from sunstroke?

The Texian artillery men scrambled. Then the Twin Sisters began to bark canisters and grapeshot. The Mexicans turned and ran. The Texian ranks roared and hooted at the enemy turning tail. But the Texians obeyed orders not to pursue them — though it was clear they wanted to. Scully's horse pranced and reared. Scully didn't blame him.

"Well, that was mildly entertaining," Quinn commented when all had quieted. "What's Santa Anna drinking in his tea lately, locoweed?"

After the brief encounter, Houston gave the order that his men who had marched all day and half the night should eat and rest. Scully wondered if this was a good idea, with the enemy within sight. But Houston had gotten them this far. He must be trusted.

Soon Carson returned from another scouting trip and slid from his horse. After unsaddling and hobbling his mount, he joined Scully and Quinn as they lounged on their saddles by the small fire, the horses grazing nearby. Mist was rolling up from the marsh.

Carson accepted a cup of weak coffee from his dad. "I'm beat."

"What's going on, son?" Quinn asked.

"What's that noise I keep hearing?"

"The Mexicans are doing what they can to throw up a barrier on the prairie between us. They're working where the prairie rises some."

"Should we be doing something?" Scully asked, trying not to sound edgy, though that's what he felt.

"We are doing something," Quinn replied, glancing at Scully. "We're resting up. Tomorrow must be the day of fighting. Unless the enemy manages to slip away during the night."

Carson shook his head and dipped his sea biscuit into his coffee to soften it. "They aren't turning tail. They're digging in, getting ready for us. They can't march eastward toward the ferry without exposing themselves to us. And if they try moving toward the ferry through the marsh, their cannon will get hopelessly mired."

Carson stopped to sip his steaming coffee. "Even if they could get by our scouts in the night — which they can't — Vince's Bridge is probably been hacked down by Deaf Smith by now. And I bet their scouts have found that out. So heading that way would let us follow and catch them in a worse position than they're in now."

Quinn smiled, clapping a hand of approval

on his son's shoulder. The same satisfaction worked its way through Scully, and Quinn put it into words. "So we finally have them cornered and Santa Anna shouldn't have chopped his army into three pieces." He held up three fingers and counted off, "Santa Anna, de Cos, and that General Urrea who beat Fannin at Goliad. You said Santa Anna had about two thousand when he was at Rancho Sandoval. Two to one are about the way the numbers shake out."

"What good will it do if we do beat this column?" Scully asked, suddenly considering a danger he hadn't thought of before. "There's two other columns out there. Will we have to beat them too?"

Quinn shook his head. "No. If we fight and can capture Santa Anna, we will have won it. Santa Anna is not only the top general, but also the dictator of Mexico. If we get him, we take the king just like in chess."

The three of them looked into the low fire. Tomorrow it would all be over — one way or the other. Scully took a deep breath. *God, let us win. Get this over with so we can breathe free.*

Yesterday afternoon Alandra had found Sugar. The little girl had been sitting in the brush near the bayou where the army must have forded earlier. She had walked the inconsolable little girl back to the camp. Dorritt had scolded and then hugged the child.

Now, she, Dorritt, and Sugar sat around the meager fire. Exhausted from nursing all day, Alandra could barely sit up. The measles seemed to be running its course. Some of the men had been well enough to leave the quarantined tent, though they still kept to this side of the camp. The doctors left behind were taking no chances of spreading the disease.

"What do you think has happened?" Alandra asked, rolling her aching shoulders. She was worn thin from worry that never quite left her, no matter what she was doing.

Dorritt shifted on the ground, as if trying to find a comfortable position. "I think by now our men should be where they were headed."

"What does that mean? Has the fighting started?" The question Alandra really wanted to ask was, When will the fighting end?

"I think we heard the start of it earlier today," Dorritt said with a tired sigh.

Alandra had hoped that had not been

true. She pressed her teeth onto her bottom lip and then asked, "You think that was the cannon, not distant thunder?"

Dorritt nodded. "I'm afraid so. I remember hearing the cannon during the Battle of New Orleans. It was far from the city but I heard the cannon. From a distance, they sound like thunder."

"But they stopped. I mean, is a battle that short?" She could not put this all together, and was breathing harder than she should have.

"Sometimes a battle starts and stops and then starts up again." Dorritt groaned softly and stretched her hands over her head.

Because of the little girl sitting beside her, Alandra did not want to say any daunting words out loud. But what would they do if Santa Anna won this war? She tried to imagine living somewhere other than Texas. Her mind came up blank, empty. Texas was her home. How could she leave it? She stroked the little girl's thin back to soothe her. And then she felt guilty about thinking of herself when so many men — not just Scully, Quinn, and Carson — might be in mortal danger.

Dorritt reached over and took her free hand. "We must not forget what the Lord has promised us."

But it was painful — hard, tight, piercing — to think that Scully would soon be facing death. And Quinn and Carson. When she had been captured, Scully had come after her and rescued her. Now, she could not protect Scully or the others. She could not protect herself. She prayed yet felt nothing but despair.

Dorritt finished reciting the psalm that Alandra had memorized as a child with her guidance:

".  .  . But the transgressors shall be destroyed together: the end of the wicked shall be cut off."

"Let that be fulfilled, Father," Dorritt said then, gripping Alandra's hand.

"Amen," Sugar whispered, the first word they had heard her utter.

Alandra wrapped her arms around the little girl, weeping silently. Tomorrow, would they hear more cannon, distant thunder? And when would Scully ride back to her, that easy grin on his face?

Scully awoke to a strangely quiet day. He roused himself and realized that he had slept long after dawn. Unusual for him. The sun was high overhead. He looked around and saw that Quinn was sipping coffee, just like he had been when Scully had sunk into sleep. Carson was there too.

"What's going on?" Scully sat up, disoriented from oversleeping.

"Not much," Quinn said, handing him a tin cup of coffee. "I wondered if you were asleep or dead." He grinned.

"All morning, the officers have been meeting over with the general," Carson said in a serious voice.

Meeting? Before Scully could ask about that, he saw that the infantry men around them were being stirred up by their officers on horseback. He gulped his hot coffee and jumped up. Their own officer, Lamar, rode up and said, "Saddle up. This is it."

Scully's heart leaped into his throat and lodged there. The three of them saddled their horses in record time. Before mounting, they loaded and checked their weapons, to make sure they would do what they were meant to. At last, all the weapons were primed and stowed within easy reach. Scully stroked the dueling pistol Alandra had given him, which he'd thrust into his belt. He was glad that he had left its mate with her.

As he swung up onto his mount, Quinn leaned forward so only Scully and Carson could hear his low voice. "Remember what

I said. When you ride into battle, think of all you have to go home to. Our ranch. Rancho Sandoval. Your mother and Alandra. Santa Anna forced this war on us. We did not go looking for trouble. If he had not slaughtered Texians in cold blood, we would have stayed at home."

Scully's pulse thrummed through him, eager and alert.

And then the order came. The cavalry was to go first, to keep the Mexicans occupied while the infantry formed up to march on the enemy. Scully watched the returning Deaf Smith gallop past them, straight for Houston.

"So much for Vince's Bridge," Quinn commented, grinning then sobering. "So much for retreat for any of us. May God give us victory."

Then the cavalry were trotting forward, as they had practiced in the weeks before this anticipated day. Scully heard the drummer begin to pound out the rhythm of the battle march. His heartbeat matched it. He pictured Alandra's face, and then her in front of the hacienda at Rancho Sandoval, her arms open wide, welcoming him.

The Twin Sisters began to bark grapeshot and canister; it hailed down over the Mexican camp. Scully saw ahead, just as Carson had, that the Mexicans had piled up baggage and anything they could to shield themselves and slow the Texians.

The infantry had formed behind the horsemen. The drummer quickened his pace to the double quick time march. Scully's spirit sped up too. Someone yelled out, "Remember the Alamo!" And the call echoed over the sleepy afternoon. Scully shouted, "Remember Goliad!" And others took up the cry.

He was holding back his horse, both he and his mount champing at the bit. And then the cry came, "Attack!"

Lamar led them, galloping forward in a charge over the prairie. The hooves that pounded the ground and threw up grass and earth pounded inside Scully as well. The Mexican cavalry lurked in a thin line of timber off to the side. That was their target. But the Mexicans just stared at them as if they couldn't believe their eyes.

Following Quinn's horse, Scully's leaped, sailing over the shallow hollow that cut the prairie in two. So close now. He slid his long rifle from his shoulder and guided his horse with his knees. He got ready to aim.

As if suddenly waking, the Mexican cavalry turned tail and bolted. Scully and the cavalry chased them till the Mexican horses floundered in the marsh. Then, at Lamar's order, the Texian cavalry swung back toward the main body of Mexican soldiers. The infantry ran straight at the enemy. Texians charged over the baggage the Mexicans had piled up.

Scully gasped at what he saw. The Mexican troops were lying about, resting. Why hadn't they heard the horses, the drums and shouting?

Now, finally, they jumped to their feet. Up from their siesta. Looking shocked, disbelieving. A few raised muskets. One blew a bugle. But most of them turned and ran for their lives.

The killing began. The Texians fired their rifles, then pistols. Then they pulled out their tomahawks or swords. Here and there a few Mexicans tried to fight back. But the Texians moved like a scythe, slashing, thrusting, shouting, "Alamo! Alamo!"

Scully fired his rifle. Then slid from his horse, his tomahawk in one hand and his pistol in the other. "Goliad!" he shouted. More Mexicans turned tail and ran. Others sprang forward to fight.

Shoulder-to-shoulder with Quinn, he fought his way through the enemy. Nearby, Texians beat down Mexicans with the butts of their rifles. Shouts. Screams. Bellows.

Pleas. Blood splattered into the air. Scully felt it splash into his eyes. He wiped it away with his sleeve.

When he looked again, a Mexican was right in front of him. Scully raised his tomahawk. The Mexican raised a saber. They lunged toward each other. The saber came down. Scully heard his own shriek of pain.

# SIXTEEN

Alandra and Dorritt froze at the same moment. Distant thunder? On a warm spring afternoon without a cloud in the blue sky? If it wasn't thunder, it must be gunfire. Cannon fire. Alandra turned to Dorritt and they clung to each other. "Do you think . . . ? Has it started?"

Dorritt clasped her tighter but said nothing. Barely able to breathe, they stood together under the canopy of ancient oaks hung with Spanish moss near the bayou.

How far away had Houston taken their men? Alandra gazed in the direction of the sound. "We must go —"

Dorritt tangled her hands into Alandra's shirtsleeves. "No. I want to go to them too. But they left us here to be safe."

Alandra tried to pull away. "We have to go —"

"That's right," barked the oldest of the physicians left behind, a crusty old man with a bald head and bushy white eyebrows. "We're leaving the young doc behind. The measles has about run its course and he can manage with the others well enough. You women, help me get the wagon ready to go. You two have shown that you know how to do serious nursing, and the army will need us."

For a moment Dorritt gaped at the man named McCutcheon, and then released Alandra's blouse. "Yes, sir!"

Dorritt and Alandra hurried along with McCutcheon and began loading one of the few wagons with boxes of bandages they had made by tearing muslin sheets and rolling the strips neatly onto spindles of wood. The two doctors brought their surgical bags and wooden chests filled with medicines and their pharmacy equipment.

Abruptly, Alandra stopped loading blankets onto the wagon. "Listen!" The four of them turned toward where the thunder had just stopped. "The battle cannot be done yet, can it?" she asked.

Dr. McCutcheon grimaced. "We're going anyway. Even if one side has surrendered, there will be wounded. We can move faster than a whole army, but it will take us well into the night to get there even by wagon."

The other doctor, Toomey, nodded.

"Come on. We have all the medical supplies and food and water." He ended the discussion by climbing onto the wagon and picking up the reins. A soldier who had just been pronounced well, had hitched up the team of two mules.

McCutcheon stiffly climbed up on the wagon seat. Alandra and Dorritt scrambled up onto the back of the wagon, finding places to perch among the supplies. Sugar had followed them, found a spot near Alandra and put her arms around Alandra's waist. The wagon began jouncing over the rutted area around the camp. Soon they were headed forward over the smoother prairie. When they reached the bayou, they found a shallow place to ford it.

Worry about the gunfire they'd heard pecked at Alandra's peace. What had happened? Who had won? She stopped her mind there. She forced herself to picture Scully, Quinn, and Carson whole and well. She let her memory roam to long past fiestas and rodeos. Scully roping a bull as people cheered. Scully watching her, frowning, while she danced with a young caballero in San Antonio. Then thoughts, flashes, images of the past two months intruded — the courtroom with her haughty relatives, the *bandidos.* But she clamped down on them, tying a tourniquet against the flow of horrible memories. Scully's low voice sang in her mind:

'Twas Grace that brought us safe thus
   far . . .
and Grace will lead us home.

She drew Sugar onto her lap, stroked the little girl's white blond hair and whisper-sang the song to her. She brushed away her own tears and clutched the child to her as a lifeline. If only she knew what was happening, if only she could dredge up some hope that she would find them well and Santa Anna defeated.

Silence came. Breathing hard, Carson scanned the scene before him. "Pa! Scully!" he called. The battle couldn't be over that fast, could it? They had barely begun fighting.

Lamar rode up. "Carson, the Mexicans have given up," he said. "Look for our wounded and help the ones who can walk toward the hospital tent."

Carson waved in reply and began moving through the black smoke and fallen soldiers who lay around him. The unnatural silence, deeper somehow after the torrent of cannon and gunfire, held. The wounded Mexicans seemed too shocked by the turn of events to moan or cry out. Had fatigue kept them asleep and unaware? Or had the Mexicans thought the weak, ragtag Texians wouldn't attack? Most of the wounded were Mexicans. Only a few injured Americans staggered to their feet or lay still, waiting for help.

Carson paused twice to rip cloth from a wounded soldier's clothing to rig up a makeshift bandage or tourniquet over a wound. Then he recognized Scully's shirt, bloodied now. Carson covered the distance and knelt down beside his friend.

A prickling chill ran over his skin and up his spine. "Scully?" He shook his shoulder. "Scully?" His throat was trying to close up on him.

Scully opened his eyes and gazed up at Carson. He reached out and put his hand over Carson's where it gripped his shoulder. "Carson," he muttered. He gasped for air. "How bad is it?"

"Bad enough." Fear rippling in cold waves, Carson stood up, took off his buckskin shirt, then shrugged out of his cotton shirt. He ripped off one sleeve, knelt again, and with care helped Scully sit up. Then he tore off the top of the sleeve and folded it into a neat pad over the deep saber cut on Scully's jaw. Only then did he notice that Scully's thigh was bleeding freely, and repeated the bandaging process.

Finally, when he'd done all he could, Carson asked, "Can you walk, Scully?"

"I think so. Let me sit up for a while first." Scully looked up and tried to grin.

"Fine. I have to find my pa." Carson gripped Scully's shoulder and then stood and began looking. "Pa!" he called. "Pa! It's Carson!"

Hearing a faint cry, he turned and saw a hand waving, his father's, from under a pile of Mexican bodies. Carson rushed over, dug in and gently pulled his father free. Quinn's shirt was soaked with blood, and Carson blanched. If his father had suffered a gut wound, there was no hope. Doctors could dig out bullets and cut off shattered limbs. But they were helpless to put a man's insides back in working order.

*Don't panic,* Carson told himself. *Pa needs help, not me having the vapors.*

As his pa had taught him, he began the examination, starting at the scalp and proceeding down the body. When he was done, he sat back on his heels and took a deep breath. His father wasn't gut-shot. But he had been pierced in the side. The wound had gone clear through front to back. Probably a sword.

His father swallowed. "How bad is it?"

"Bad enough." Carson destroyed the rest of his shirt binding up his father's wounds. Then, as he shrugged back into his buckskin jacket, he rose and called, "Scully! Come! Help me!"

Scully rose, staggered a little. But leaning on the butt of his rifle, he limped through the littered battlefield to Carson.

"Pa's hurt. We need to get him to the hospital tent. Stay with him while I get my horse."

Not waiting for Scully's agreement, Carson ran down his horse. Then he and Scully managed with some help from two other soldiers to lift Quinn to lie facedown over Carson's saddle. Then Carson led the horse while Scully clung to the saddle horn and limped along beside, favoring his right thigh.

"Let's find a doctor." But what Carson wished more than anything was for his mother to be there. He trusted her doctoring more than that of the camp physicians. Then again, fortunately she was far from this place.

As he steered the horse back toward the Texas camp, it looked like they'd won. But he didn't feel very triumphant. *Dear God,*

*just let the war be over. I want to go home.*
*We all do.*

Night had come, but under the nearly full moon, the two doctors driving the hospital wagon had pressed on. Fortunately, they had come to the savaged Vince's Bridge before dark. Since someone had taken an ax to the bridge, they had been forced to find a path down the steep bank and a place to ford the wagon. The trip across the Vince's bayou wasn't one Alandra wanted to repeat again.

Finally, ahead through the shade of deepest night, she glimpsed many campfires within a stretch of timber. The solemn treetops stood against the silvery moonlight. Their party had made good time with the mules, which had been at rest for two days. Dr. McCutcheon slapped the reins and hurried the mules over the last mile of turf. They drove into the camp, seeing the white Texas flag against the night sky. They drove directly to a large tent illuminated from inside with candlelight and oil lamps.

Dr. McCutcheon stopped, tossed the reins to a few soldiers who had hurried forward. "Unharness these mules and give them attention." Bags in hand, he and Dr. Toomey hustled inside the tent and were met by the physicians who had gone ahead earlier with the army.

Alandra and Dorritt slipped down from the wagon. Fortunately Sugar was sound asleep. Alandra was chilled with fear and the night air. Some soldiers came forward to unload the medical supplies. One of them said to Dorritt, "You're that half-breed Quinn's wife, right?"

Alandra's irritation ignited. Why did everyone always use Quinn's parentage to define him?

"Yes, I have the honor to have married Desmond Quinn." Dorritt's tone was mild and her words were balm to Alandra's heart.

"He's inside the hospital tent, ma'am. And his friend and your son," the man said. "Thought you should know."

The news slapped Alandra in the face like a wet rag. Dorritt grabbed her and they hurried inside, hand in hand. "Quinn! Carson! Scully!" Dorritt called in a low voice as they picked their way through the men, lying on blankets or the bare grass. "Quinn, I'm here."

Alandra found she couldn't speak. Men suffering from measles were a world apart from men bleeding from cannon fire, gunshot, and sword wounds. The spectacle of rows of moaning and weeping men unnerved her. She clutched Dorritt's arm and tried not to show her revulsion and panic. The smell of sweat and blood brought the gorge up to her throat. She tried to hide the fact that she was beginning to retch.

Near the rear of the tent, Carson rose from the ground. "Ma, I'm here with Pa and Scully."

"Thank God, you're all right!" Dorritt exclaimed as she reached Quinn. She released Alandra and hugged Carson, kissing his forehead and stroking his hair, murmuring soft words of joy and gratitude.

Hanging back, Alandra did not want to look down where Quinn and Scully lay. Fear seized the back of her neck and shot down her spine, nearly freezing it. *No. No. I don't want to see them wounded . . . dying.* Still, she forced herself to look. Quinn's midsection had been wrapped tightly with a large bandage, stained with blood.

"Alandra?"

She heard Scully's voice and turned to look down at him. He was trying to sit up, and she knelt beside him. "Scully," she said, and folded him into her arms.

# SEVENTEEN

Finding Scully alive lifted Alandra, but seeing him marred by blood from head to knee crushed her. She clung to him. And looked to Carson.

Alandra looked to Dorritt, kneeling by Quinn, who was unconscious. Dorritt's expression was impassive. She asked only, "What happened, son?"

"A Mexican officer ran him through with a sword. He told me."

Dorritt moaned and covered her mouth. Alandra moaned silently, *No, no, no.*

"Ma," Carson urged, "don't give up hope. It went clean through, front to back. Pa must have leaped to the side and the thrust didn't hit his vitals. The doc here who bandaged him said he thinks it just cut through muscle."

Dorritt squeezed Carson's hand, then turned to her husband and began examining his dressings.

Alandra had been embracing Scully all through this exchange. Now she felt him try to return it. His weak embrace pushed her fear up another icy notch. "Why are you here?" he asked in an unexpected sharp tone.

"These women are here because we needed them to help with the wounded," Dr. McCutcheon barked, coming up to them. "Now, has one of the physicians seen to your wound?"

"Yes, sir," Scully said, wincing.

"Well, if I know women, your wife will have to see if it was treated to suit her." McCutcheon looked down into Alandra's face. "Do that quickly and then we must get busy. The other physicians say that most of the wounded are Mexicans who haven't received treatment yet. We'll probably be working all night and into tomorrow."

Then the doctor waved toward Carson. "Your little sister is out sleeping in the wagon. Go take care of her."

Carson looked to Alandra, who mouthed, *Sugar.*

Carson put on his hat and turned to go. "I'll be outside, Ma, if you need me."

"Come back around dawn," the doctor continued. "You women, see to your men first, but then I must have your help. We may actually manage to save a few lives if we act quickly." As McCutcheon drew away, he instructed Dorritt to come to him and told Alandra to help Dr. Toomey.

Alandra moved back from Scully. The low light made it hard for her to see him clearly. But she saw him shiver, probably from the ground chill. She could feel it herself.

"What happened?" she asked, moving to lift the bandage over the side of his face.

He caught her wrist, stopping her. "The doc already stitched me up. A saber cut to the side of my face — caught me from the ear to chin. And someone managed to put a bullet through my thigh. It didn't break my bone."

He sounded irritated with her. Alandra lowered her hand, but did not give in completely. "I'll want to give both a fresh dressing tomorrow." Though she was shaking inside like jelly, she made her voice firm.

He wouldn't meet her eye. "I thought they were going to keep you away from this."

His irritated tone left her floundering. What was she doing that was wrong? "Was the battle that short? We could hear the cannon firing and then they stopped —"

"Mrs. Falconer," Dr. Toomey called, interrupting them. "I need you *please*."

Hands on his shoulders, Alandra urged

Scully to lie back down. Scully, a good man, did not deserve pain and suffering. "I must go and do what I can. You try to sleep. I will come back when I have a moment."

She rose, but then bent down and stroked his cheek. He pulled away.

"Good night," she murmured. "I will not be far." She stroked his cheek again, even though he did not acknowledge her. "Sleep. You heal faster if you rest."

He lay on the blanket, turning his head away. Alandra glanced down at Dorritt, who was kneeling with her hand on Quinn's head. Alandra leaned closer and heard Dorritt praying. Of course her aunt would be praying.

Her reaction was the opposite. She did not feel like praying. She felt like cursing. Even if she knew little of how to curse. She suddenly understood why Job's wife had told her husband to curse God and die. She wanted to shake God, not pray to Him. What was He playing at? Did they mean so little to Him? Dorritt had always taught her that God was good, faithful to those who trusted in Him. That the wicked would be defeated.

Now, as she picked her path through men bloody, battered, gasping, and groaning in pain, she wondered what part of God's love this was. Just how many righteous had to be wounded or die before God decided to cut off the wicked?

The appalling night went on. Alandra held an oil lamp over patients while Dr. Toomey probed flesh for bullets and stitched up ragged flesh. She learned how much opium could soothe and how much could kill. She bathed gore from wounds and threw up twice. But she did not leave. She did not desert the poor men lying there, suffering, dying.

Most of them were Mexican, and she tried to speak kindly to them in Spanish. They clung to her hands and begged her to pray for them, for their souls. They told her the names of their wives, their sweethearts, their mothers, as if she could somehow communicate with them, tell them of the passing of their loved ones.

Tears streamed down her face and she did nothing to stop the flow. If she did not weep for these poor souls who had been marched thousands of miles from home to die far away from their families, the very rocks would weep for them.

For many of the patients, the doctors could do nothing. They were given a portion of opium and carried out to another tent to die. Alandra wished there had been some priest present to give them the last rites to ease their passing. But there was none. So to comfort them, she prayed for them, reciting the Latin prayers she had been taught as a child. She wept with every word.

Finally, the night she would never forget at last ended. All the patients had been treated or assigned to the death tent. As the thin light of dawn glowed through the tent canvas, she staggered toward Dorritt, who sat huddled between Quinn and Scully. Alandra rubbed her arms against the chill and had trouble feeling her legs and feet, numb from standing so long. This long night had been a preview of hell.

Alandra sank to the cold ground near Dorritt and wrapped her arms around her knees. Pressing her face into her skirt, she rocked like a fretful child too overdone to go to sleep. Glancing over, she saw that both Quinn and Scully were asleep. But both were shivering.

After a wound, a high fever always set in. One blanket would not be enough to warm Scully. But she did not have a second blanket here. She thought of all her fine blankets at her hacienda, blankets lovingly woven by the wives of her farm workers.

And here she had one ragged blanket for Scully wounded and trembling on the bare earth.

She pulled herself together then. How many times had Scully warmed her when she shivered? Afraid to disturb his dressings, she lay down behind him and wrapped her arms around him. His whole body shook against hers. Tears threatened to start again, but she would not allow herself to weep.

Glancing over, she saw that Dorritt had also folded Quinn in her arms and that her lips were moving. Tía Dorritt was praying. Alandra did not need to hear the words to know what the prayer was — Psalm Thirty-seven.

She turned her face away and buried her nose in Scully's nape. When she closed her eyes, she saw again in her mind the men she had seen carried out to die. What if Scully died?

She clung to him, trying to stop his trembling. The heat of his fever penetrated her clothing. She was trying to warm him but his body was warming hers. Was that not just like this man? She needed and he gave. "I'm sorry," she whispered. "I'm sorry."

She overheard Dorritt's praying.

Alandra had heard of people whose hearts hardened. She had never understood that. But now she did. Her heart was hardening inside her, turning rock hard. Scully was a good man, a man of strong if quiet faith. He had rescued her from the renegade Comanches, married her to protect her inheritance, saved her from the ship, and ridden to war to run the butcher Santa Anna out of Texas. And what did he receive for his faith, his goodness, his courage? He lay on the ground wounded and perhaps dying. And she was powerless to save him, repay him. *This is not right. This is not just.*

Dorritt's whispering went on:

"For evildoers shall be cut off: but those that wait upon the Lord, they shall inherit the earth

For yet a little while, and the wicked shall not be . . ."

*For a little while? What is a little while?* And why must the wicked prosper at all? How much was flesh and bone expected to bear? *I want it to stop now. Must I lose everything and everyone in order to satisfy you, God? Make it stop.*

She bit her lips to hold in the wail trying to work its way up and out.

Dorritt was speaking louder: "Don't give up, Quinn. Feel the baby moving against you. You must not die. You must live. I don't want to go home without you to raise this child without you."

Alandra clung to Scully, no longer believing that God heard Dorritt. No longer believing that He even heard her railing against him. She had reached her limit. Her heart was marble. *I am only human, made from dust. I will wither and die like grass. And now I know God does not care. I am done praying. Have your way, God. Cut off the wicked when you feel like it, but I no longer care to know you.*

Still lying against Scully, Alandra looked up to see who had shaken her shoulder. Carson knelt down beside her, handed her a cup of steaming coffee and one of the tasteless sea biscuits. Still, her empty stomach leaped and growled at the sight of food. She edged herself into a sitting position. One had to be truly hungry to welcome a sea biscuit.

She dipped it in her coffee and began gnawing. After riding all day, fording two bayous, and then tending the sick all night, she felt as if she had caught her heel in a stirrup and had been dragged for several miles.

"How are my pa and Scully doing?" Carson asked.

Alandra glanced over at Scully. He had stopped shivering, but his breathing was labored. And she knew she would have to foment his wounds at least twice today. It was the only way to draw out the infection. And infection could still kill him and Quinn. The stain and smell of blood lingered on her hands and clothing. Disgusting her.

Letting the steam from her cup warm her face, she asked, "What happened here, Carson?"

"It was a bloodbath. We caught them before they could cross the San Jacinto River at Lynch's Ferry, just like Houston planned."

She asked a question that had bothered her all last night, "Why are there so many Mexicans wounded and so few Texians?"

Carson snorted his disapproval. "Santa Anna must have got cocky. Didn't think we'd attack him first. The Mexicans didn't even seem to see or hear us coming. And we were in plain sight and in broad daylight, shouting. As we crossed the prairie out in the open, it was as if we were shielded from them seeing us." He shook his head as if he still couldn't believe it.

Alandra tried to wrap her mind around this. How could Santa Anna, the arrogant general, have blundered so? "Where's Santa Anna? Or was he killed?"

"He hasn't turned up. It was a mess. There was a bayou at the rear of the Mexican camp, and many of his men drowned trying to escape across it. I hope I never see such a day again."

"Is it over?" Alandra sipped her bitter coffee.

"You mean the war?"

She nodded, hoping he would say yes.

"It is if we can find Santa Anna and hold him. Remember, he's not just the general. He's the dictator of Mexico. He's got the power. So if we have him, *we've* got the power."

Alandra stared into Carson's blue eyes. She was completely cold inside, dead except for her hatred. She wanted Santa Anna caught and punished — executed. She inhaled. "Then I hope someone finds him, and fast."

A soldier came up to her. "Are you Mrs. Falconer?"

"*Sí.*" Alandra looked over at the man.

"Dr. McCutcheon told me to let Mrs. Quinn sleep, but he needs you to come and foment General Houston's wound."

Alandra scooted forward, suddenly thinking of how she must look, bloodstained and rumpled, wearing trousers under her skirt. She longed for Rancho Sandoval, her room and the luxury of a long bath with rose-scented soap. If she rode up to her hacienda now, would anyone even recognize her?

Carson rose. "I have to go see to Sugar. I don't want her to come in here. She's been through enough."

Alandra nodded. "I'll be back soon." She drained the cup and handed it to him. The hot coffee and biscuit had at least revived her enough to start again. She leaned down, pulled the blanket around Scully and stroked his back once, hating to leave him. "When he wakes, Carson, tell him I will be back soon. And get him some coffee and food."

Carson nodded. Then Alandra walked away beside the soldier who kept looking at her. *Well, let him look. In rags or brocades, I am still the* doña *of Rancho Sandoval and Mrs. Scully Falconer, the wife of a brave man.* She lifted her chin.

She found Sam Houston lying on a mattress under an oak, with his wounded limb propped up. He was sleeping. Alandra noted that his boot had been cut off and his ankle bound with a bloodstained dressing that needed to be changed. She found that the doctor, who she was told would return soon, had left her a dish of herbs to use to foment wounds and draw out the infection.

If she did not foment the wound, gangrene would set in and the foot might have to be amputated. She set the man who had brought her to boiling water while she mixed the herbs and made a poultice with herbs wrapped in unbleached muslin to lay upon the wound. She soaked the poultice in the hottest water she could bear, then laid the poultice onto the wound.

Houston yelped and woke up, uttering an oath.

Alandra looked up. "I apologize, General, but I must foment this wound, and hot water is a part of that."

Houston closed and opened his eyes. "Forgive my outburst, ma'am. I didn't know a lady was present."

His calling her a lady when she plainly was not dressed as a *doña* bolstered her lagging spirits. And this man, this general, had done the impossible. He was David and Santa Anna had been Goliath. "Think nothing of it, General. I would forgive you anything in honor of your victory here against a much larger enemy. Lie back now.

This will take some time, and I'll have to repeat it again later."

As she was speaking, two men approached the oak tree and Houston. At the sight of one man's face, shock burst like a bubble inside her.

# EIGHTEEN

Slowly, she rose and pointed. "General Santa Anna." Her voice rang out in the sudden silence like an accusation.

"What?" Houston swiveled and looked at Santa Anna.

"We meet again, El Presidente," Alandra said, her words vibrating with heart-deep disdain. She folded her arms and sneered at him. He was dressed like a common soldier and his face was ashen.

Santa Anna stared at her. "You have the advantage of me, señora."

She lifted her chin. "I am Mrs. Scully Falconer and *doña* of Rancho Sandoval." She held onto herself tightly. She wanted to spring forward and scratch out the man's eyes. How many good men had died because of this butcher?

Appearing dazed, Santa Anna made no reply to her, but addressed Houston. "I have come to surrender. I am General Antonio

Lopez de Santa Anna, and a prisoner-of-war at your disposition."

Alandra looked to Houston. The Texas general only took a moment to size up the man. By a motion of his hand, Houston gestured at a large tool chest that sat nearby and asked him if he'd like to sit down. Santa Anna did so, leaning forward. Crossing his arms, he pressed both of his sides with his hands.

Anger billowed within Alandra like steam from boiling water. She drew in air, shaking with outrage. Houston looked up at her. "You are sure that this is Santa Anna?"

She glared at the Mexican. "I have no doubt." Her infuriated words felt hot in her throat. "I was forced to entertain him at my rancho before he slaughtered the brave men at the Alamo. This is the dictator of Mexico." Sour acid flowed up into her mouth. She could have spit it in his face.

Ignoring her, Santa Anna looked to Houston. "My nerves are shattered. I see you have a doctor present. May I have some opium?"

"So your nerves are upset? Did not enough men die yesterday to suit you?" Alandra turned away, her revulsion pulsing, mounting.

To master herself, she knelt on the damp

earth and began treating her patient, General Houston. The moist ground soaked into the knees of the trousers she was still wearing under her skirt. Another reminder of how Santa Anna had brought so many to misery. A foolish thought, but true. Why did God allow Santa Anna to stand here unharmed while Houston lay here in pain? Evidently Diablo took care of his own.

The doctor returned and handed the Mexican general the opium he had asked for. As soon as Santa Anna swallowed it, he began negotiating with Houston for his liberation. Gritting her teeth, Alandra made herself focus on soaking the general's poultice in hot water and reapplying it.

"What is to be done with you does not lie in my power," Houston declared, nearly snarling with the pain she was causing him. "Texas has an elected government and your freedom is in their hands."

"I don't like to deal with civilians," Santa Anna snapped. "I abhor civilian governments. I would much rather deal with a military man. And, General, you can afford to be generous; you are born to no common destiny." Santa Anna made a flourishing wave toward himself. "You have conquered the Napoleon of the West."

Alandra hissed a mocking sound. Her

hatred of this arrogant man reared inside her like a great serpent. She could not keep silent. "You dare flatter yourself even while you try to charm another. That will not work here."

Houston smothered a chuckle but grinned broadly. "You see, General Santa Anna, even the women in Texas are fierce. And I cannot agree with you. My victory yesterday was not my doing but the achievement of the brave men who obeyed my orders."

"This dictator will not understand men like my husband or my uncle Quinn, sir," Alandra said as she fingered the general's wound, working out the ugly infection. "I spoke to many of the dying Mexican soldiers last night and prayed with them. Many were Indians from Yucatan who had never wanted to fight. They had literally been dragged from their villages and forced onto boats at Vera Cruz." Her hatred of this dictator ballooned inside her once again, as she thought about the injustice he'd brought about. "How many of them will ever be allowed to return to their homes?"

Houston's gaze connected with hers. He smiled, but managed to ask her politely with his expression to let him handle the rest of the negotiations. She pursed her lips and nodded. She trusted this man.

Lifting himself on one elbow, Houston demanded, "Sir, how do you expect to negotiate after your actions at the Alamo?"

"General Houston, by the rules of war, when a fortress, insufficient to defend itself, is summoned to surrender, and refuses, and causes the shedding of human blood, the vanquished, when it was taken, are open to execution." The man sounded as if he were reciting from a military text.

Alandra listened to the man's defense of his indefensible actions and ground her teeth. Did he think he could hide behind such deception?

Houston did not appear impressed either. "That may have been the rule in the past, sir, but it is a disgrace now in the nineteenth century. And, General Santa Anna, you cannot give the same excuse for the massacre at Goliad. The men there surrendered but were betrayed, and slaughtered in cold blood!"

As Alandra continued working out the infection, she remembered Scully telling her about Goliad and then about his parents being killed by Indians as he hid in the well. How did humans like this Santa Anna think they could carry out these wretched crimes and never be held accountable?

Santa Anna looked away. "If they capitulated, I was not aware of it. General Urrea must have deceived me. I had orders from the Mexican government to execute all that were taken with arms in their hands."

Houston replied, sounding grim, "General Santa Anna, you are the government. A dictator has no superior."

"But I have the order of our Congress to treat all that were found with arms in their hands, resisting the authority of the government, as pirates. And Urrea has deceived me. He had no authority to enter into any agreement; and, if I ever live to regain power, he shall be punished for it."

Did the man have no idea that his trying to place blame on others would be scorned by the free men standing there, listening. Alandra snorted as she had heard Quinn do many times when he was told a lie.

Houston sounded as if he had heard enough too, as he changed the subject, asking Santa Anna if he would like some refreshment and sleep. Santa Anna said he did, but as he rose from the tool chest, Houston stopped him. "I want you to write orders to your other generals to fall back to Monterrey. I will choose the Mexican couriers. In the orders, instruct your generals that you will not be released until all Mexican troops are off Texas soil."

Santa Anna bowed and was led away to write the orders, then to eat and sleep.

Alandra finished wrapping the general's ankle in a fresh dressing. She looked up at the doctor, who was gazing down at it too. He said, "I think, General, you will need to go to New Orleans and have further surgery. I'm sure that there are more bone fragments from the shattered ankle still in there. And none of us are as skilled in surgery such as you need."

Houston exhaled long and loud as he lay back down. "This isn't the first time I've been wounded in battle. Just keep gangrene from setting in, and when I can, I'll take your good advice. Thank you, Doctor."

Alandra said, "I will be back later. Now I am going to go do the same for my husband." She gathered up the supplies.

Before she left, however, General Houston took her hand. "My thanks, and I hope the man you've married knows what kind of woman his wife is." He grinned. "I expected at any moment for you to call Santa Anna out."

She nodded and left. Her outrage at Santa Anna's refusal to assume blame still simmered. The man had been defeated and reduced to wearing a common soldier's uniform to avoid being identified and killed on sight. Still, he sought to justify his reprehensible actions. And refused to accept any responsibility for butchering unarmed men. Did he think the world was meant just for him and what he wanted?

*Do you think the world was just meant for you and what you want?*

It was a still, small voice, her own voice. But it slammed into her with astounding force. She staggered and nearly fell. The doctor, who had been behind her, hurried forward and took her arm. "You must sit down for a while, ma'am. You are overdone."

She nodded and let him help her to a nearby willow tree, where she slid down to the ground and leaned against the rough trunk. "Do not worry about me, señor. I will be better soon."

He nodded and left her with apologies. Many others needed his services more. Under the drooping willow branches, she stared around at the quiet, greening prairie and wondered what had just taken place. Leaning her head back, she stared up into the limitless sky.

*Do you think the world was just meant for you and what you want?*

She closed her eyes. She ached all over with the deepest fatigue she had ever known. Her clothing was caked with dirt and blood.

And she did not have the strength or will to face her own words. But she heard them again, scolding her, prodding her conscience. She did not want to look at herself. Did not want to see that she was as self-centered as Santa Anna. Did not want to admit that she thought the world should suit the *doña* of Rancho Sandoval.

*It is not true. I did not seek to control a nation.*

But she had thought that regardless of the revolution, she should have peace and comfort. Others could suffer far from her as long as she did not have to see them and suffer the same hurt. That sounded so harsh. But was that not the truth? She knuckled her burning eyes like a fretful child. All of Texas could be under siege and in deadly peril, but not she, not Doña Alandra Sandoval.

She recalled Scully's words: *It's not just us. Texas is bleeding. Texas is on its knees.* He had spoken the truth. But had she thought her life was to remain untouched while Texas bled? That she was privileged? Above everyone else?

She rubbed her taut forehead as if to rub away this ugly truth. But it would not be erased. Dorritt had taught her what God thought of the proud. Not much.

Pride went before a fall. God had not ripped everything from her — her inheritance, her home, her peace of mind and safety. He had not abandoned her here hungry and desolate.

Evil men, wicked men, had moved against her. Fernando had wanted more land, wealth, and the power they brought. Mendoza had tried to wreak revenge on her. And Santa Anna had wanted to force every Texas knee to bow to him and call him lord. And since he had already seized control of the nation of Mexico, that pride, that arrogance, had unleashed this evil time, a war. And thousands had died and thousands had suffered, and would continue to suffer because men they loved had been lost here in Texas.

*And I expected to be left alone, untouched. But I am not immune. I am not apart, but a part of Texas here and now. The fact that my rancho is one of the largest in Texas does not make me exempt from evil, from war, from history.*

This was a violent time and she — along with the rest of Texas and Mexico — had suffered because of it. None of them would ever be the same for having lived through this ordeal. Where she sat on the ground, more wetness was seeping into her trousers and skirt — the *doña* sitting on the ground like a peon. And she did not care. What did appearances mean today?

Santa Anna had dressed as a common soldier to avoid being captured. But in the end he had realized that he had no other course than to surrender. He was not a man who could handle disaster. Even in defeat he had tried to claim superiority. *I am the Napoleon of the West.* Had he forgotten that Napoleon had died alone and in exile?

But General Houston had looked at Santa Anna for what he was. Hosuton had also looked at her and seen only her strength and spirit. He had called her a Texas woman, a fierce Texas woman. And that was all she wanted to be, nothing more.

A breeze moved the long spring green willow branches hanging above her. With a gentle rushing sound, the willow sighed around her. She breathed in deeply.

She had railed at God last night. She had demanded to know when the evil would end and why it had to be at all. Now she regretted her attitude with all her heart. God had not caused the evil. Wicked men, rebellious men, had done that.

*Forgive me, Father. I forgot for a time. If all men obeyed you, war would not come. All this evil came upon not just me, but all of Texas. Yet when I prayed you would send Scully to save me, you did. And I prayed that Scully and Quinn would come through the battle, and they are still alive. Though thousands have prayed to you, you have not disdained my prayer. I am sorry for being so thankless.* She hid her face in her hands, rocking like a lost child.

Carson had told her that it seemed as if the Mexicans had not even seen the Texians marching across a prairie in the midday sun. A miracle? Perhaps. And against overwhelming odds, the Texians had defeated the butcher at last. And Texas would be a free land with a government ruled by law and citizens who had rights. No more king or dictators.

She wondered for a moment if Santa Anna realized why he had lost to a much smaller army made up of civilian soldiers. Had he realized yet that a man like Quinn, who was fighting to protect his family, his home, and his rights as a free man, fought like a hundred of the poor souls Santa Anna had dragged from their homes and impressed into arms?

No, no doubt he did not. He had fallen for the Devil's lie. Santa Anna had thought he could slaughter and go free. Now, instead, he begged for opium to ease the humiliation of defeat. And went on lying.

She rested against the bark and began to feel stronger. The truth could make one free, and it could evidently also give strength to those who were weakened, as she had been. She tried to think, plan, be practical. What should she do? What would God have her to do? Wonderful new ideas, new plans, began slipping into place in her mind. Her eyes opened wider.

Santa Anna was in the hands of the Texian government. The war was over. But both Quinn and Scully would need careful nursing to heal. And then they all faced getting home safely, finding Sugar's family, and helping Texas return to normal.

She imagined riding up to her hacienda with Scully at her side. And all her people were rushing out to welcome them. A smile curved her mouth and new warmth began. There was much to do, so much new liberty in Texas — and it was for all.

She looked up through the green willow leaves toward the sun climbing higher. Arriving home starting fresh, that's what she would look forward to. With Scully. They would pull their lives back together, with God's blessings. There was much to do.

But would she lose her rancho through that awful will? Had this victory made her land safe? For a moment the fear of losing

Rancho Sandoval flushed the warmth from her veins, filled them with cold water. She shut her mind to this dread. *I must believe that God will save my land. And my husband.*

Later, Scully woke to find sunshine lighting the tent and Alandra doing something to his wound. "What?" he mumbled. He didn't like the way he sounded. He sounded weak.

She was lifting his head and holding a cup to his lips. He wanted to scold her and tell her he could do that himself. But bone-weariness, like a huge snake, had swallowed him whole. He could barely speak and moving took an amazing amount of effort. So he submitted to her helping him drink.

When the cup was empty, she lowered his head. "Your wound is infected and that causes the fever. That is why you feel weak. It will pass."

He felt her applying a hot poultice to his wounds and stifled a cry. He didn't want her to have to do this. He didn't want a lady to have to see what must be a horrible sight, his flesh ripped and torn. He tried to stop her hand with his.

With ease, she slipped her hand from his loose grip. "I am fomenting your wounds just as Tía Dorritt taught me. I will keep doing this every day until the infection ends.

Then the fever will leave you and you will gain back your strength."

He found he couldn't fight her. He was so drowsy and limp. And the poultice was at the same time agonizingly hot and blessedly soothing. He could almost feel the throbbing, hurtful swelling being drawn out. What could he do? He didn't want her to have to do this dreadful task, but he needed her nursing. He nodded and muttered, "Thanks."

She bent and kissed his forehead. "You will be well soon." She whisper-sang into his ear the same words of "Amazing Grace" he had sung to her. But he liked to be the one singing them, not the one sung to. He knew what his second ma would have said to that. Foolish pride.

"Santa Anna has given himself up," Alandra said. "The war is over. We won."

"Good," Scully muttered, seeing Quinn asleep nearby. With great effort, he patted her hand. Heartfelt gratitude flowed through him. "We have all come through alive."

"Yes, *querido.* Do you want something for the pain?"

He shook his head. "Don't like opium. Getting easier." He wasn't lying really. With Alandra applying the poultice, his wound did get some ease. His eyelids were so heavy.

He finally gave up and let them close.

Alandra watched Scully fall asleep as she continued drawing the infection out. When she had done all she could do for now, she got up, stretched, and walked outside.

Carson was watching over Dorritt, who was sleeping on a blanket under a nearby oak tree. Alandra walked over and sat down beside him. "I can't believe it's over. Shouldn't we be shouting and celebrating?"

"We're all just too plain tired for excitement, I guess." Carson picked up a stick and began whittling.

"Scully's wounds are some better." A memory from the past, her brother suffering weakness for years and then dying from the effects of a gunshot wound, twisted inside her, hot and tight. She gripped the gnarled root of the oak, feeling the smooth old wood, which had refused to stay underground.

Carson rose, slipping his knife and stick into his pocket. "I'm going hunting, see if I can bring back something better to eat than sea biscuits."

Alandra smiled, thinking of fresh meat, a sign that everyday life was returning. Regular meals. No sea biscuits — what a wonderful idea.

"Tell my parents when they wake up. I'll

find a few other hombres to come along."

He turned to the little girl and told her to stay with Alandra. Sugar ran over to him and wrapped her arms around his legs. "Sugar, I promise. I'm just going hunting and I'll be back soon. The war is over. You don't have to worry." Carson patted her back and then pried off her hands from around his legs.

The little girl watched him walk away and then went back to the rag doll and began playing again. Little children all loved Dorritt and were drawn to her. Why did this child prefer Carson to Dorritt? Why did she prefer a man over a woman? That wasn't the usual way. Alandra found herself dozing on and off, leaning against the oak.

"Ma'am?"

An unfamiliar voice woke her and she looked up.

"Ma'am? Are you Miss Alandra Sandoval?"

She studied the man, tall and handsome with wavy brown hair. She recognized him. She rose and held out her hand. "Mr. La-Croix." Dorritt's brother-in-law.

He grinned and shook her hand. "It is you, then. I saw Miss Dorritt lying here and thought my eyes were playing tricks on me. And then I recognized you. Why are you here? I thought you all would stay out west and not get into this fray."

She could not begin to explain to him all that had happened. "I have come with the Quinns. And my husband Scully Falconer. Your sister-in-law will be most happy to see you unharmed." Her fatigue made her slide down to sit again.

Stooping to be at eye level with her, he sat back on his heels, facing her. "I'm surprised I didn't see you before. But there were nearly a thousand of us marching here so I suppose I shouldn't be surprised."

"Where did your wife and her family go when they left Buena Vista?" she asked. Dorritt stirred beside her, waking.

"They headed back to Louisiana —" Then Dorritt sat up and he broke off. "Miss Dorritt! Dear sister-in-law! And what has happened to your good husband?"

Alandra watched Dorritt greet her sister's husband, Henri LaCroix. She listened to the two of them catch up on what had happened to Quinn and other family news. When they went into the now much less crowded hospital tent to see Quinn, she followed.

She sat down on the ground beside her husband. Pressing her wrist to his perspiring forehead to judge his fever, she prayed that his strength would return in full and soon. Again she thought how far they had come over the past two months. They had lived a lifetime.

She looked down at her hands, which had gone without gloves for many weeks. Her nails were broken and the backs were tanned from the sun. Now her fingers were stained with the iodine she had used when nursing. These were not the hands of a lady.

She took a deep breath and reminded herself that Tía Dorritt had always taught her that being a true lady had nothing to do with soft hands and white skin. And today she had come to terms with God over this truth.

Today she had learned that she was a woman like any other. Being a grand lady, owner of thousands of acres of land, did not grant her special privileges in real life. She gazed at Quinn and Scully, still pale and perspiring from their raging fevers. *If I am a lady in any sense, it is because such a fine man has married me. I am Scully's lady.*

She dipped the cloth she had in a basin of water and began sponging Scully's face. She would not allow herself to think that he or Quinn might not heal, might not return to full strength.

When her mind tried to envision going

home without either or neither of them, a black bottomless abyss opened in her heart. It threatened to suck her into a despair beyond anything she had ever known.

After nearly a month of intense nursing and now three days of walking and riding, Alandra could hardly believe it, but Buena Vista was just up the road. The first leg of their long journey home had been reached. Henri LaCroix had been released from the Texas Army. and when Quinn and Scully were deemed well enough to travel, he set out with them.

She rode Scully's horse, and her husband sat in front of her. She could feel him resting back against her and tried not to worry that he still fatigued so easily. Quinn was unable to ride for any length of time, so Carson had rigged up a canvas travois for him.

She wished they were already at home at Rancho Sandoval, where her husband could rest, eat nourishing meals, sit in the sun in the courtyard and heal deeply and completely.

*Her husband.* Everyone called her Mrs. Falconer and treated her as such. But in the midst of the crowded camp, she and Scully had barely shared a private word. They whispered a bit every day but had not addressed the fact of their marriage. Or the annulment of their marriage. Alandra looked ahead. When they reached home, they would be forced to confront the issue.

Alandra increased the pressure of arms wrapped around Scully's waist. Resting her cheek against his back comforted her. In the weeks since the battle, full spring had exploded. The Texas bluebonnet, daisies, and wild petunias in red, pink, and white flourished in grass made green from all the winter rain. The same rain that had made them miserable as they slogged through its resulting mud was responsible for all this beauty.

The lane to Buena Vista opened to them, and they turned onto it from the road. It was late in the golden afternoon. The house still stood charred and desolate. But she could see that one of the jacales had been rebuilt, and that smoke was issuing from the chimney of the stove in the detached kitchen out back.

Scully felt his own spirits rise in spite of the lingering weakness that he tried to hide from Alandra. As they rode up to the house, he expected to be met by Amos and Nancy, and indeed the couple came running toward them. "Praise God!" Amos shouted. "Miss

Dorritt and Mr. Quinn have come back safe! Hallelujah! Praise Jesus!"

Nancy was clapping and hopping up and down like a child. "You come back. We prayed you would." Then she began weeping. Amos put his brawny arm around his wife. And then from the house came two white women, an older white man, a young man around Carson's age, and a little boy and girl.

Exclaiming, Dorritt slid from her horse and embraced them. "Mother! Jewell! I didn't expect to find you here!"

Mr. LaCroix was welcomed with hugs and shouts too as Scully helped Alandra down and they waited to be introduced. Scully had never met Quinn's family by marriage. But he had heard about them from Ash, who clearly didn't think much of them at all.

The older lady was Mrs. Kilbride, Mrs. Quinn's mother, and the older man was her stepfather. The younger woman was Mrs. Jewell LaCroix, Mrs. Quinn's half sister, and the little boy and girl were hers. The young man was Mrs. Quinn's younger half brother, Scott. It was hard to keep them all straight, so Scully just nodded and smiled. Alandra was known to them from previous visits and she received a warm welcome.

When asked by Quinn, Mrs. Kilbride said that the two men wounded at Goliad had headed for home a few weeks before. And then there was a sudden silence. Then Jewell spoke up. "Dorritt, Amos, and Nancy told us that you were here when Houston burned our house." The woman sounded as if she personally held Mrs. Quinn responsible.

"Yes, I was," Dorritt replied, "and there was nothing we could do. The fire spread through the treetops. If a spring shower hadn't put it out, we'd have been forced to run for our lives." Dorritt turned toward her mother. "My husband is still suffering the effects of severe wounds from the battle and he needs bed rest and some good food."

"Of course, of course," the older woman said. "Come. We'll take him to the kitchen. That's the best accommodation we have right now."

Scully and Alandra hung back at the rear of the party. Scully wondered how long they would be stopping here. He had to admit he could use a few days' rest before traveling again. San Antonio was a week's ride away, and with the travois slowing them, they would be moving at an armadillo's pace. After rushing eastward, the trip home would drag on for at least two weeks. And they had to do something about finding Sugar's family, which might add more days.

Suddenly he just wanted to sit down where he was. Alandra must have sensed this because she looked up at him and put her arm around his waist. "It is only a bit farther."

He hated this weakness, this having no energy. But he forced a smile for his wife. *My wife.* He wondered when he and Alandra would ever have a private moment to discuss what they were going to do when they returned to Rancho Sandoval. Did she want their marriage to end?

He knew he wanted her for his wife. He knew that everyone here accepted him as her husband. But did Alandra? She'd been through so much. Would their marriage become real or not? He prayed that it would.

# NINETEEN

A week had passed since Scully and the rest of the party had arrived at the burned plantation. While Quinn still traveled on the travois, Scully and Alandra took turns riding and walking, as Carson and his mother did. Four more had joined their party at Buena Vista. Amos and Nancy, now free, were coming to work at the Quinn ranch. And unfortunately yesterday, when they left the plantation, Jewell LaCroix, Mrs. Quinn's half sister, and her children had been persuaded to come home with her sister's family, and Mrs. Quinn's younger brother Scott Kilbride had also joined them.

Scully was not happy about the addition of Jewell LaCroix to their party. He wondered how Henri LaCroix could stand being married to such a spoiled and complaining woman. It didn't surprise him that LaCroix had encouraged his wife to stay with her half sister while he rebuilt Buena

Vista with his father-in-law. Scully hoped that when the rebuilding was done, the man would come and remove the irritating woman from earshot.

"I cannot believe it is taking this long to get to your ranch, Dorritt." The woman had said this over and over that morning.

Mrs. Quinn finally turned to her. "Jewell, if I hear that once more from you, I will send you back to Buena Vista with our brother."

Jewell stopped walking and planted her hands on her hips. "Fine. That's exactly what I want." She turned to her brother, who was on horseback. He had come along as added protection for the women. "Scott, we are going home now. I don't know why I let Henri talk me into this trip. I don't want to walk halfway to Santa Fe." And with that, she turned around and started back the way they had come. Ignoring Amos and Nancy, who were walking at the rear of the party, she lifted her nose and marched between them and away. Her son and daughter ran after her, calling, "Mama!"

Scott called after her, "Stop!" But of course the woman did not halt. He looked to Mrs. Quinn. "What should I do, Dorritt?"

Mrs. Quinn gestured with her hand. "Go with her, Scott. You know she must always

418

have her way. She never changes."

Scott swung down from his horse and hugged her. "Please write when you can. I know Mother will worry about you." Then he leaned down to the travois and shook Quinn's hand, and then Carson's. "God be with you. I better get her home." With that and a wave to Scully and the others, the young man caught up with his sister.

"Poor Henri," Quinn said, and closed his eyes. "But what a relief."

Scully couldn't help himself. He chuckled. "Whew!" Then they were all laughing, and it felt so good to laugh. Amos and Nancy looked relieved. Amos was free, but had signed a paper promising to pay for Nancy over the next ten years. Mrs. Quinn had insisted the couple stay together. Her step-father had grumbled loudly but finally had given in.

"Let's get going," Carson urged. "I think Sugar's cabin is only a day's ride from here."

Scully could see Alandra wanted to ask him how he was but didn't want to make a big deal out of it. He nodded and murmured, "I'm fine." Of course, he wasn't fine, the weakness still plagued him. But at least he could ride. Quinn still didn't have the strength to ride or walk. It was a worry. To them all.

Two days later Carson called out, "Here it is! This is the lane to the house where we found Sugar."

Alandra gazed at the small grove of live oaks and pine.

"Are you certain, son?" Dorritt asked, reining her horse.

"Yes, here see the mark I carved into the tree."

They all looked to the X etched into the bark of a cottonwood. Alandra glanced at Sugar, who was walking beside Quinn. The little girl looked frightened. "Carson," Alandra said, "why don't you get down and hold Sugar's hand?"

He followed Alandra's gaze, and seeing the little girl's expression, did as she'd suggested. "Don't worry, Sugar. You will be all right. We are here with you."

The little girl took his hand, but looked at the ground and, of course, said nothing. Alandra wondered again why she did not look happy to be home.

At the end of the short track, they reached a small log cabin. "Hello the house!" Carson called.

No answer came.

Carson led a plainly reluctant Sugar to the door. He knocked and waited and called again, looking around.

Alandra scanned the cabin yard and was not impressed. It was not the usual neat cabin and barn. It looked rougher. But then, it had been empty for over a month, and spring was bringing back weeds along with the wildflowers.

Carson pushed the door and it opened. Sugar refused to go inside. He entered and immediately returned. "It looks like no one has been here since we were, Ma."

No one seemed to know what to say to this. Alandra had been certain Sugar's family would have returned by now. Many Texian families had already returned from Louisiana. And their party had not been the only travelers on this road. Along the way they had spoken to many others returning home.

"What should we do?" Carson asked.

"Carve a message somewhere it can be seen easily," Quinn said. Sugar ran to Quinn and climbed up beside him on the travois. She had taken to Quinn too.

Carson approached a birch tree near the cabin and spent several minutes there and carved: *Girl at Rancho Sandoval.* Alandra had joined him, and he turned to her and said, "I hope you don't mind, but your ranch is so well known. And if they come to you, you can send them on to our place."

"That will be fine," she agreed.

"We should reach your rancho in about three days," Dorritt said, and sighed. "Alandra, I will be so happy to see your hacienda. Not long now, and we'll be home."

Alandra's longing to be home again had grown stronger every day. She felt it as a physical pull, as if she were the hand on a compass and her hacienda was due north. Closing her eyes, she drew in a deep breath.

And then glanced sideways at Scully who was mounted. While they traveled the road home, she did not have the courage to broach the fate of their marriage. In her courtyard, listening to the spring trickling in the stone fountain, she could face whatever might come. In her courtyard, she could ask him whether he wanted to annul their marriage or not. This thought brought a sharp pang. She pushed the ache aside or tried to. She pictured herself there in the courtyard. Just a few more days.

Recognizing familiar landmarks since dawn, Alandra walking, gripped Sugar's hand, trying to hold in the excitement expanding like hot air inside her. Riding beside her, Scully looked down at her, and she tried to control her smile, which was trembling at the corners of her mouth.

"I don't know about the rest of you," Carson said, turning in the saddle to look around at everyone, "but can't we hurry a little? We're almost to Alandra's."

"Yes, we can," Quinn answered. "And I'm not arriving there on this blasted travois." He called out, "Whoa!"

Everyone else glanced toward Dorritt, who was walking beside Quinn. She nodded her agreement, and Carson reined the horse. Quinn rolled off the travois and then, with Carson's help, mounted the horse that had been pulling the travois. Dorritt climbed up behind him.

Alandra wished Scully would ask her to ride the last few miles behind him, but she didn't say anything. Ever since she decided to wait until they reached her home to discuss their marriage, their arrival had come to mean even more to her than returning to the familiar setting. Now the journey of the war would end, and her life with Scully would begin — if he wanted her.

And then they came over the rise and there it was — Rancho Sandoval, laid out before them. As they moved closer. Alandra looked for her people to pour out from the hacienda, the barn, the jacales, to welcome her. Whenever she returned from a trip, they had turned out to greet her. But today no one appeared. The ranch was quiet, still. She looked at Scully. "Take me up with you! I cannot wait any longer."

He rode over to her, reached down and swung her up behind him. Then he nudged his horse and they were galloping up to the front door. The others kept up with them. When they reached the door, Alandra gasped. The house looked deserted, empty, abandoned.

She slipped down from the horse and approached the door, which had been tied shut with a strong rope. Fear whirled inside her. "Ramirez! Maria! Paloma!" She began calling names in the eerie stillness. The only reply was the whoosh of the wind blowing around the adobe walls.

What might she find on the other side of the door? What had happened here? She pounded on it, then began working at the knot. The doors had never been tied shut like this. Never.

"Wait!" Scully called out. "Let me."

Alandra stepped back, her eyes moist. "What do you think has happened to everyone?"

"I don't know, but we'll find out." He

424

worked the knots out of the stout rope and then pulled open the double doors and stepped inside. He turned to them and held up his hand. "Wait here till I look around inside."

But Alandra looked past him into the courtyard bright with the sunshine. The fountain sounded loud in the stillness. Entering the courtyard, she saw that all the wrought-iron furniture was gone and the sheltered plants were limp from lack of water. She moved toward the corridor from the courtyard to her bedroom, then ran down the hallway to her room. As she passed the dining room and drawing room, which were empty. Even the portraits of her mother and father had been taken away.

Her bedroom had been stripped. It was completely bare. She stood in the doorway and could hardly breathe. Where was everyone and everything? Tears filled her eyes and she blinked them away.

She turned, then, and stumbled back to the courtyard. The Quinns and Amos and Nancy waited there, looking uncomfortable. Across from her, Scully returned from the opposite wing.

"Is that empty too?" she asked.

He nodded, looking grim.

Her mind rebelled, imagining the hacienda

as it had looked, as it should look. She gazed into Scully's eyes. "Everything, everyone, is gone." She was shocked. How could this have happened? Her knees weakened and she staggered over to the stone fountain and sat down on the stone wall around the wide pool.

The others approached her slowly. She read the confusion and sympathy on their faces, and put her hands over her eyes so she would not have to see it.

"Your relatives must have stolen everything before they left." Scully's voice was strong, loud, angry.

Alandra looked up, feeling herself shrinking. "That is what my lawyer advised me to do. When I left San Antonio after the court hearing about the will they brought from Mexico City, he told me to take my personal belongings and some cattle and leave, that I would not win my case." *And then I was kidnapped on the way home and —*

"So they beat you to it?" Carson said, sounding disgusted.

"I cannot think," Alandra said, smoothing her hair back, then leaning forward and propping her elbows on her knees. The joyful reunion she had anticipated for weeks had been snatched from her. But how? Why?

Quinn walked slowly over to Alandra as if

each step cost him pain. He eased down beside her and rested a hand on her back. "There is some reason for this, some sensible reason."

Scully plainly did not know what to say to her. He hovered near her, looking as if he wanted to hit someone, break something.

Dorritt spoke up, "We — all of us — will just go on to our ranch. I'm sure that Ash and Reva will know what happened here."

"No," Alandra said. "No." She could feel the others waiting for her to go on. But she could not put what she was feeling into words, except *no.*

"Lonnie," Carson coaxed in a soft tone, "you can't stay here. There's no furniture, no food —"

"I am not leaving this hacienda." She jumped to her feet and turned her back to them. "I am not leaving my home."

Scully walked around to face her. The concern on his face snapped her anger in two and she wilted. "Oh, very well. I know I am being foolish." Then she straightened and turned toward them.

Her bravery and kindness of putting others first did not surprise Scully. "No, we'll stay here for at least a few days." He turned to Quinn. "I hope you don't mind, but I'm done in with this traveling. Why don't you all go on home? I'll stay here with Alandra. We need time alone anyway." *And we certainly will be alone here.*

"Scully," Alandra said, coming closer to him, "I will go with you to the Quinns. I know there is no food here —"

"I can hunt for supper. I've been doing that for weeks now, and we have our blanket and such. Your relatives didn't manage to take the roof, doors, or shutters with them. We'll be under a roof for the first time in months. You shouldn't have to leave your home again." *Not after all you've been through.*

"You do not mind?" she asked, gripping his arm and looking up at him almost shyly.

He patted her arm, feeling awkward with everyone watching. "We'll be fine. And in a few days, we can go on to the Quinns' rancho and see what they have found out."

She stood on tiptoe and kissed his cheek. Before he could respond, she had turned away.

The two of them walked everyone outside. The Quinns looked like they didn't like the idea of leaving them. They milled about for a long time talking, until they ran out of cautions and promises. Scully, with Alandra close to his side, but the two of them not touching, finally sent them off with waves and many good-byes. Then they stood in the doorway and watched their friends until they were out of sight.

Finally, Scully turned to Alandra, feeling awkward in their complete aloneness. "I'm going to ride around and just check out the area right around here." He waved his arm in a wide circle. "And if I can bag us dinner, I will. Then I'll put my horse in the barn and come inside. All right?"

She touched his arm. "Please do not go far."

He didn't like how uncertain she sounded. He put his hand over hers. It always surprised him how small her very capable hands were. "Don't worry, I have no desire to go very far. I think we have traveled far enough, don't you?"

"*Sí.* I am going to go to the kitchen and see if anything we can eat has been left there. And I may go to a few of the jacales and see if any sign remains to tell us where or why everyone has left."

He noticed that they were both speaking in low tones, as if someone might overhear them. Or perhaps the barren state of the rancho made them cautious, as if they might wake some sleeping evil or unseen danger. "All right. I'll be back soon. Don't you go far."

"I will not," she promised him with a smile.

He noticed her lips tremble. Mounting, he rode toward the paddock and around it. When he looked back, he saw she was still standing in the doorway, watching him. He waved and then turned away. He'd make a quick survey and get back to her. He couldn't think why all this had happened. How could he make this right for her?

Scully sat next to Alandra on the bare stone floor in the courtyard. Her nearness made it difficult for him to speak, so he had begun watching the stars appear overhead in order to avoid looking at her. He had wanted to be alone with her for months now, and here she was, so close, yet his tongue had turned to wood.

He couldn't bring himself to speak all the words he had been saving up for her. So they sat under the overhanging roof and leaned against the adobe wall, looking at the stars and the flickering flames in the clay fireplace. He had built a small fire there in the courtyard for cooking and warmth. How should he bring up the matter of their marriage? How could he start?

For once, they weren't hungry and exhausted from walking all day. They had eaten the few thin black-eared jackrabbits he brought back. Alandra had added to the meal from the great covered crocks of pickled peppers she had found. She'd also found some cornmeal and lard hidden or overlooked far back in the larder. So they enjoyed a decent meal.

As if leery of disturbing the deep quiet around them, they had spoken very little. This hacienda was usually full of voices and the footsteps of people coming and going. The stillness now felt uncanny, as if a plague had carried everyone else away, leaving only them.

It occurred to Scully that he should have expected something like this. But he had counted on the loyalty of Alandra's people, her vaqueros and the families who worked in the fields. He had counted on their sheer numbers to keep Alandra's relatives at bay. Now, looking around at the courtyard, he recalled how welcoming, how beautiful, how special it had been. And, he hoped, would be again.

The deep blue of evening turned into the black of night and covered the open sky above them. Early summer had warmed the air. And he was aware of the coming bedtime, aware that they were alone for the first time in months. There were no beds in the house, and they only had the single ragged blanket that they used while sleeping side by side for over two months. But more than that, he still did not know how to bring up the sleeping arrangements.

Then Alandra said, "Since you left for the war, we have not had a moment to speak together alone. Now I must ask you if you wish to end our marriage or not?" As she spoke, she looked down at her skirt, which she was pleating between her fingers.

Though she had broached the subject, the real matter that had to be settled between them, Scully found it hard to speak. But of course, he knew he had to answer her. He cleared his throat, said, "I want to do what you want."

"And I want to do what you want." She looked at him sideways with a slight smile.

"What do you want?" he asked, feeling his way forward.

She shook her head in a determined way. "No, you must tell me first. You are the one who did me the kindness of marrying me to prevent my relatives from pressuring me into marriage with my cousin. You wed me only to save my land and protect me. So you must go first. Do you wish us to remain husband and wife?"

He didn't want to have to put his feelings

into words. He didn't think he was good at that, and this was so important. How could he make sure he said the right words? Women could be touchy about a man saying the right words about love and such. He took the coward's way out. "Everyone considers us married. Otherwise, they wouldn't have left us here alone."

She shook her head at him. "This is not about what others think, Scully. You and I have lived outwardly as husband and wife since February. This is May. Except for the Quinns and Señor Veramendi and the priest in San Antonio, both of whom will probably move to Mexico now, no one else knows of our marriage. My people, wherever they have gone, would never tell anyone. You can still depart a free man and leave me with my reputation intact."

He wished she would give him some hint of whether or not she wanted him to stay or leave. What would it feel like if she didn't want him to stay? He hedged again. "I don't want to put any pressure on you."

"I do not feel pressured by you. Here there are only the two of us." She pointed to herself and then to him. "We may speak freely, and no one else will ever know what we have said to each other. I wish to know the truth. A marriage must be built on truth

433

and honesty, do you not think so?"

Alandra wished he would just put into words what he wanted. How hard this truth-telling was. Both of them were the kind of people who did not want to upset anyone, but now one of them had to speak up and tell the truth, whatever the result.

"Scully, you will not hurt my feelings if you tell me the truth," she told him. "Truly you will not." In fact, she knew she was not telling the complete truth herself. It would hurt her very much if Scully said he wished the marriage to be annulled. But if that was the truth, the words must be said, spoken aloud.

"Why can't we just stay married then and not have to talk about it?" he asked, sounding irritated.

She leaned closer to look at him. Why was he trying to avoid her questions? She tried not to let her own irritation nip at her. From the small fire in the courtyard, the flames flickered, casting a golden glow and moving shadows over his features. He was staring intensely into the fire, but then he looked at her sideways. There was longing in his expression.

So that was it. If she had not been raised with Quinn as an uncle, she would have misunderstood the reason Scully was evading her questions. He was an Anglo man, and they did not want to talk about feelings. They just wanted to do, not talk. "Does that mean that you wish to stay married to me, Scully?"

"Yes."

Just yes and no more. She smiled to herself. But tonight she knew they had to be sure of this, because marriage was for life, and it affected generations to come. She rested a hand on the adobe wall between them. "Scully, I never knew my parents. My father died before I was born and my mother a few months after. But their love endures in these walls. My brother used to tell me about my parents. How they fell in love and how they defied his family and married and left Mexico City to start a fresh life here."

With the back of her hand, she stroked the cool rough wall again. "My brother always said that their love built this house. He taught me that I must never marry just to make a good match, that I must marry a good, honest man because I love him."

Scully was looking into her eyes now. She moved to kneel beside him and sat back on her heels. He appeared surprised. "Scully, you are a good, honest man. You are also brave and loyal. Why would you think I

435

would not want to stay married to you?"

"You're the one with the land."

She had expected that to be the sticking point. "Ah, that is true. I am the one with the land, or maybe I do not have the land. If I do not own this land anymore, this hacienda, will you leave me then?"

"Of course, not," he said hotly, flushing.

"So you have not married me for the land or for this beautiful hacienda?" She smiled so he would know that she was just teasing him. "Scully James Falconer, you are a good honest man. And I do want to stay married to you. But only if you love me. This house was built by love and to be home to a husband and wife who love each other. Do you love me?"

# TWENTY

Scully knew he had to be a man and pluck up the courage to say it out loud. To do less would show a lack of respect for her. He drew up his resolve and said, "Alandra Sandoval, you are a good honest woman. And I do want to stay married to you. But only if you love me."

"Then you do love me," she said, moving nearer.

He nodded, trying to look away, but finding himself unable to take his eyes from her.

"And I love you." Close now, she lay her hand on his cheek where the new scar shone red. "When did you know you loved me, *querido?*"

He wished she would stop talking. He wanted to pull her close and kiss her. But he sensed that this was an important time for her, for them.

He cleared his throat again. "When Carson caught up with us and told us you'd been kidnapped and were probably in Matagorda. I had never felt such a . . . consuming anger. I burned with it. I wished I could have flown to you. And beat down, bloodied, everyone who had frightened you, who had hurt you."

At his mention of being kidnapped, she lowered her eyes. Her hand on the deep groove of his scar, she knew that being carried off by the *bandidos* had left a scar upon her, upon her spirit too. She fought the fear that spurted inside her, and with it, the urge to run away. But she stayed where she was, her pulse racing.

He moved onto his knees and put his arms around her. "I'm sorry. I wish I could have spared you that. I wanted to kill that Mendoza for putting you through it."

She gave a tiny dry laugh. "His *companeros* did that for you." She let him draw her to sit across his lap as he settled back, leaning against the adobe wall. He stroked stray hair back from her face. She rested her head on his substantial shoulder.

"When did you know you loved me?" he asked, his voice low and rough.

"When I was kidnapped, I prayed that you would find me. Not Quinn or Carson, though they are as close as family. You were the first one who came to my mind. I knew you would never stop looking for me. But when I was carried down into the hold of that awful ship . . ." The cold fingers of memory stroked her, and she shivered. She put her arms around him.

He hugged her close. "No one will ever do that to you again."

She lifted her head and kissed his face. Then she placed small kisses along the line of his scar.

"Don't do that. You're a lady. You shouldn't even have to look at something so ugly."

She looked into his green eyes. "The only lady I ever wished to be like was Tía Dorritt."

"She is a fine lady," Scully agreed. Her nearness stirred him more and more.

"But some people still judge her because she married a man whose mother was Cherokee. She is known in San Antonio as the New Orleans lady who married the half-breed. When I hear people say that, I want to slap them."

"I know what you mean. They make her sound like she's someone odd, out of the ordinary." He brought her against him.

"Yes, she is extraordinary because she does not see people as others see them." Alandra looked down. "I did not tell you, but I witnessed Santa Anna surrender to Sam Houston."

"You did?" Scully's eyes widened.

"It was a moment of history for Texas. And it also taught me something of the utmost importance. It taught me that though I was the *doña* of Rancho Sandoval, that did not entitle me to a life above the lives of others, did not entitle me to a life without sorrow or suffering or consequences."

It was something Scully had always known, and that she'd just discovered it surprised him. "That's right," he murmured.

She smiled and fingered the waves in his hair above his ear, sending shivers through him. "Yes, you know that." She pursed her lips, the lips he wanted to kiss so much. "Santa Anna was not content to be just a man. He wanted to be the lord of all Mexico, and especially of Texas. And even in defeat he would not admit that he was to blame for the slaughter you witnessed at Goliad and the one at the Alamo. He quoted some military text in his defense. I could see that Sam Houston despised him for this. I also despised him. His arrogance had unleashed death and misery on thousands."

"As you recall, I didn't think much of *el*

*presidente* myself." He grinned ruefully.

She beamed at him. "I remember. You did everything but challenge him to a duel." Then she waggled her left hand. "See, no one could pry your ring from my finger. So we must stay married." She chuckled.

He touched her nose with his index finger.

She laughed out loud. *"Mi esposo fuerte y valiente.* My strong valiant husband. I do love you so. *Estoy enamorada de ti."*

"Is that how you say it in Spanish?"

She nodded.

*"Estoy enamorado de ti,"* he whispered into her ear. "Can we stop talking now?" *And start the loving?*

There was much she still wanted to share with him. She had plans for the future, but perhaps she would never be able to put those plans into action. Perhaps she had lost Rancho Sandoval and her people.

But she had learned that she could be content in whatever circumstances she found herself. And the circumstance of finally being alone here with the man she loved and who was her husband was the best she could imagine. *"Sí."*

She leaned toward Scully's mouth and began a soft kiss there. He made a low sound in his throat, and it made her smile. He pulled her tight against him and she reveled in the strength of him, his resilience. Just weeks ago he had been weak and feverish. Now he was himself, again strong and powerful.

The delicious first kiss finally ended and the next began. Scully found it hard to catch his breath. She was so beautiful, so soft. And she was his. After all the nights she had lain in his arms, his waiting, his longing, for his bride was over. "How do you say 'wife' in Spanish again?" In fact he knew it, but wanted to hear her say the word.

She paused and, nose-to-nose, looked him in the eye. *"Esposa."*

Her warm breath fluttered against his face. He grinned and said, *"Mi esposa fuerte y valiente."*

She smiled and then leaned forward for another kiss.

He claimed her mouth with his and dug his fingers into her black heavy hair. Everything about her stirred him. And he knew he would never forget this night, their wedding night.

Two days had passed since they had returned to Rancho Sandoval. Scully and his bride stood outside the big double doors. This morning he was going to ride around to pick up any stray longhorns, in order to start their herd again. He found himself smiling.

He couldn't remember a happier time in his whole life. Alandra and he had decided to set up housekeeping here in the hacienda, even though they might be forced to leave it sometime in the future.

He leaned down and kissed her, and when he tried to pull away, she tugged him back and kissed him again. "I have work to do today, woman," he growled, and nuzzled her neck.

She laughed and tugged down his hat brim. "I have work to do today too, cowboy."

He finished the kiss, then swung up onto his saddle and gathered his reins while his restless horse pranced. The horse needed a good run today. "I'll be back as soon as I can." And he meant it. He waved to Alandra and galloped away. He didn't know if the fact that Texas was now independent of Mexico would have any effect on land titles or not.

He and his wife had decided that if they were forced to leave, they would return to the Quinn ranch, where he would work and save so they could buy their own land and start a ranch nearby. *My wife.* He liked saying those words. *My wife.* After years of being alone, he had a wife.

Alandra kept her eye on Scully as he rode away. She would go inside soon and sweep the courtyard, then take a walk through the fields that had been planted with corn. Thank heavens her people had gone ahead and done the planting while she was gone. She hoped that the cornfields might bring some workers back.

Then she saw something large on the horizon, moving toward her. Scully had stopped and was also staring. It was a crowd of people in wagons and horseback. Scully turned, spurring his horse back until he reached her. He swung down from the saddle, tied up his horse, and took her hand.

"Who is it?" she asked, worried.

"Our friends."

"Oh." Alandra tried to take it all in.

Then her vaqueros rode up and, as if it were a rodeo, sprang with style from their horses. They exclaimed their joy at seeing her again and greeted Scully with smiles, back-slapping, and repeated shouts of *"Felicitaciones!"*

Then came the Quinns, Ash and Reva and their son, and Ramirez and his son Emilio on horseback. And several covered wagons driven by more of Alandra's people. She gripped Scully's arm tighter, her face growing wide with excitement.

When everyone had reached them, there was a time of confusion, hugging and kissing and shouting with joy. Finally, they all quieted and looked to Scully and Alandra. He sensed that they were expecting them to say something. He looked to Alandra, letting her know he wanted her to do the talking.

She smiled and spread her arms wide. "Amigos! Friends! How wonderful to see all of you. My husband Scully and I did not know what to think when we found the hacienda empty and everyone gone. What took place here?"

Ramirez moved to stand near her. "After Señora Quinn left to go rescue you, Antonio, Emilio, and I decided that we needed to do more to protect your interests, *doña.* So Antonio and Emilio and the other vaqueros drove most of your cattle onto Señor Quinn's land."

Scully nodded. That made sense. Alandra called out her thanks to the two young men.

Ramirez continued, "Then several days after you left, your relatives returned. I would not let them enter the hacienda. They were very angry. They ordered their outriders to force me to back down. But, *doña,* your vaqueros outnumbered them and we stopped them from entering."

445

Her housekeeper Maria spoke up. "We were certain they wanted to steal all your fine furniture." She made an angry sound and shook her fist.

Ramirez nodded. "They said that they would go to San Antonio and bring soldiers back with them and take what was theirs."

Antonio, Ash's son, took over the story then. He grinned. "I said to Ramirez, they can't steal what they can't find."

Everyone grinned and nodded.

"So we stole everything first," Ramirez's son Emilio crowed, "and took it to Señor Quinn's!"

Alandra shouted with laughter. And then the men driving the wagons jumped down and drew back the canvas cover to reveal the dark wood and leather and wrought-iron furniture from the hacienda.

*"Gracias, gracias, mis amigos,"* Alandra repeated again and again.

The three Quinns came to stand with Scully and Alandra. Scully put his arm around his wife and beamed at her loyal people. Alandra was weeping, but smiling. Then she stepped forward and held up her hands. Everyone quieted and drew nearer to hear what she had to say.

"Amigos and amigas, your faithfulness to me and my family have moved me deeply.

*Mil gracias,* a thousand times thank you."
She paused as if controlling her emotions.

She looked up and went on. "Texas is free
now. When this rebellion first started, I was
too wrapped up in what was happening here
to think about what was at stake in this
revolution. But now, after traveling with the
Texas Army and meeting General Sam
Houston, I have come to understand what
it means, what it brings to us, all of us."

Scully noticed that no one spoke, not even
the small children. Around a hundred
people were giving his wife their complete
attention.

"Your families came out of Mexico City
with my parents. You came to herd our
cattle and till our land and serve us. My
late brother" — almost everyone crossed
themselves, showing respect — "taught me
to deal with our peons the way my parents
had, with honesty and fairness."

Many made sounds of agreement and
nodded.

"But Texas is now free, and that means
that you are free too. You have always
worked, and we have made certain that
everyone had food, clothing, and a roof to
call their own. We have even paid you in
silver each year so you could buy some of
what you needed for your families. But you

447

have never owned the land. And you would never be able to own land because you would never have enough money to do that."

The crowd of people were quiet now, frozen.

"I own over seven thousand acres of land. Today, I vow that to each family that came from Mexico City with my family, I will give the legal deed to one *labor* of land."

There were gasps around them. A *labor* was 177 acres. Women put their hands over their mouths, and most of the listeners had tears spring to their eyes.

"Texas is a free land with free people in it. I will still employ you, but you will also have your own land to do with as you wish. I will situate the lands so that they lie along the eastern boundary of my land, near enough for you to come and go. The Quinns and the Falconers" — Alandra looked to Scully — "will discuss how this will be done in the best way —"

Many of the peons dropped to their knees. Some appeared dazed, their startled expressions filled with gratitude and yearning. The sight moved Scully in a way he hadn't thought possible.

"Please do not kneel," Alandra implored them, gesturing with her hands for them to rise. "Please! *Por favor!* You should kneel only to God. I am only a woman."

"You are our lady," Maria declared. "And more." She began weeping then, wiping her eyes with her rebozo, as the people kneeling before them slowly rose.

Alandra held her arms wide. "You are my friends. Your actions to protect me and my belongings speak of friendship. I hope that will never end. But I do not want to keep you here if you wish to go and prosper elsewhere.

"And one more thing that must change is that your children must learn to speak English and also how to read it. Texas will now be an Anglo country. And the language will be English. You have become citizens of Texas. Tía Dorritt taught me English and taught me about how a democracy works. You must learn this also. And I will teach your children and then they can teach you, their parents, and later their own children."

Alandra paused and looked from face to face. "Santa Anna had more men, more cannon, more weapons, more arrogance than the Anglos. But I saw what happens to a dictator when free men take up arms to fight tyranny. The Anglos were men fighting for their land, their families, and for their rights as free men. Santa Anna lost. Sam

Houston and his army of free men won."

Scully's throat began to thicken and his heart beat faster with each word his wife spoke. He hadn't thought of it that way. He had just wanted to defeat the dictator who thought he could slaughter hundreds and go on doing that scot-free. But now his wife made him see what he had actually been fighting for and why so many Americans had come to Texas to fight.

"I know that the Anglos think they are better than Mexicans," Alandra said as she lifted her chin. "Better than us. Better than Quinn because his mother was Indian. My father's family opposed my father marrying my mother because she was a mestiza, half Indian. That is how Rancho Sandoval came to be."

His wife looked from face to face. "The Anglos are not better than us. But we can learn from them. We can learn how to be free. And we can make certain that our children learn that too. Shall we?" she asked. "Shall we be free?"

The vaqueros shouted, *"Sí! Sí!"* And the men and women exclaimed, *"Si! Si! Viva la liberación! Viva nuestra doña!"*

Scully couldn't stop himself. He pulled his wife into a hug and shouted his approval too. Then he whispered into her ear, "I married one fine woman all right."

She turned and kissed him.

# Epilogue

Later that year when the days were growing shorter, a courier rode up to the double doors of Rancho Sandoval. He was allowed to enter, and found Alandra sitting in the courtyard by the warmth of the clay fireplace. He gave her the letter he had brought from San Antonio. She offered him refreshment. With a bow of thanks, he went to the kitchen to eat.

She took the thick letter wrapped in parchment to her office, slit under the wax seal, and began reading:

*August 10, 1836*
*Mexico City*

My granddaughter Alandra,
I am your father's mother. I have been trying to communicate with you since my son Benito and my grandson left Mexico City much earlier this year. But

the rebellion made it impossible for me to do this. I finally made a visit to the American ambassador, a dreadful man, but he has promised that he will forward my letter to New Orleans and that in time it will be delivered to you.

The document that Benito is going to use to try to take your land is outdated. I have enclosed here a copy of the final will of my late husband. You will see that he renounced his claim to Rancho Sandoval in your favor. He regretted disowning our eldest son and forcing him to sign that awful document under duress.

Our son Benito has been a disappointment. You see we sent our best son away and kept the good-for-nothing one. Before his death, my husband wanted to right the old wrong. And so he drew up this document which I have put before the courts here.

I was shocked that Benito would try to deceive and rob his own flesh and blood. Though after watching him cheat and steal his whole life, I do not know why it should have surprised me.

Hold the copy of this document. If anyone from Mexico disputes your claim to your land, take this copy with you. It proves that you, as the child of our beloved son, are the rightful heir to Rancho Sandoval in Texas.

I am very sorry that we have never met and will not meet in this life. I am a very old woman and spend my days sitting in my courtyard thinking of what might have been. Do not live your youth like that. Be generous. Love freely. Do what is right in the eyes of God and you will not suffer the same fate.

Your grandmother,<br>
*Alicia Maria Alandra Sandoval*

Alandra looked over the enclosed document. She heard footsteps, and then her husband sat down beside her. "I heard a courier has come."

She nodded and read him the letter. Scully shook his head. Alandra leaned her head on his shoulder. "Is everything ready for our trip tomorrow?" Dorritt would be giving birth any day now, and Alandra wanted to be there for the event.

Scully laid his hand on her abdomen. "You're up to traveling?"

She smiled and laid her hand over his. "I am well. Do not worry about our little one. He is fine."

Scully kissed her, and she let his lips play over hers. So much sadness and danger this year and now so much happiness. *Be gener-ous. Love freely. Do what is right in the eyes of God.* Her grandmother's advice was so close to Tía Dorritt's:

The Lord knoweth the days of the up-right: and their inheritance shall be for ever.

# HISTORICAL NOTE

Researching the Texas revolution proved to be an eye-opener for me. I had of course heard about the Alamo, where two of the giants of the American frontier — Davy Crockett and Jim Bowie — gave their lives. But I had never really grasped what was at stake in the realm of the advance of human rights. The revolution of course was sparked by an extreme culture clash. The Americans who settled in Texas believed that they were free men with God-given inalienable rights. This was something which the Mexicans did not understand because of the Spanish colonial system and the lack of any democratic practice in Spanish or Mexican society.

Into this clash came the infamous Santa Anna, who actually said everything I included in his exchange with Sam Houston. This self-proclaimed Napoleon of the West spent the rest of his life trying to disavow the massacre he ordered at Goliad. Sam Houston, for all his foibles, did not suffer such delusions. He managed to pull off a monumental coup with his victory at the Battle of San Jacinto. In this battle, which only lasted eighteen minutes, Mexico lost Texas, and in the end, all of the Southwest.

Now to own up to the two historic events I took dramatic license with in this story. Did you notice them? First, I allowed Señor Veramendi to remain alive to help expedite Alandra's marriage to Scully. My sources weren't conclusive whether Veramendi died with his daughter of cholera a few years before 1836. However, dramatically having a Tejano with a daughter who had married Jim Bowie, an *angloamericano,* added more meaning and depth to the scene. Secondly, of course, the massacre at Goliad did not take place the very next day after the Texians surrendered to General Urrea. That took place on Palm Sunday, 1836. Again, I am very careful of history, but I am writing fiction; and bending history to increase drama is permissible. And General Urrea did not want to follow Santa Anna's orders, but felt compelled to obey the top general and dictator.

The next book in this series will focus on Carson Quinn and the unlikely woman he falls in love with and Sugar's history will be uncovered. If you've enjoyed these books, please drop by my Web site www.LynCote .net or drop me an e-mail at l.cote@juno .com.

# DISCUSSION QUESTIONS

1. Do you think it was different personalities or cultural differences that put Alandra and Scully at odds in the beginning of the story? Why?

2. How had Dorritt and Quinn influenced the way Alandra viewed life?

3. When did you realize that Scully had a deep faith in God?

4. This story says a lot about greed and revenge. What does God say will happen to those who pursue these? Were you surprised about Mendoza's end?

5. What or who had shaped Scully's faith in God?

6. The hymn "Amazing Grace" was special to Scully. Is there any hymn that is special

461

to you? Why?

7. Alandra thinks she knows what her adult life will be. But history intervenes and changes her life. Have you experienced this? What events, and how did it change the direction of your life?

8. At fourteen Carson had to grow up fast to face a war. How do you think this will influence his future?

9. What did you think of Alandra's grandmother's advice?

10. What do you think Sugar's story is? What happened to her to leave her abandoned and afraid?

# ABOUT THE AUTHOR

**Lyn Cote** married her real-life hero and was blessed with a son and daughter. She loves game shows, knitting, cooking, and eating! She and her husband live on a beautiful lake in the northwoods of Wisconsin. Now that the children have moved out, she indulges three cats — V–8 (for the engine, not the juice), Sadie, and Tricksey. In the summer, she writes using her laptop on her porch overlooking the lake. And in the winter, she sits by the fireplace her husband installed with the help of a good neighbor during their first winter at the lake.

Lyn's inspirational novels feature American women who step up to the challenges of their times and succeed in remaining true to the values of liberty and justice for all. The story of America is one of many nationalities and races coming together to forge our one nation under God and Lyn's novels reflect this with accurate historical detail, always providing the ring of authenticity. Strong Women, Brave Stories.

Lyn loves to hear from readers, so visit her website at *www.LynCote.net* or e-mail her at l.cote@juno.com.